Even if Nothing Else Is Certain

A Love for Certain
Novel • Book 2

For my husband.
Every girl wants a best friend who believes in her and encourages her to follow her dreams. How lucky am I to have one who does. Luckier still to call that friend my husband.

Even if Nothing Else Is Certain

A Love for Certain
Novel • Book 2

Amy Willoughby-Burle

FIRESHIP
PRESS

Chapter 1

Ruby

March 1937

Spring in Certain, Ky was like stepping through a thin spot between this world and another one. Maybe spring was like that everywhere, but I wouldn't know having not been anywhere else. Here it was like one season overlaid on the next and if you looked you could almost see them rippling on top of each other. Some people might have thought they saw the product of the wind, but I knew better. I was good at seeing the blending of what was and what could be.

Bare tree limbs and muddy ground were overlaid with patches of too green grass and outlandish yellow daffodils that always seemed like they'd popped up too soon. Or like some child from the future had dropped them as she ran home. Pear trees bloomed billowy white like snowballs made of flowers and the pink blossoms of the Redbud tree burst open, too excited to wait for the rest of spring.

That was me. I was a redbud blossom, a billowy white pear petal, a yellow daffodil finding myself out of step with the rest of the world around me. Putting on a show to cover the fact that I had no idea where

I belonged. Growing up an orphan will do that to you.

I wanted to think that the lingering years of economic depression were a thin spot. That at any moment we would step out of this time and into something better. *The Hazard Herald* told of rebounds in the economy dashed by a new recession. Wasn't that the epitome of getting kicked when you were down. Just when things started to get better, they got worse again.

My gramma had told me about the thin places between this world and heaven. She believed Certain was one. Heck, she believed that the living room was one. Anywhere you wanted to see Heaven was a thin spot according to her. I could wait a little while for Heaven, but I sure did feel like something was on the horizon. I felt like I was about to stick my hand out in front of me and part a curtain onto a different world.

My gramma wasn't technically my grandmother. I didn't know anything about my first family. They'd left me at a church in Lexington when I was a baby and I'd grown up in the orphanage there. Well, I spent the first five years of my life in the huge stone, four story building with so many rooms I was lost half the time. There were so many children I couldn't know them all, but it was the loneliest place I'd ever been. Everything was clean because we all had to clean it. And there were fancy paintings on the walls and everyone's clothes were pressed. The caretakers spoke very properly and the teachers tried to make us into clever citizens. But it wasn't home. Thankfully, God had taken me out of there and sent me to live with who I call, because they were, my real family. Gramma and Grampa. They were older when they took me, but I didn't care. They were my family. So, I'd really grown up in Certain and that cold stone place in the city became only a bad dream whose edges were mostly blurred if I didn't look too closely.

Our cabin in Certain was small, our clothes were wrung out in a wash basin and hung to dry on a string tied between two trees. My dresses were mostly clean and often somewhat wrinkled, but they were warm and smelled of sunshine. You couldn't get lost in our four rooms if you tried and there wasn't a fancy thing to be seen for miles around. It was the most magical and perfect place I could ever want.

Now, for the first time ever, though, it felt lonely. Grampa had been in Heaven for some time, but Gramma had only passed just last year. I still expected her to greet me when I woke up every morning with a smile and a call of "Good morning, my Lovely." She'd called me that all my life and even though I was twenty-nine, and a grown woman getting more grown by the day, I still miss that childhood name.

Gramma had always made me feel loved and special and she was the one who introduced me to the most magical things of all. Books. Books were a thin spot as well. Except they were a thin spot you could touch, open up and press to your face, smell and feel and fall asleep with under your pillow where their words drifted off the page and into your dreams.

I didn't want the realism of some of the newer authors. I knew all too well how life could knock the wind out of you and drop you to your knees. It was a gift that our little library here in Certain was filled with cast-offs and donations of well-worn old books read so many times the words were a little lighter on the page somehow. And shouldn't that be what a library was anyway, the preservation of imagination across time.

Proud to be a Pack Horse Librarian with The Works Progress Administration, my saddlebags were filled so tightly with fantastical beings and other worlds that it was a wonder Patty didn't sprout the wings of a griffin or a unicorn's horn as we traveled along the Hell for Certain Creek delivering peepholes into other places born of imaginations so wild I didn't see how the mere mortals they inhabited could even fall asleep at night without floating right out of their beds, through their windows, and into the moonlit night of possibility.

I was almost giddy at delivering Peter Pan and Wendy, Dorothy and Toto and her band of friends, Toad, Rat, Mole and Badger and precocious Peter Rabbit and cohorts into the hands of the children along my route.

And the house I knew that would relish them the most was also the house where my best friend, Mattie Barrett, lived. She'd been Mattie Mobley up until about two weeks ago when she married Certain's widowed *grizzly bear*, Daniel. Talk about a magical tale.

I was content as I rode across the fields and through the creek beds delivering my books. Even coming up the craggy leg of The Hell for Certain Creek toward Mattie's house I told myself I didn't want anything else but to bask in the glow of my friend's happiness. I was fine being single and living alone. Being a working girl doing an important job. Being beholden to no one and free to come and go as I pleased.

Who was I kidding? I did like being independent, but it was the being alone part that wasn't optimal. And I was doing an important job, but it wasn't the one I dreamed of.

I ducked through the canopy of tangled tree limbs that made a gateway of sorts into Mattie and Daniel's yard. I was greeted by a half dozen hens and one ornery rooster all coming up to me for the snacks they'd become accustomed to while Mattie and Daniel were on their honeymoon and the kids were staying with their Aunt Ava.

"Yes," I said to them, pulling a small bag of feed and seeds out of my saddlebag before I dismounted. "The food lady is here." I sprinkled the food onto the ground, eliciting much clucking and bonking as they called to each other about the food right in front of them.

It took all of about three seconds for the children to come running out the front door of the small cabin making even more noise than the chickens. Ella, Marie, and Hugh came racing toward me clambering for their books.

"Here you go," I said, handing them my best selections of the fantastical and magical.

Marie held *The Wind in the Willows* tight to her chest as if the book was already making itself at home in her heart.

Marie's older sister, Ella, held her hands open ready to receive whatever story I had for her as well. "What did you bring for me?"

"It's called *Peter and Wendy*," I said and placed the book gently in her hands. "It's just about the best thing in all the world."

Ella shifted the book to one hand and touched the dark green cover and golden lettering with the other. "It's so beautiful," she said. "It looks magical."

"It is," I said, raising my eyebrows and lowering my voice to a whisper. "Fairies, pirates, and boys who can fly."

Little Hugh piped up. "I want to fly."

Who doesn't, I thought and patted him on the head.

I was so busy talking to the kids that I hadn't even noticed my friend, Mattie, walking toward us until she spoke.

"Beware Captain Hook," she said and bent her fingers forward to make a hook with her hand. She laughed and drew me into a hug. "I missed you, Ruby," she said.

"I missed you, too," I said, hugging her tightly and then pulling back with my hands on her arms giving her a once over as if I hadn't seen her in months. "How was your father? How was Asheville? Did you love it so much you didn't want to come back?"

My secret fear.

"It was lovely, but of course not," she said, looking me in the eyes. "There's nowhere else I want to be but here."

I admit I was terribly relieved. I had worried that spending time back in the city, back with society and fancy clothes would remind Mattie of just how little we had here in Certain these days. Times were rough all over the country still, but I doubted anywhere was as bad off as we were. But then again, when you've never had two nickels to rub together in the first place, bad off is relative.

Daniel walked up beside her then and put his arm around her waist. He kissed the top of her head and nodded to me. "Thank you for feeding the chickens, Ruby. You got some eggs I hope."

"A plenty," I said. "For one lonely person anyway."

Mattie smiled a small knowing smile at me. "You'll find your love; I have no doubt. In the last place you expect to find him I predict."

"That could be anywhere then," I said, since I wasn't really looking.

"Maybe you'll find him along the creek on your way home even," Mattie said and chuckled.

"I bet I will," I said. "I've always wanted a bunny rabbit of my own. Then again, I'll most likely find a toad like the one in the book I brought for Marie."

"You can kiss him and turn him into a prince," Mattie said. "Like I did." She elbowed Daniel who only looked at her adoringly.

"That's a whole different book," I said, and sighed.

Mattie giggled loose from Daniel's sweet hold and put her arm around me. "You'll see the value of love, yet. I promise."

Chapter 2
Cole

Love makes all the decisions where it counts. The want of it. The need of it. That longing in the heart. But sometimes the heart is a haunted house. Filled with dark corridors and tightly closed doors, cracked glass windows covered in cobwebs. The grass is overgrown and there's a faint whispering of something rusty and squeaky off in the distance. Fear has its name on the mailbox. It's scary in the heart. All our ugliness, our shame, our despair. It's all there.

And for me, it was all there in Certain, Ky.

Why on earth had I come back to the town that had run my family out on the rails fifteen years ago. Well, there were no rails, just a long and winding road out of town. I swear my father would have ridden off and left me here had it not been for my mother. I wished now that she'd let him.

With nothing left and nowhere else to go, I'd come back to the only place that had ever felt like home to me. I'd been living along the Hell for Certain Creek for near about a week … too afraid yet to go into town. Mostly my stay had gone well, but a storm was rolling in.

Certain, Ky spring storms were not new to me, but I had forgotten how oddly beautiful they could be along the creek. Of course, when I lived here last, I was barely a teenager watching them from the safety of my living room as it were and not a grown man sitting out on the creek bed under a lean-to hoping it didn't blow away. And me with it.

I huddled up under the makeshift structure deciding there was nothing to do but trust my skills and the good Lord himself. I had done alright finding downed limbs and vines and twines and all manner of other material to make what on a non-stormy day seemed a pretty safe and roomy shelter. And one that blended in well if you didn't want to stand out. The three-walled structure was open in the front. Today I covered the pitched roof with some old tent fabric I'd picked up along the way and had staked into the ground on all three sides. I'd been living pretty lean the last couple of years going from place to place, alley to alley, and to a cheap motel if a buck or two came my way. I didn't have much, and I didn't need much, but a tent always came in handy. Even if it was a bit worse for the wear. It kept the rain out, mostly.

In the lean-to, I could stretch all the way out lengthwise and although I couldn't stand up straight inside it, I could sit and have plenty of headroom. Having to pull all my belongings inside, as sparse as they were, made it feel a little cramped, but better that than having everything soaked for the next day or more.

I liked the way a storm came in. The first slight darkening of the sky like whispers of warning.

Look up, do you see something changing?

The rustle of the leaves was the answer.

Yes.

There weren't many leaves yet to rustle as spring was still in its early stages, but the limbs of the trees along the creek swayed and rattled. When I was young, I had always liked to stand outside and feel a storm come in until Momma saw the first flash of lightning or heard the sky crack suddenly and would yell for me to come inside. She hadn't been around for me in a long time now though, so with no one to call me in, I sat in the wild outside of my pitiful campsite and watched the storm brew. I was past grown anyway and who needed their momma at nearly thirty years old.

I sighed off the sadness and focused on the beauty of the storm. I loved the way the air swirled as if confused about which way to blow. Little circles of wind turning the branches one way and then the other. The branches swinging back so that it looked like the tree was trying to swat away the storm. The sky had darkened from bright noon to what looked like early evening even though it wasn't. The wind curled around itself and began to talk to the trees.

My favorite part of a storm back then was the first pings of rain on the tin roof of the newspaper office we called home just up the creek in Certain. It sounded like the storm was tapping out a song. Then and now, that was the point where I closed my eyes to finish feeling the storm come in. Sometimes you can sense better with your eyes closed.

I breathed in deeply and waited for the rain. There it came. Slow and low like a stranger sneaking up. I soaked up the familiar smell of rain and creek and moss.

Not all my memories from Certain were bad ones. Just those to do with my father. He was a swindler. And by the time I figured that out, I'd already been in his midst long enough to not know any better way of being. He'd pulled one heck of a scam in Certain and I had come back to undo what he'd done. Or at least I wanted to. I had something with me that the people of Certain wanted and they had something I wanted … a place to call home.

I'd been on my own since I was a teenager. Long story there. I'd gone from odd job to minor scam and back to odd job so many times my head hurt. My last job in the mines had been the closest thing to steady and true work I'd ever done. That had fallen through, too. I'd been up to no good and it served me right. I was just doing what my father had always told me, *"Look out for yourself, Cole. Ain't nobody else looking out for you."* As a kid that was about the most daunting thing I could imagine. I sure hoped it wasn't true. So far, it seemed it was.

Now, the rain fell persistently and I knew I was in for a storm indeed. I opened my eyes and drew my legs up closer to my chest so that my boots wouldn't get wet where my feet stuck out of the lean-to. The rain dropped into the creek leaving circles on top of circles like a million pebbles plunked in all at once. I felt like the fourteen-year-old kid I'd been when we left Certain fifteen years ago.

But that boy had had hope. This man didn't. I'd run out of money, luck, and everything in between. All I had left was a stack of deeds that didn't belong to me and a wild idea that I might be able to come home again. Why else would I have ended up back along the Hell for Certain?

Chapter 3
Ruby

"Hello," I called out as I didn't see Mr. Gibbons at the register when I walked into the Certain Grocery across from the library and the church. "I'm just going to go ahead and shop for a couple of things."

"Go right ahead, Ruby," his comforting voice called out from the top of the stairs that led to his living quarters. "I'll be right down."

I loved the way he knew my voice. A calm came over me just being in there and knowing that he was upstairs. Mr. Gibbons and my grampa had been childhood friends and being around Mr. Gibbons made me feel like Grampa was here too. Childhood friends have a way of shaping who you are like nothing else does. They open all the doors to who you might be and help you figure out which of those doors to go through and which ones to shut. I had a friend like that here many years ago. I still wondered about him from time to time.

"So, what are we after today?" Mr. Gibbons said, appearing beside me. His white hair and kind smile never failed to make me breathe out with relief as if something had been bothering me, but now that he was there, everything would be OK.

I perked up. Mr. Gibbons was one of the few people who not only didn't mind me talking about wild plants and all their uses, but he seemed downright interested. He carried a couple of my medicinal tinctures in the store and would sometimes trade goods for a big batch of wood sorrel or chickweed if he was in the mood for some fresh greens. I made a chicory coffee that he didn't love, but when the real stuff was scarce, he'd take some of that in trade too.

"Today I'm harvesting pine needles" I said, holding my hand out in protest of the face I knew he'd make. "I know you don't like the taste of the tea, but the medicinal value of the pine tree as a whole is enormous."

He smiled and put his hands in his pockets, leaning back against the counter as if he had nowhere to be. "Do tell."

I shook my head. "I know you're just humoring me. You've heard it all from me before."

He nodded and straightened back up. "I really don't like that tea. It tastes like eating a Christmas tree."

"I'll also be collecting some wood sorrel just for you," I said. "That's actually why I came by. I wanted to see if you had any lard."

Mr. Gibbons' face scrunched up. "That sounds like a terrible combination. I think I'll just eat the sorrel raw."

I shook my head at him and he chuckled. He knew me well enough to know what I was after.

"But," he said as if just figuring it out, "if you end up with soap to spare, my shelves are getting low. The sorrel for the lard, I'm guessing?" He winked at me.

"Deal," I said as if there was a chance he'd say no.

"Are you still working on your field guide," he said and reached out for me to hand him the scrapbook I was making and that he knew I had in my satchel bag.

I flipped to the newest page. "I'm doing a section on edible trees."

"Hence the pine needles," he said in confirmation.

"And," I said, pointing at the drawing Adaline, fellow librarian Ava's daughter, had done for me, "did you know the soft buds can be used to make an antiseptic?"

"I did not," he said and looked like that was genuinely true. "We'll

17

have to carry that in the store as well when you've made it."

"Deal," I said again as he flipped through the book, looking with interest over the pages he'd already seen a dozen times. Mr. Gibbons could make a person feel special with the simplest of gestures.

Making scrapbooks was one of my favorite librarian activities. It was a bit like foraging for edibles and medicinals. Finding information on any given topic a little here and a little there and putting it all together to make something useful.

Claire Thomas appeared on the other side of the big front window outside the store and a scowl instantly wrinkled my face.

"You know what I like best about foraging in the woods?" I asked once she and her porcelain skin and shiny red hair had disappeared from my sight.

"The free snacks?"

I nodded caught off guard. "Well, yes, but I like best that the wood sorrel doesn't care how I look."

Mr. Gibbons had my number and his eyebrow raised up. He had seen Claire pass by too. "Ruby Foster, I'll have you know you look positively lovely today and every day. Those eastern redbuds and wildflowers have nothing on you. You'll be the prettiest thing in the forest."

I pressed a hand against the wiry knot of hair at the back of my head. I had never been one to fuss and muss with my looks. I was about as plain as they came. And who needed to be fancy to ride a horse to deliver books up and down the hills. I smiled to myself thinking of Mattie and her first weeks here from Asheville. My new best friend was the real sort of fancy that Claire thought she was. Mattie was only fancy on the inside these days as her socialite attire had been boxed up and sent back across the mountains, but what was on the inside shone through far more.

"Thank you, Mr. Gibbons, but you don't have to flatter me."

He closed the scrapbook and set it on the counter so that he could take my hands in his. "Not that outside beauty matters a lick my dear, but you do not give yourself credit. How can those big hazel eyes, freckle covered cheeks, and soft brown locks be seen as anything but lovely?"

"You're too kind," I said.

"I try," he said and shrugged. "But I am truthful. God made you just like he wanted you to be, Miss Ruby, inside and out. All you have to do, my dear, is be brave enough to be who He made you to be."

I sighed. Was I brave? Was I being the person God made me to be?

I guess I'd need to figure out who that was first. Or maybe I knew, but was too afraid to announce it to the air. I knew I was supposed to want to get married and have a bunch of kids. And maybe I wanted that. But I liked having my independence too. I figured when the Works Progress Administration came up with the idea for the Pack Horse Librarian program that they had to know the kind of women interested in that job might be the independent sort. The sort of woman who would ride alone through the rambles and ruckus of the Hell for Certain Creek delivering books to the masses was a special breed of lady. Well, there aren't masses in Certain really, but a handful of citizens along the way at least. And a few of them were even a bit dangerous if you rubbed them the wrong way. A librarian would have to be ready and able to brave the elements, maybe fight a bear, OK I'd not seen a bear but likely only because it had seen me and my horse, Patty, first. This sort of woman would get rained on and covered in snow. She'd have to fix a thrown horseshoe and who knew what else. Of course, that type of woman would be a rule breaker, a tradition bucker, a … loner. I sighed heavily.

All the better as I've always been more at home in the out-of-doors than the in. As a child my gramma called me "a princess with a frog in her pocket." I wondered sometimes which she saw as the more prominent thing … the princess or the pocket full of frogs.

Thinking about my gramma's comment I asked Mr. Gibbons, "Do you think an unladylike lady is an oxymoron?"

Mr. Gibbons burst into a fit of laughter. After a full minute, without one ounce of exaggeration on the time, he gathered himself together, wiped the tears from his eyes, took in a deep breath and said, "Your grandmother thought it was the most delightful thing to see you tromp around in your ruffled dress and bare feet picking up bugs and reptiles and holding them out for passersby to marvel over. Or so you expected them to."

My mouth fell open. "How did you know I was thinking about Gramma just then?"

Mr. Gibbons put his hand on my arm and winked. "I have known you all your life, my dear. Well, once you got here that is. Your grandmother and grandfather and I were The Three Musketeers. Long before our Daniel Barrett and the Collins boys decided to call themselves that. We let them have the nickname ... your grandmother and I."

"Since my grampa was gone by then?"

Mr. Gibbons nodded and smiled that small wistful smile that memory will allow, but only for a moment as to keep your throat from tightening up beyond control. I touched his arm and he smiled more fully at me.

A smile came across my own face as I thought about friends and nicknames. "Maybe Mattie and Ava and I will steal The Three Musketeers away from them and give it back to you."

"Steal away, my dear, but keep it for yourselves," he said and winked again. "Give those boys a run for their money." He patted my arm and I knew I was being sent on my way to enjoy my adventure. "Get whatever you need and I'll put it on your account, dear."

"Thank you, Mr. Gibbons," I said. "Other than the lard, I'm only getting some parchment paper so I can keep things sorted."

"Be safe out there," he said, pointing me toward the item I needed.

"I'm used to being alone," I said, which wasn't really the truth, but it felt like it. Maybe that was a crazy thing to say. I had always had people around me, and I knew those people cared about me, but I felt lonely in my heart sometimes.

"You're never really alone," Mr. Gibbons said and winked at me. Then before I could ask what he meant, he nodded me on my way again and said, "Have a lovely afternoon and come tell me all about whatever you find out there."

Outside, I tucked a jar of water into Patty's saddlebags on one side and my field guides and parchment paper on the other before hoisting myself into the saddle. Somehow, she knew we were off on an adventure and not planning to ride our usual book route along the creek. Patty was a good horse, but like me, she got a little bored riding the same path all the time.

For the longest time I'd ridden a wonderful horse named Molly, but she'd gotten a little old for hard work and was now enjoying her retirement on the Lawsons' farm way outside of town. Patty and I had made fast friends over the last months. We both knew every rock, every tree, every tuft of moss, every squirrel and groundhog along the way. But on the days we went foraging, Patty was a new horse. Her chestnut coat and blonde mane were somehow shinier on those days as if the joy in her heart was coming through her very pores. I felt like that too. She and I both were in our element when there was something new to discover.

Once we got deep enough into the trees or down by the creek where riding was tricky, I walked Patty through the woods and along the creek bank. We walked slowly so we could look carefully at the ground around us. I could swear she was looking too.

I'd planned to hit a patch of pine trees I was familiar with on the way home to harvest the actual medicinals I was after this trip, but for now, I was just scanning the ground cover for wood sorrel for Mr. Gibbons of course and maybe some plantain or some jewelweed if I saw any. I probably wouldn't pick those last two unless I got stung by a bee or fell into some poison ivy. I just liked to see what I could see.

It had rained something fierce the night before and there were still patches and puddles of water to muck through. Maybe not the best foraging day to some, but I preferred the cool after a spring rain to the heat of a long sunny day. And perhaps I was a little fantastical in my thinking, but it always seemed like the plants were more radiant, like the rain made them magical somehow.

"Stay, girl," I said to Patty, seeing a patch of interesting area I wanted to inspect. I pulled an apron out of the saddlebag and tied it on. I liked to make a basket of sorts out of the material, using it to collect plants as I walked. "I'm going to go down to the creek, Patty, you stay here and snack on the grasses."

Head down and eyes scanning as I collected sorrel, I reached the edge of the Hell for Certain Creek before I knew it. The water at this section wasn't too deep nor was the creek all that wide. It was certainly not the spot the fabled explorer had deemed "Hell for Certain" as the waters rose around him. A person might get their whole foot wet and even up their ankle if they weren't careful right here. It was a spot I knew well from a long time ago. I didn't come this way much anymore and I hadn't realized where I was. My heart skipped and bounced back into rhythm.

I held my apron bunched in my fist to keep my stash of sorrel in, stepped on out into the creek in my big work boots and walked through to the other side of the Certain. I hadn't been on this side of the bank at this spot for quite some time. It used to be my favorite place. I was so busy looking up into the tree canopy and trying not to let old memories lodge in my throat that I didn't notice the campsite until I fell over a circle of stones with wood and ash still fresh enough to tell me the owner was still close by. The lean-to and canvas bag I landed near told me the same. I scrambled to my feet assuming the worst of persons must be about somewhere. Some criminal hiding in the woods. A mysterious drifter, at the very least, come to Certain to, well, I would say rob us blind, but he wouldn't have gotten much before we got to that state.

I should have just hightailed it back across the creek and to Patty and taken my leave, but two things kept me from doing so. One was that my sorrel was now everywhere. Whoever's site this was would surely know someone had been there and Certain was the nearest place that someone would have come from. But it was unlikely that a criminal hiding in the woods would come into town to take his vengeance on the person who made a mess at his campsite with wood sorrel. That wasn't a very plausible plot. I had read enough of the books in our library to know that. So, I guess the real reason I didn't run right away was number two, curiosity. I couldn't resist the pull of a mystery.

I gathered the sorrel, putting it back into my apron. There were still some sprigs lying about, but they blended in well enough. Then I set about taking a careful look at the campsite. I didn't know what a criminal's campsite would look like, but I didn't think it would look like this. This site was neat and tidy—except for the items I'd displaced when I fell—and it was well-established even in its sparseness. Whoever this person was, he wasn't just passing through, hiding out 'til the cover of darkness. Someone lived here.

I knelt on the ground and ran my hand over what looked like some kind of army bag. US stamped on the cover flap. The name Cooper was poorly stitched along the seam. A soldier? My bookish mind began to wander, pulling from my childhood memories of the war. I remembered many of the fathers in town volunteering and the mothers begging them not to go. I was only a little kid at the time and hadn't been in Certain that long, so many of those memories are like fog across the creek to me, ghost-like and unsteady. Those years were dark and full of things most people try to forget: war, flu, fear. Had there been a time in Certain when things actually were certain? What a strange name for our town once I thought about it.

Could some long-lost father have come back? I knew of a couple of kids whose fathers never came home. I scooted closer to the small pile of belongings sticking out from under the edge of the lean-to. I opened the flap of the sack and pulled out a leather notebook. Inside the front cover was written "Property of C. Cooper. Not to be read by anyone else."

The familiarity of the name and the tone brought a smile to my face and then a sudden thudding in my heart. It couldn't possibly be.

"Cole?" I said out loud as the memory of another Certain hardship flooded back. A terrible time for our town and a friendship lost from which I'm not sure I ever recovered. I tucked the book to my chest as if it might be the boy himself and then set it down beside me to search through the bag. Nothing else told me anything I wanted to know. A comb, a knit cap, an old copy of *Popular Science* and an old Bible that looked like it was about to fall to pieces. Was it read that much, I wondered? I wanted to read more of the journal, but it clearly said I shouldn't, so I slipped it back into the sack and closed the clasp.

There was no way a Cooper, even my Cole, would come back to Certain after what happened. For all I knew this was an outlaw after all and he'd stolen this whole pack and everything else here. He was probably on his way back up the creek from fishing for his supper and there I'd be, caught rifling through his things. Rifle being an important word. I didn't see a gun anywhere, which surely meant he had it with him and I was about to have it trained on me if I didn't get back to Patty and back up the creek from whence I'd come.

Just then I heard the tell-tale cracking of twigs that announced someone's arrival through the thicket. I rushed away as fast as I could, holding my apron tight, careful not to trip over anything else. I splashed back through the creek and hoped that if the person, which I was sure it was, heard me they might think it was a raccoon or something else not to be worried over.

When I got back to where I'd left Patty, she was nowhere in sight. Probably bored with this whole outing and heading back home without me. I really should have just kept on going, but I heard a voice coming along the way in time with the twigs cracking. Not talking to me for sure, but to himself I imagined. I tucked myself safely behind a thicket along the other side of the creek and tried to spy. I saw someone come into the clearing of the camp. He was mumbling, but not necessarily unhappily. Just the way someone who has spent a lot of time alone might do as they talked to themselves. I should know.

He looked around the campsite and then looked across the creek. I jumped back a little and almost fell. He didn't seem to see me. I trained my eyes on the man across the creek. He kept turning away or slipping behind a branch or tree trunk so that I couldn't get a clear view of his face. I tried to deduce what I could. The man's wavy dark brown hair, a little too long for the current style, gave away that he had been out here for a while. As he moved in and out of view, I caught a glimpse of the little divot in his chin. My heart kicked in my chest. Cole had that divot too. But this wasn't a boy of fourteen. This was a man, sturdy and tall. He looked about my age from what I could tell. Cole was only months older than me. It was possible. He'd be almost thirty by now. But he was long gone.

"It's just your overactive imagination," I whispered to keep myself in check. "You read too many books." *And you want too many things you can't have.*

I shouldn't have, but I kept watching him, whoever he was. He walked to the creek and splashed some water on his face. A face, now that I could see, was easy to turn into the older version of Cole. But then again, wishful thinking can turn anything into anything. He began to unbutton his shirt and I took in a short breath. Embarrassed to be looking, but too interested not to, I promised myself that I'd stop spying before I saw anything I shouldn't see. And with all the branches in the way, even if they were still sort of bare, it would be an obstructed view at best. My justifications didn't keep my cheeks from growing hot. I noticed that he only used one hand to unbutton his shirt. He fumbled a little, but he got it done. His hand was bandaged all the way to the wrist, and not very well I could tell, even with him moving in and out of view.

While I was looking to see if I could tell what was wrong with his hand, I saw that he was shimmying the shirt over his shoulder. I didn't mean to see his muscled upper arm, but it came suddenly into view and when I blinked my focus grew sharper. I wanted to keep watching, but it wasn't proper. Gramma would have had my hide if she were here to know about it.

Knowing I was invading the man's privacy, I turned and sought out Patty, finding her a little way up the creek drinking some water that ran over a section of rocks close to the bank. She whinnied when she saw me like I was the one who had wandered off.

"Shh," I said. "He'll hear you."

She whinnied again.

My hands shook as I pulled the parchment paper out of the saddlebags and wrapped the sorrel loosely in it. The plants were crushed beyond repair and there was no way I'd present them to Mr. Gibbons but I had to keep myself busy doing something and that something couldn't be letting myself imagine that Cole Cooper might be back in Certain.

Chapter 4
Cole

Coming back into my campsite after a long walk, I knew right away someone, or something had been there. I could swear that my satchel had been turned with the clasp down when I left and there it was now clasp up. I would have thought maybe a raccoon came searching for something, but if it had been one of those sneaky critters the satchel would be open at least. I'd seen those little sly buggers open a clasp or flip a lock. Only thing was, they couldn't usually figure out how to close it. Or they didn't care to most likely. There were crackers and a piece of jerky in the bag that I knew a raccoon could smell and surely would have tried to get. I suspected a much bigger varmint instead. One that's got a lesser ability to smell and a bigger ability to cover their tracks.

"Nothing missing," I said out loud as I rummaged through the contents of the satchel to take inventory. Crackers and jerky still accounted for. Not an animal. Leastways not a hungry one. Some person must have come across my campsite. I figured it would happen sooner or later. I thought I was off the beaten path enough to stay hidden, but then again, if I found this spot surely somebody else would too. It had been a particular haunt of mine when I was a kid, a special place my best and only friend had come to often. I had come to hide here once before and that friend had found me. I made a promise that night that I didn't keep.

My mind flicked back in time. The Hell for Certainers; Adventure First, Reason Never. The memory of our secret club made me smile; something I hadn't done in a while. Ruby had been my best friend and I had left her standing right here waiting for me all those years ago. I hadn't let her in on my real secrets and they'd gotten the best of me.

That had been a long time ago and this section of creek was probably somebody's homestead now. Certain was a small town, too small for me to think I could go undiscovered. If I really was here to set things straight, I needed to get it done and disappear before anyone else discovered me. The only thing that had kept me from my original plan of going into town, returning the land deeds my father had swindled years ago and hotfooting it out of town was that I had nowhere to hotfoot it to. I wanted to stay in Certain and so far, I hadn't come up with a version of my plan that would allow that to happen.

I babied my stupid injured right hand as I undid my shirt so I could wash it and me both in the creek. It had been my own fault that I got cut. Probably more accident than intent, but then again in a bar fight it can go either way. Don't try to punch a man with a knife. Better yet, stay out of bars and don't try to swindle people. This foray back to Certain was part me trying to right a wrong and part me trying to get my life back in order all together. I was back at the starting point. Back in the last place that ever felt like home.

I really needed to see a doctor and get my hand bandaged properly. I could move all my fingers but my thumb, which was the worst one not to have mobile. It felt like something was torn in the meaty part between the thumb and first finger. I'd been cut bad there. The cut had healed, but something wasn't right. Certain didn't have a doctor when I was here last, but maybe they did now. Maybe I could go into town, see someone now that I was back.

"You're not back," I said out loud to keep myself focused. "This isn't your home. It never really was."

I blew a mournful breath through my lips and went about washing in the cold creek water. Just enough to blow the stink off a bit before I put my shirt back on. I needed to return the deeds my father had stolen and then disappear before anyone was too much the wiser. That was the smart plan, but the lonely kid in me was hoping I'd somehow find a place to belong again. I'd never had a proper home, but Certain was about the closest to it. I was twelve when we moved here and fourteen when we left. I had figured out that my father was running the scam of his life here in Certain, but there wasn't anything I could do to stop him. He was smart, but he was also evil. Most of the time his scams were fast and we were long gone before anyone knew what hit them. This time he was running a long game. I guess he was making sure I wouldn't grow a conscience and rat him out, so he made me part of the scam that time and I was too ashamed to tell anyone, even Ruby, what was happening. I couldn't make things right then, but I could now. That's what I was doing here. Trying to fix what he'd done.

"We're gonna make a fortune here" he'd said not long after we arrived three days after my twelfth birthday. I had wondered how that was possible in the small town of Certain, but Dad had a plan. He always had a plan. And that had been back before the economy tanked. We were here for almost three years. The best years of my life. But of course, every kid thinks that the years of twelve, thirteen, and fourteen are the best years of their life. Those are the magical years. The "run wild and free in the woods" years. The "sneak out at night and lay out in the yard looking at the stars" years. The "heart fluttering, have your first kiss with the girl next door" years. And yes, I'd had all those things right there along the Hell for Certain Creek. And every one of them had been shared with Ruby Foster. The last one, that heart fluttering first kiss had happened right here along the creek bed the night my dad got us all run out of town.

I needed to get my nerve up before I could face the town again, especially Ruby. Right now, I just needed a place to be alone. I had enough supplies to last a few weeks so long as the fishing held out. I had a pole and spear I'd made from some thin but tough branches and so far, that was getting me by. Although, truth be told, I was getting mighty tired of fish. I knew there was a store up in town, but that was going to take some courage to visit. Especially since it was right next door to the newspaper building where Dad had run his scam and where we'd lived in the upstairs rooms. I didn't even know if that store was still open with the way the world had crashed and burned—especially around here. I didn't know what had become of the newspaper either—especially since it wasn't real to start with.

Whatever was going on in town, I would need to be ready to face some old ghosts before I ventured there. I was a little too chicken now. I would need to be some other kind of brave bird, an eagle or at the very least a blue jay. If I was something smart like a crow, I'd just fly into town, drop the deeds at the church and fly for the hills.

I wasn't nearly as smart as a crow.

Chapter 5
Ruby

I tried to forget about the campsite along the creek over the next couple of weeks as I went on with the regular routines of my life. Whoever it was, was surely long gone. It was ridiculous to think that it had been Cole. Cooper was a pretty common last name and it really could have been anyone. The bag could have been bought off someone else or given over in charity. Whoever it was surely didn't have much to their name. And sure, the man looked like what I thought a grown-up Cole could look like, but that could have been my wild imagination wishing for times long gone to come back again. Cole and I had only been fourteen and I hadn't seen him since, he would be twenty-nine years old by now and could look like any given person I might see anywhere, or nowhere.

And besides, if it was Cole, wouldn't he have come into town to see me? It was probably a drifter and I was lucky I hadn't been shot. Startling up on a stranger was a dangerous thing to do. Heck there were people in these hills who'd known me forever that might not think twice about taking a shot if I'd walked up on a still or some other operation they wanted to keep hidden. Best I put it all out of my overly curious mind.

Instead, I thought about work which was the way I distracted myself most of the time. So, I was glad that even though I didn't have a route today, I was needed for Repair and Report at the library. I loved my job delivering books along the creek and up into the hills and down into the hollers, but there was something about repair and report day that sometimes I thought I liked even better. It was the day that Ava and Mattie and I would sit around the library and gossip. I mean work. Routinely, we had to gather to repair damaged materials, report on any new families or people who'd left or died, problems or good news along the routes and just about anything else that came up. We'd sort and catalog new materials and set aside things our patrons had practically read to death so we could trade them with other libraries in the surrounding areas.

Mattie wasn't working as a librarian anymore now that school was back in session and she was officially teaching full time, but she always came to repair and report as soon as school was out next door at the church. We seemed to "repair and report" more than some of the other libraries and that was just fine with me. Ava and Mattie were like sisters to me. Sisters I desperately needed. We each did. Mattie was an only child just like me, and Ava had lost her real sister several years ago. Now she and Mattie were sisters-in-law, well sort of, since Daniel had once been her brother-in-law and before that he was a brother at heart in the Collins family after his parents passed away. Talk about a story.

I never knew my own parents. I didn't even know my real name. I didn't know if I'd even had one before Ruby. So maybe that was my real name. Gramma and Grampa had never had kids of their own and were getting too old to, so when someone from the orphanage asked if they could take me, they said yes without a second thought. Gramma always made sure to tell me that part when she told the story.

"I said yes, before she'd even finished asking me," Gramma would say and kiss the top of my head. Even after I was taller than she was and I had to duck down to let her.

I asked her once why I called her Gramma and not Momma.

"I'm too old a lady to have a little daughter, but I'm just the right fit for a gramma," she had said. "And besides, a gramma gets to spoil her granddaughter way more than a momma spoils her baby."

And that's what she proceeded to do, spoil me. Yes, poor people can spoil their babies too. Spoiled with love, affirmation, and encouragement.

Spending time repairing at the library also kept me out of my empty house. At first, I didn't mind the house being empty. It gave me privacy to grieve. But lately it was finally starting to feel lonely, like even the old ghosts that had once been there had found better places to be and suddenly it was just me rattling around. Alone. Afraid to make my next move. Afraid to fly.

I held my arms out to my sides and shook them side to side, seeing if my wings worked.

Ready to spend some time with Ava and Mattie, I led Patty around to the pen behind the rectory-turned-library and saw that Opal was there which meant that Mattie was inside. A smile broke across my face. I situated Patty, who was very glad it was repair and report day and not another long haul through the wilds of Certain on the paths she was already tired of traveling. I gave Opal a pat before heading up the front steps to the library that had once been Daniel's house years ago. Daniel had recently made a lovely sign that hung to the right of the front door. Certain, Ky Library Est. here 1937. It had been quite an undertaking, moving the books from the church, where they used to be kept, to the house and the school desks and supplies from the house which Mattie had used as a school to the church, which was now the school, making the house the new library. Whew! We had two lines of folks moving things along one way and the next. Many hands make light work indeed. After all that we'd moved the beds that had once been upstairs out to Daniel's cabin where he had finished an addition to his old homestead knowing that Mattie would be coming to live with him as soon as they were married.

The best part had been seeing all the townsfolk come together to make it happen. Of course, Daniel had also made a sign for Mattie that now hung beneath the Certain Baptist Church sign. Certain School of Innovation Est 1936. He told her to give him a little time before she up and moved everything again.

"I'll give you enough time to build a proper school and then I'll ask you to change the sign."

"Deal" he'd said. "I think." He had winked at her. Daniel would do just about anything for Mattie. I wanted that one day.

I opened the door to the library and went in to the sound of Mattie and Ava talking from the kitchen. I could smell coffee and honey buns. Ava had been baking. That was always a good thing. I was glad we hadn't dismantled the kitchen. It made the library feel like a home.

"Ruby," Mattie said suddenly when she saw me, startling me just a hair. She thrust a newspaper at me. "Look what came in the boxes of books from Lexington."

I took the paper from her. It was dated January 30th. Today was April 12th. **F.D.R. Appoints Flood Commission** it read in bold black letters all the way across the top.

"It's about the flood in Louisville," I exclaimed the obvious and sat down quickly at the table with them so I could study the paper.

We got news from other cities whenever we were lucky enough to get it. Mr. Gibbons had had a subscription to both the *Lexington Herald* and the *Louisville Courier-Journal* but he'd let them go when things got hard. Not knowing things in a timely manner made us insular but in the regular run of the day it didn't seem to matter. We were Certain, Ky getting along as best we could. Besides, the last time we'd had a newspaper it had been run by Cole's father, Mack Cooper. He'd used that paper to ruin us. So opening it back up was not something anyone was keen to do even if the old printing press was still in there gathering dust.

When we did get an actual paper, it didn't matter if it was weeks or months old, we devoured it word for word, front to back and every inch in between.

I pointed to what Ava and Mattie had probably already read. "It says officials set the number of dead at 190." My heart sank. We'd all heard about the flooding of the Ohio River earlier in the year, but details were few and far between and probably not that accurate. "This is awful." I flipped through the paper skimming over the other things I would pore over later as I looked for more about the flood.

"There's a list of people who died," Mattie said and put her hand over her heart. "I don't know a one of them but just seeing their names breaks my heart."

"Look at this picture of all the people sleeping on cots," I said and turned the page to face them. They nodded having already seen it for sure, but they looked again and hurt along with me for the folks who were suffering.

Ava shook her head. "Doesn't life always kick you when you're down? Things are tough enough for people without getting washed up in a flood."

I placed the paper on the table and sat back. "That's all I can look at for a minute." Why was it that bad things happened in places where things were bad enough already?

We don't always understand God's plan, Ruby Bear. My gramma's voice came back to me clear as a bell. Sometimes I loved it when her voice rang so clear in my ears and sometimes it near about dropped me to my knees. I was glad it was a comfort this time seeing as how I was sitting here in the kitchen with eyes on me, even if they were the friendly sort.

Mattie piped up freeing me from my own mind. "Maybe we can get permission to donate some of the books we don't need any more to the worst of the areas hit. I'm sure they're not ready for that yet, likely still trying to get the basics back together, but one day they'll want their libraries filled up."

"Oh goodness," I said, the thought having not occurred to me. "Do you think they lost their books?"

"A good amount, I'm sure. I hear some of the towns along the river were all but wiped out. Water to the roofs."

The most surreal image of books floating down the streets and out to the river came to mind. My attempt to shake off the thought was aided by a sudden noise from outside the library.

"That's a car horn," Ava said, already standing up. "Who would stop outside the library and honk?"

Mattie jumped to her feet just as Marie and Ella, Daniel's oldest children, came bustling down the stairs and out the front door. I hadn't even known that Mattie's new stepdaughters were here. They must have come in with her from school. Both of them ready for any excuse to be at the library.

Mattie shook her head in an unnecessary apology. "We were supposed to stay in town and have a girl's day after school while Daniel and Hugh are fishing, but all they wanted to do was come to the library and read."

Ava beamed. "That's my nieces for you and isn't it grand?"

"I don't know what other day we'd have had anyway," Mattie said. "Not much to do here but read."

I smiled at the memory of me as a girl, always huddled up somewhere with a book, so much so that Cole used to call me Reading Ruby.

"We'll never get to our next adventure if you don't put that book down," he would chide.

"I'm on an adventure right now," I would say and shoo him away.

That was back when I thought I'd have him forever.

"I know that horn," Mattie said, bringing me out of my remembering and making a face I didn't know how to read. Good or bad, it could go either way. "It's my father," she said.

"Back already?" Ava questioned, clearly wondering if this was a good or bad thing. "He was just here for the wedding."

Mattie's eyes bugged out and she wiped her hands on her skirt. She stood up straight and blew out a hard breath.

"I don't know why I get so worried to talk to him," Mattie said. "I always feel like he's going to try to make me come home." She shook her head and laughed at herself.

"The kids sure seem to think it's a good thing that he's here," Ava said, trying to reassure Mattie it seemed.

Mattie patted Ava on the shoulder and laughed. "You do like to see the bright side. I suspect they're just as excited to see his fancy car as anything else."

Ava chuckled back and nodded her head. We all walked toward the door, Mattie in the front and Ava and me close behind like we were flanking her sides in case of emergency. Although what sort of emergency a wealthy father was, escaped me.

Mattie hesitated at the porch before taking the few steps down to the street. Dirt road as it were, but still. Ava and I followed. I had met Mattie's father at the wedding, but there was so much going on that day that I didn't really get a chance to talk to him. He seemed taller now than I remembered. His hair thicker and whiter. He didn't seem to mind Ella and Marie jumping all around.

"Where's that handsome little brother of yours?" Mr. Mobley asked, looking around as if Hugh might be in tow somewhere.

"He's off fishing with Da," Marie said and changed the subject. "Did you bring us anything?"

"Marie," Ella said her name in sharp shock, "That's not polite at all."

"It's just a question," Marie said and put her hands on her hips. "It's OK to ask questions. Momma Mattie done told us that in school, right?" She looked back at Mattie as if she'd expected her to be there, which she was.

Mattie shrugged at me. "I suppose I did."

I winked at her and reached out to take hold of her hand. I knew it made her nervous to have her father here. She wanted to impress him and to show him she was happy and well cared for. His showing up without notice was stressful for her. I could read it on her face. That's the way it was with friends.

"Pop," Mattie said and stepped forward. "Did I know you were coming?"

"Only if you're psychic these days," he said and pulled her into a hug.

Ava and I looked at each other and sighed. Whatever brought him back so soon after the wedding wasn't the end of the world.

Mattie looked around as if something was wrong. "Pop, where's your driver?"

"You're looking at him," he said, holding out his arms and smiling widely.

"You drove yourself here?" She looked around nervously as if danger was coming up the road behind him. "It's so long a ways and the roads are so awful."

"I love to drive," he said and pretended to tip an invisible hat. "Remember when you were little and we used to drive around on a Sunday afternoon to see what the rest of the folks were up to?"

Mattie nodded, but it didn't seem like it was a particularly good memory.

"Anyway," he said and cleared his throat. He went around to the trunk of the car from whence he pulled a small mahogany box about the size of both his palms put together.

Marie elbowed Ella. "See, he did bring us something."

"That ain't no more for you than it is for the man in the moon," Ella said and rolled her eyes.

"Ella," Marie said like an exasperated mother, "we have been over this a million times. There ain't no man in the moon."

Mattie's father burst into a fit of laughter then and once he'd revived himself from its throes, he handed the box out to Mattie. She looked confused but she took hold of it. Mr. Mobley held up one finger to the girls to signal them to wait a moment and then he winked at a still-confused Mattie. Mr. Mobley opened the box she held out in her hands and took out a shiny gold necklace with a small green stone dangling from inside a pendant at the end of it. He motioned Marie over and slid the necklace over her head. Marie's mouth fell open as she and Ella huddled together to look at the gem and the gleaming gold.

"And there's another in here for you, young lady," he said when Ella looked up to him, trying not to be obvious, but obviously hoping that she had a necklace coming too.

"I told you," Marie said and pressed the stone to her chest. She rushed to Mr. Mobley and threw her arms around his legs. "Thank you, Momma Mattie's father."

He burst into a new fit of laughter. "I do believe that I now hold the honored title of Grandfather if you would like to call me that."

I knew this made Mattie happy and when I threw her a look, she was already looking at me waiting to catch it. That she was already smiling at me before I had looked over at her struck hard in my heart. So much so that I took a step back from it. Me. She was looking at me, waiting for me to look at her, knowing I'd know how she felt and already waiting to share it with me. Such a pure and unplanned moment that I was a part of. I supposed I shouldn't have been so taken aback, I knew we were friends and that's what friends do, but I think up until that moment, I knew our friendship from my side of it. I knew her worth to me, but not mine to her. I should have, but in that moment, I realized that I hadn't. I felt connected where I had always assumed I was hanging on. The connection now was a thread I could feel. I could almost see it shimmering between us.

The girls squealing took me from my sweet reverie. And none too soon in case someone caught the water gathering in my eyes. Tomboys did not cry.

"Why don't you call me Grandpa Mobley," Mattie's dad was saying to the children. He then looked over at me. "And you Miss Ruby, how about a trinket for you?"

I was startled at his remembrance of my name. Sure, it had only been a short time that he'd been here for the wedding, and I suppose I was a person of honor in the wedding party, but still I was surprised that he called little old me by name. I was about to shake my head no and offer a nice decline, but then he pulled a pin from the box and held it out in his hand and so help me, I gasped. Whether they were real emeralds and amethysts, or costume gems didn't matter as in the palm of his hand he held a glittering green and purple stalk of lavender, smaller shoots branching out from the tall center, the whole thing about the size of my palm.

"I thought this was something that you would like," he said and winked at me.

"Yes," I stammered, wondering how he knew my fondness for plants like these. "I love it, but I couldn't accept it," I said, stepping back so I wouldn't be tempted to reach out and grab it like a hungry child spotting a biscuit.

"No thank you isn't an option," Mr. Mobley said and stepped closer. "It's a gift and a gift must be accepted."

I reached forward gently and took the brooch into my hand.

"Thank you, Mr. Mobley," I said, pressing the gemstone plant to my chest. I swear I could feel the lavender calming me already. Peace and grace.

I was just unfolding my fingers from the treasure to look at it again when Mattie spoke.

"Pop," she said and breathed in expectantly, "why exactly are you here giving out Mom's jewelry? I mean, don't get me wrong, it's a lovely gesture that I know she'd approve of, but…"

He held a hand up to stop her and sighed. "You never did shy away from being forthright."

"Which I get from you," she said, and her expression softened. She wasn't angry, just curious.

"Times are very lean," he said as if this was breaking news, "and I want you to have these both in memory of your mother and also as barter if you need it."

"Pop, these are worth a small fortune for sure," she said, "but you can't eat them and food's about all that anyone has need of bartering for these days."

He nodded and looked around as if he might spot some hungry people lining the street that would prove Mattie's point. Across the street, as if on cue, Mr. Gibbons opened the front door of the grocery and stepped to the side to let Mrs. Sully out into the sunshine. The bag she held was noticeably light and concern wrinkled her brow.

"Well," Mr. Mobley said and sighed again. "Perhaps there's something more I can do, but for now, please accept these."

"Thank you, Pop," Mattie said. "The memories alone will be worth more than you can know. Might I ask why you didn't bring them when you came to the wedding?"

He smiled and shook his head. "You got me again, young lady." He shuffled his feet which made Mattie frown as if she'd never seen such a thing. "Like I said, times are lean," he continued. "I didn't want to be tempted. I've brought them here for protection."

"From who?" Mattie said and closed the box as if that "who" was just behind her.

"From myself and the temptation to sell them," he said and looked at the ground. "This downturn has caught up with me after all. I hear tell from the President that things are getting better, and I sure hope that to be the case, but the hole I'm in is deep. I've been digging it for the better part of ten years now."

"But I thought you weren't affected by the crash," Mattie said and pulled the box of memories closer to her.

"I sure did my best to make it seem so, my dear," Mr. Mobley said, "But it's been many years of losing, a few of almost getting it back again, and then another kick in the pants with this recession as they call it. I didn't say anything at the wedding because it was your special day and," he paused, looking embarrassed, "I was trying to keep up appearances so no one would suspect anything. I've been good at that a long time now."

"Pop," Mattie said and handed me the box of jewels as she moved closer to him. "What are you saying? How bad is it? And why didn't you tell me this before the wedding. I never would have accepted those dresses and all the food you had sent in. Pop, I wish you'd told me."

"I didn't tell you, Pudding, because I knew you wouldn't accept the dresses and all the food I had sent in," he repeated with humor as if hoping she'd find it humorous too.

She didn't. I could tell by the way her hands went to her hips.

"You look just like your mother," he said, his eyes glistening.

Mattie reached back her hand and I knew she wanted the box. I knew she was going to give it back to him and so I dutifully put my lavender back inside and gave it all to her. Ella and Marie however clutched their necklaces to their throats.

Mr. Mobley put his hands on his hips and I saw who Mattie really looked like.

"I will not take that box and I will not take those jewels from off my grandaughters' necks, so don't you even try to convince me." He turned then to me. "Ruby, you take that brooch and you pin it to your overalls straight away."

I looked at Mattie, my eyes bugging out. She sighed and gave the box back to me. I wanted to open the box and grab the plant, but I didn't dare. I swear I could feel it wilting in the box, begging for the sunlight.

"Open that box and take the precious plant out before it dries up and withers away," Mr. Mobley said as if he could sense it too.

I opened the box and grabbed my sprig of lavender, almost able to smell it somehow. Across the street at the grocery Daniel raised his hand to get our attention. Little Hugh jumped from the wagon they'd pulled up in and was about to dash across the street, but Daniel caught him up in his arms.

Daniel was standing behind Mr. Mobley's line of sight and he made a gesture to question the man's appearance in town. I shrugged. This was not mine to gesture back about. Daniel set Hugh down and hefted a box from the wagon with one hand and with the other pointed at the store and I knew he meant for me to tell Mattie he'd gone inside.

"Da," Marie squealed seeing him and everyone looked across the street.

He waved and held up his finger to gesture he'd be right back.

"I was hoping to save face with my new son-in-law for a little longer than this," Mr. Mobley said.

Mattie reached out her hand and took his in hers. "Daniel is the last person to judge anyone for anything. Stay with us for a while."

"I don't have anything with me, I'll be ok. Let me go back and get some things taken care of and I'll be back in touch with you."

"Stay for dinner at least," Mattie all but pleaded.

Mr. Mobley looked like he was considering a great quandary. "It will be too dark soon to drive all the way back home, I suppose," he said.

I watched them go back and forth. It was obvious to me that the longer they volleyed the more Mr. Mobley really did want to stay. I wondered if he needed to stay. Want and need were two very different things. We knew that better than most. I looked to Mattie. What she said now would make all the difference.

"Next time," she said, and my heart sank for him, but then rose as she continued, "remember to bring some things with you. We'll make do tonight, but there's no way you're getting back in that clunker and driving all the way to Asheville today."

Mr. Mobley's eyes flashed relief for just a moment and then he pretended to puff himself up a bit in show. "Did you just call this fine piece of machinery a clunker, young lady?"

She smiled at him and winked at me. Included again.

"You're just in time to see the addition that Daniel has put on the house," Mattie said, pulling her father to her. "You'll have a bed to yourself and perhaps a half a moment's peace once the children stop jumping up and down with excitement."

"Are you staying, Grandpa Mobley?" Marie asked as excitedly as Mattie seemed to think she would.

"Looks like I am," he said, a broad and relieved smile etching across his face. "At least for the night."

I knew right then that Mr. Mobley was going to be Certain's newest resident even if he wasn't ready to accept it. Mattie hugged her father and although I was happy for her, my heart thudded with jealousy. Alone was hard. It called too much attention to itself and talked over you when you tried to make pleasant conversation about other people's good fortune.

I breathed in deeply and exhaled slow and quiet. I opened my hand to look at the lavender glittering there. While Mattie and the girls circled around Mr. Mobley, I pinned the jeweled plant to my dingy overalls. I pressed my hand to it as if I was hiding it for a moment. This pin was a sparkling representation of what I truly wanted and to have all the world see it, was a bit frightening. Maybe it just looked like a fancy piece of jewelry that happened to be in the shape of a pretty plant, but to me, pinning it on my chest meant that my foraging and my tinctures and my talk about medicinals and healing herbs was not just the hobby I pretended it was. It was an announcement of what I really wanted to be. A healer. A nurse. I didn't think I could be those things and to announce it so spectacularly seemed awful rash. Heck, there weren't any nursing schools around here and I sure couldn't go off to England to study to be a midwife like the nurses in the Frontier Nursing Service, or FNS, over in Hyden.

When I looked up, Ava caught me in her piercing blue-eyed stare. She winked at me, and the blue became the gorgeous sky and the jewels on my chest threw their color into it. Maybe I could dream about being a nurse at least. What hurt was there in that? I could imagine myself riding alongside one of the FNS nurses. Maybe as a courier. You didn't have to be trained as a nurse for that. I saw the nurses come and go all the time around here. It wasn't that far-fetched to think I could be part of it. Was it? I touched the pin on my overalls and imagined a bejeweled FNS patch alongside it. They weren't really bejeweled, but they might as well be for all I'd see one on my dingy overalls.

Chapter 6
Cole

Coming to town was always going to be a risk, but I'd decided to finally take it. I couldn't go on living along the creek just outside of town forever, dreaming of the day I might be accepted back into the fold. I knew once they saw me and assuredly once I said my name that I'd be run out again. It had been a pipe dream and I needed to face reality.

So my only actual option was to drop the deeds and the letter I'd written at the church and take my leave. I hoped for an empty street and a clear shot into the church and out. When I rounded the corner by the grocery store just across from the church I was stopped in my tracks. Outside the church and the parsonage was a whole passel of folks standing beside a fancy car. I quickly stepped back glancing left toward the old newspaper building. It was still there, but it looked closed. Memories threatened and I looked back across the street at the group of people. There was no way I was getting to the church unseen.

Then I spotted Ruby and panicked. I pressed myself up close to the exterior of the grocery store and watched. There was a sign up now that said the church was also a school and I could see another sign saying that the old parsonage house was a library. I suppose things had changed since I was here. But not Ruby. I'd recognize her anywhere even after all these years, but I really recognized her here in Certain. She was so Ruby here. So bright and wild and free. I still saw that. It looked like she'd made some friends since I left judging by the other women around her that seemed familiar and friendly with her. I'm not sure if that made me happy or sad. It wasn't like I wanted her to go friendless after I left or anything. That would be an awful thing to want. But I didn't want her to forget me.

That was the worst fear. Being forgotten.

I watched Ruby and the other ladies and some kids talking to an old man in a fancy car. Boy Howdy, my dad would have coveted the mess out of that automobile. The last time he'd gotten his hands on one though, he'd killed a lady. He liked to say he didn't, but I know he did. He'd been running a con over in Asheville at the time. I didn't know he was a con man then, I just thought we moved around a lot for his job. Which I guess was true.

He said he'd been waiting on an "associate" when he noticed the car sitting along the curb. He didn't know how to drive back then, but he thought he did. He thought he could do anything he set his mind to. Thing was, his mind was set to greed and that's about as close to being blindfolded to what's important as a man can get.

"I'd give anything to have an Overland," Dad had said that afternoon in town when he'd spotted the car along the street. I didn't know at the time that Overland was the make of the car. I didn't know what he was talking about.

"Take a spin with me, Cole," he said, raising his eyebrows and running his hand through his thick dark hair. I had that same hair now.

I had backed away. "But this ain't ours." I offered what I thought would be an obvious statement to bring him to his senses. I was naive back then. All little kids are.

He winked and whispered to me, "When has that ever stopped me?"

I looked up and down the street, willing the owner to come flying up to us and demand that we step away from his automobile, but no one seemed to notice us. They all went here and there and didn't so much as nod. I figured the owner was probably sitting up in some fancy office in one of the tall buildings along the street.

"Stop worrying over every little thing, Cole," Dad said as he opened the door and slid into the driver's seat, so slithery I almost heard a hiss. "Life is an adventure and today's adventure is taking this car for a drive."

I knew adventure. I lived for adventure. This was not adventure.

I shook my head and backed farther away as he pressed buttons and looked all around trying to figure out how to start it. He looked at me and gave a thumbs up and I knew he'd figured it out.

"Suit yourself, bucko," he said when the engine roared to life. "I'll take her for a ride and come back and get you. Be right here, you hear me?"

I nodded and he stepped on the gas. I waited there for him until after dark. My mother found me sitting on the curb eating an apple a passerby had given me thinking I was a street urchin. Mom didn't tell me what had happened, but I saw the papers the next day and read about the accident involving the wife of a prominent town citizen. There was a picture of the car taken from behind, but you could tell that the front was smashed in. I could also tell it was the car my father had stolen for his adventure. I don't know how he avoided jail other than we left rather suddenly and moved to Certain not long after. A town that no one would find even if they were looking. One of those towns no one wanted to be in for longer than it took to leave.

Except for me.

And that was how the universe turned itself around to deliver me Ruby. Or me to her. I wasn't sure. But the stars had aligned again, and I was back. OK, so it wasn't so much the stars sending me anywhere as it was my sense of duty and if I'm being honest, my exhausted loneliness. As much as Certain hated the Coopers, it was the last place I'd felt what love was.

Ruby was love. Sure, that sounded sappy, but sap was all I had left.

There was no hope of getting to the church with that group of people in front of it and I knew I wasn't ready to be face to face with Ruby, so I ducked into the old grocery store. It was largely as I remembered except the shelves were even more bare. It had never had much of anything, but now it had a little of nothing.

The bell dinged as I went in and I ducked. Strange reaction in hindsight, but telling, nonetheless. Right away I spotted Mr. Gibbons. He looked almost exactly like I remembered him. As if time had not pushed him here and there like it had me. Of course, I was only fourteen when I left and time turned differently between then and nearly thirty. Gibbons was that age where time had taken a break from showing its face on yours.

"Howdy do, son," he called and for a moment I took his greeting to mean that he recognized me, and my heart quickened in my chest. I was at the point of no return. But then he spoke again, and things changed. "Who do I have the pleasure of greeting in my store today?"

He didn't know who I was. Not being recognized wasn't in any of my scenarios. Then, before I knew what I was saying, a name that was not really mine fell out of my mouth. "Henry Hall, sir," I said and looked down to see the words rolling across the floor.

What was I doing? Telling lies the first chance I got. Like I hadn't learned a thing from my father. Or maybe I had, which was even more terrifying.

"Well, Henry, welcome to Certain," Mr. Gibbons said.

He winked at me and my heart galloped again. Taller and leaner than I had been when I left, my face covered in stubble from irregular shaving since I couldn't really see what I was doing, and fifteen years from child to adult might very well have left me unrecognizable. At least at first glance. I needed to get out of the store and back to the creek before this lie grew legs. This wasn't what I meant to do.

Before I could come up with something to say, a man and a small child came in the front door.

"Brought you another batch of Mattie's lotions, Mr. Gibbons," the man said. "One day maybe she and Ruby will go into business together."

"For now, I'm happy to have something new on my shelves," Mr. Gibbons said to the man and they occupied themselves unloading the little jars of lotion.

Grateful that someone was taking Mr. Gibbons' attention, I made myself busy looking at the sparse shelves, planning to sneak off as soon as it didn't seem weird.

"How's married life, Daniel?" Mr. Gibbons asked and clapped the man on the shoulder.

I couldn't see the man's whole face, but his smile was happy and wistful at the same time.

"As lovely as I remember it," he said, and I knew there was a story behind those words.

I picked up a box of saltine crackers and tucked it under my arm. As the men talked and the little boy who had let go of his father's pant leg ran around the store, I moved toward the big windows at the front. I couldn't stay in there much longer, but I was afraid to go back out. The lack of vehicles in the small parking area out front, save for the buggy that must have been Daniel's, gave me a full view across the street. I knew Ruby couldn't see me, but still I found myself looking sideways to watch her. Her hair, wild and frizzy as ever, blew up and off her shoulders as the small breeze came and went around her. She hated her hair back then and I wondered if she still did. I thought it looked like a soft, chestnut-colored cloud. I didn't dare tell her that for fear of her bursting out into a fit of laughter at my gushing. I watched her talk with the other ladies and the older man. I couldn't make out the words but just to watch her saying them gave me a thrill wondering what her voice sounded like now and if I would recognize it. She held something in her palm that kept catching the sunlight and tossing it back out in an array of colors that sparkled and danced. It was like she held magic in her hand.

"Henry," I heard a voice say and then say again with more urgency, "Henry?"

I looked up. It was Mr. Gibbons and he was talking to me. Or at least he thought he was.

"Sorry," I said and dragged myself from the window. "I was," but I didn't have anything in mind other than the truth of what I was doing, so I didn't say anything more. The truth could be a dangerous thing, especially if you were already caught up in a lie.

Mr. Gibbons didn't seem fazed by my stumbling. He just held out his arm to me and motioned me over.

"Daniel," he said, "Meet Henry. He's new in town. Or passing through." Mr. Gibbons tilted his head. "I didn't get his story. Nonetheless, here he is."

This Daniel held his hand out to me and I reached out and shook it. He was a might taller than I was and he had that look about him that suggested he could be a very different man from the smiling and friendly figure before me if he wanted to be. I hoped he didn't.

Mr. Gibbons kept up his introductions. "Henry Hall, this is Daniel Barrett."

I hoped my eyes didn't open wide in acknowledgment like they felt like they did. I knew that name. Barrett. I knew who this was. Daniel was a few years older than me, but I remembered him. I remembered Zachary and Liam and Ava and Emily. I had to bite my lip to keep from asking about them. I knew the story about his father and how he'd ended up living with Pastor Collins. He was near about grown and already going around with Emily by the time I was there. Is that who Mr. Gibbons was referring to him being married to?

Mostly I knew that people around here didn't care for the Barretts. Reduced to some old gossip and such by the time we got here. I bet Daniel was glad that the Coopers had taken the heat off his family. I hoped he'd had a happy life since I left.

Daniel nodded at me, "Welcome, Henry. How long you here?"

Gibbons elbowed him, but playfully. "Don't run the young man off already. Perhaps he's here to stay."

I passed the tin of crackers from one hand to the next trying to come up with what to say. I really should have planned this better. I should have had a line ready, like Dad always did. He was a smooth talker. I was not. Or I could have just told Mr. Gibbons who I was and why I was here. There was no scam in it. Just fear.

I cleared my throat and gave a truthful answer. "As long as y'all will have me."

That seemed to be the right answer as Mr. Gibbons clapped his hands together and looked at Daniel as if he'd won a bet. My underlying suspicion that they wouldn't have me for long had apparently not translated.

Daniel smiled and nodded and then opened the door to my next lie, which was not his fault of course. "So, Henry, what do you do?"

His little son, Hugh, as I had heard him call the boy, had run back over to him and Daniel scooped the boy up in his arms, holding him against his hip even though the little fellow was a tad too big it seemed.

All three of them, Daniel and Hugh and Mr. Gibbons, looked at me awaiting my answer.

"I'm a reporter," I said, appalled at the words passing over my lips. What on earth was I saying? And then I just kept talking. "I was over in Louisville doing a story on the floods which is what brought me back to Kentucky, my old home state, to check on some family," I lied again.

What? Was I out of my mind? A reporter. I had wanted to be one. I thought at first when my father bought that old printing press that I might see the dream of being a writer come true. I got to be a writer, but the dream was a nightmare. I should have stopped while I was ahead, or at least not too far behind, but I just kept talking.

"I finished the story some time ago, visited with family, and was headed out of town when my car broke down."

"Goodness' sake," Mr. Gibbons exclaimed. "Where is it?"

"A town over," I said, shaking my head like it was too much to go into. That was a trick I'd learned from my father for moving past a potential inaccuracy when you didn't know what you were talking about and someone else might. "I was walking along the road hoping to catch someone's attention, but I think I took a bad turn and got lost. Ended up down by the creek somehow." I shrugged and laughed at myself. Making yourself seem the fool causes people to pity you which makes them go out of their way to help you. Another trick from my dear old dad. I was starting to feel a bit sick to my stomach at how easily the act came to me.

What I needed to do most was shut up, but no, I just kept right on going. The little boy smiled at me like he was hearing a grand tale, which he was.

"I walked all the way across the water there," I said, pointing toward the creek I knew was off in the woods. "Got turned around again and ended up here. I was so glad to see a store that I rushed right in."

The little boy squirmed in his father's arms and spoke excitedly. "I like to walk in the creek too. There's all kinds of wigglers and things to catch if you're looking."

Mr. Gibbons drew in a breath. "You just walked into town right now?"

I nodded and sighed as if it had indeed been quite an ordeal just experienced. "Just now."

Daniel looked concerned. "And you have nothing with you? What happened to your belongings?"

This was the sort of thinking on your feet that Dad loved. It was making me a little nauseated. And I knew that the more I talked, the more they looked at my face, the greater the chance that they'd realize who I was.

"That's the darndest tale," I said, and let me say this, should anyone ever begin a story with that phrase, you can be darn tooting it's a big fat lie. "About the time my car broke down and I was standing out beside the road with my thumb in the air, a brand-new Ford Coupe came to a stop and out jumped two men who headed for me like they were my saving grace, calling out to me like I was in desperate trouble and they were there to help."

I paused to try and come up with the next part of the tall tale. When Dad had done that same pause, it was very dramatic and people leaned in closer, their breath held and their eyes wide. I didn't have said flair. My audience was more squinty-eyed than anything, but their faces told me that I still had their trust, at least for a few more well thought out sentences.

"Well, what happened, son?" Gibbons said, waving his hand for me to carry on.

Hugh wriggled away completely having lost interest in my lie perhaps or hopefully yet had become more interested in a basket of penny candy he saw from up high in his father's arms. With Hugh run off, Daniel folded those arms across his chest. They were formidable arms and I noted that I didn't want to be on the bad side of them.

"Well," I said and exhaled, "their demeanor caused me to let my guard down and step away from the car and into the road to greet them."

"And," Mr. Gibbons said in wait.

Daniel said nothing.

"And," I went on, "don't you know that they ran straight past me to the car, which was quite disorienting when you think you're about to meet in the middle and carry on a conversation, and they took my suitcase and my camera and even my hat that I had left sitting on the driver's seat and then they raced back past me and got into their car and drove off."

Daniel raised an eyebrow. "They ran right past you?"

"Oh, I know what you're thinking," I said, now listening to the story as if I was outside my own body, wondering just like Mr. Gibbons and Daniel as to what would come next in this tall tale of woe. "You're wondering why I didn't reach out to grab my things or at least chase them to their car as it did take them a moment to get my things inside it and leave."

Daniel nodded. "That is indeed what I'm thinking."

Mr. Gibbons was then looking back and forth between me and Daniel.

"Perhaps it was just my genteel upbringing," I said, inwardly shaking my head, amazed at the depth of my own deception, "but I was so flabbergasted at their actions that I was rendered motionless. Certainly, it was a joke." I paused again, coming to the end, which I had learned from Dad, required just one more line to invoke a much-needed sympathy if your grift had any hope of working. "Sadly," I said and put a pitiful look on my face, "the joke was on me."

"Let us help you retrieve your car at least?" Mr. Gibbons said, and my heart sank as I didn't think I could go any further with this lie.

Then like a sound from the heavens saving me, the bell over the door jingled yet again and all heads turned toward it. In walked a woman so beautiful that you'd think she was a Hollywood starlet. Her skin was creamy and clear, and her hair was red and it shone like a light was aimed at it. She was dressed as meagerly as the next person in Certain that I had seen so far, but she held herself in such a regal way that she might have been mistaken for wealthy.

Daniel cleared his throat and said, "I guess we'll have to hear more of your tale later."

I caught on the word "tale" and wondered if the word "tall" had been implied, but his voice had not given way to any sarcasm or scorn. This

Daniel Barrett was a tough one to read.

Mr. Gibbons motioned for the young woman to come over. "Claire, may I introduce you to Henry Hall," he said and nodded for me to extend my hand which she shook. A formidable shake. "He's a reporter from over in Lexington," Mr. Gibbons continued and I all but faltered on my feet. I had said Louisville, but that was a lie too so what did it matter? I'd been to Lexington, so that was true enough.

Claire's formerly neutral countenance turned into a smile. "A newspaper man," she said and stepped closer to me. She smelled of rose water. "We had a paper once."

"Did you, now?" I asked and started backing toward the door. The time for me to leave was long gone.

Mr. Gibbons clapped my shoulder and I literally jumped. "We're going to try to keep him," he said. I felt like a puppy found along the side of the road. Which, of course, was exactly what I was. "We've still got that old press. Perhaps we could convince him to stick around and start it back up?"

"The paper here was quite a fiasco," Claire said and the tension that fell across the room was palpable. "Surely you remember?"

"It's been a long time," Mr. Gibbons said. "Surely we're past old hurts and ready to move on."

Claire scoffed. "I don't think so," she said and then nodded her head at me. "Welcome to Certain, Henry," she said and before she went on about her shopping, she looked at Daniel and her smile faded a bit. "Daniel," she said to him firmly, aiming a steely glare at him.

"Claire," he returned and then nodded an obvious goodbye to me, "I'll see you around, Henry."

He turned back to Mr. Gibbons who had appeared back at the register. Daniel purchased a box that was prepacked with items and then nodded to me again as he called for his son and they made their way out the door.

Claire brought a couple of items to the register as well where she slipped little looks at me as her purchase was totaled and paid. She turned to leave without acknowledging me further. I let out a hard breath at not being recognized again. I remembered her well, though.

She had grown up pretty, but she still had that tough exterior that I also remembered. What I was gathering quickly was that if I remembered all these people, surely, they would remember me. The cover of anonymity was surely about to blow off.

Mr. Gibbons' voice brought me back as close to reality as I was going to get in the midst of this current deception. "Claire Thomas," he said. "She's not a fan of reporters. Last newsman we had around here really did a number on this town."

This had been a colossal mistake. I needed to get myself out of the store and fast. I remembered when Dad needed to make an escape, he did his best to get the other person to leave first.

"Say, I was wondering," I said, as if I really was, "Do you have any more of these saltines in the back? I could eat my weight of them."

"What you see is what we have," he said, then held up a finger as if something had occurred to him. "Wait here, I have something that you might like to pair with those dry old things." He turned then and went behind a curtain that likely led to the storeroom.

I knew I might only have a moment or two tops, so I put the tin of crackers I had on the counter and made haste for the door. Outside, I saw that Daniel and Hugh had joined the crowd of people. I ducked my head and turned my face away from them as I hurried around the corner and back toward the creek.

My disappointment at flubbing up the visit to the grocery told me just how much I'd really wanted to be able to come home again after all. All my work to convince myself I could just drop the deeds and leave was just fooling myself. But one thing I knew for sure was that Certain didn't want a Cooper conman back in town and I had just shown my colors. Which was the greatest disappointment of all.

Chapter 7
Ruby

Spring had finally triumphed over the lingering fingers of winter and the world was green and glowing again. Ava and I were back in the library making scrapbooks and catching up on things. We usually sat around the kitchen table, but we had been busy in the fiction section shelving new books and just ended up sitting on the floor by the new shelves that our own personal carpenter, Daniel, had crafted. He had tried to argue with Ava that he didn't have time to make new bookshelves, but he was all talk. He would build a whole new library if Ava or Mattie asked him to. I didn't need a man to build me a library, but I did hope for one who would value me the way Daniel valued Mattie.

"The pin looks lovely on you," Ava said as she hand-stitched a scrapbook together with a leather thread she had fashioned from an old hat band. "I love the way it catches the light."

"I think it looks silly pinned on my overalls," I said and laughed at myself. I might have thought that, but it didn't stop me from wearing it and overalls were the staple of my wardrobe.

"Nonsense," she said and waved her hand at me. "It's actually just the adornment they need."

I touched the gemstone sprig of lavender that Mr. Mobley had given me and marveled at Ava's ability to always see the best of things. It was silly for me to pin the brooch to my dingy denim but I, too, loved the way it caught the light and I couldn't imagine leaving it at home in the drawer all by itself. Such a beautiful thing should be allowed out.

The front door flew open and Mattie stumbled in carrying a box that was almost too big to fit through the door. She nearly stepped right on me.

"Goodness," she said, startled, "what are you two doing in the floor?"

"Reliving our youth," Ava said, setting the scrapbook down beside her and making a pretend show of struggling to get up. "If Ruby will help me up, I'll help with that box."

"That box I've already managed to get inside," Mattie said, laughing.

"That's the one," Ava said.

I never knew what to think about Ava. She was so solemn sometimes and so full of humor at others. She had a long story to tell and no one to tell it to it seemed. One day, we'd get her to open up.

Mattie dragged the box more fully into the room and we all stood around it.

"Well," I said, nudging it with my toe for effect, "What's in it?"

"I don't know," Mattie said, looking concerned.

Ava and I both stepped back and Mattie harrumphed at us. "It's nothing dangerous," she said and laughed. "It's addressed to my father."

"And what address is that?" I asked, seeing as how he had been "staying a little while" for quite a while now.

"It was sent here to the library, but under his name," she said. "I don't even know that I have an address." She wrinkled her brow, having never really thought about it, it seemed. She then moved her hands out in front of her as if making the words that came next appear in the air. "Perhaps my address is, The Barretts, The Other Side of the Hell for Certain."

"And Mr. Mobley?" Ava asked. "Is he staying at that address as well?"

"Why do I think that whatever is in this box will answer that question," Mattie said.

"I bet it's all his underwear," I said and burst out laughing which made Ava burst out laughing. I loved when I could make her laugh.

"Dear Lord, I hope not," Mattie said. "Besides, it's way too heavy."

"It could be a lifetime supply," I said.

"Stop it," Mattie said and playfully pushed me. I loved it when she did that. "You're the worst." Which meant I was the best and I loved when she did that too.

"Yes, please," Ava said and put her hands to her cheeks. "No more talk about Mattie's father's underwear."

I smiled knowing I had made them both happy.

"New topic, then," Mattie said and pushed the mystery box aside. "Did you all hear about the newspaper man we have in town? Doing a story on something, I think?"

Ava's head popped up from where she was examining the box. "In this town?"

I was equally as incredulous. "Not possible. We've got all of twelve people in Certain. That will never warrant a story."

Ava waved her hand at me, shooing away my exaggeration. "There are probably more than twelve people here in town right now."

I raised my eyebrow. Who was exaggerating now. "OK, perhaps the population is more like fifteen."

Ava waved me off.

I looked at Mattie who just stood there looking back at us. "Well," I said, "tell us more about this mystery reporter and what his story is."

"Tea first, I need to sit down," she said, looking a little piqued. "Then gossip."

"Obliged," I said, already heading for the kitchen to get the kettle going. "Open that box," I called back over my shoulder.

In the kitchen I set about getting our tea ready. A mystery man in town, huh? And ever so coincidentally, I had run across another mystery man along the creek. The town wasn't big enough for two mysteries at once. Could that same man still be around?

I couldn't get the notion out of my mind that it was Cole Cooper I had spotted along the creek. I'd been too chicken to go back and check. Mostly because I didn't want to find out I was wrong. If I didn't check, it could still be him and he might still come to town to see me. It was more likely a drifter, maybe even a dangerous one and it was best that I didn't let my curiosity get the best of me. And if it was Cole, what did it mean that he hadn't come to see me?

Besides, what on earth would Cole be doing back in Certain after everything that had happened to send his family running for the hills? That had been Certain's darkest hour, at the time anyway. The town had almost folded after what we called the Cooper Debacle of '22. I wanted it to be him, though. So badly. The man I had seen at the creek was a far cry from the boy I'd hoped would return to me right in that same spot the night his family had left town. This man was taller and broader. His face rougher and his jawline more rigid. But I had a feeling that if I was close enough to see them, that his eyes would still be as soft and gray-blue as they ever had. I had noticed he held his hand to his chest when he walked and didn't use it to unbutton his shirt as if the hand was injured. I shook the shirt removal out of my mind and I wondered what might have happened to his hand. The more I thought about the man, the more I turned him into Cole in my mind.

The tea kettle screamed and near about scared me to death. I rushed to take it off the stovetop and managed to bang it into one of the teacups which almost fell to the floor but I caught it in time.

"You OK in there?" Mattie called out.

Not really, but it didn't have much to do with the tea.

"I'm fine," I called. "So, what was in the box?"

Mattie and Ava came into the kitchen then with their arms loaded with books. Not a surprise, but these were strange-looking books. Mysterious and formidable. Some of them were thick and big like you might uncover in the dusty basement laboratory in a horror novel. *The Island of Dr. Moreau* maybe or *Frankenstein* perhaps. Books that held the secrets of science and maybe even how to see beyond them. I could feel my skin tingling with a sudden excitement.

"My father's personal collection per the note inside," Mattie said, setting the books down on the table. The thud rattled through the floor and all the way up to the teacups on the counter. "I had no idea he had these. No wonder that box was so heavy."

"Your father's collection?" Ava asked. "Who sent them if he's here?"

Mattie shook her head and relaxed down hard into a chair. She sighed heavily as if she'd been working all day. "I imagine he got the housekeeper to send them." She tilted her head. "If he still has a housekeeper. Or a house. I'm not really sure."

"Is your father a doctor?" I asked, reaching right away for an odd-looking volume on the top. "*Bilz, Nouvelle Methode*," I said, realizing after I said it, that the e on the end of that last word was probably silent. "New Method," I said, opening it up to reveal pages like I had never seen in a book, especially like this. It had pages that folded up and out and all of them were alive with vivid color drawings of the human body inside and out. It was terrifying and enthralling all at the same time. "It's in French," I exclaimed, realizing that as well.

"How do you know French?" Mattie asked.

"I don't," I said, rather disappointed that I wouldn't be able to read the book. "But it looks like French." I turned the book around to her and she nodded in agreement.

Ava looked over my shoulders as I flipped the pages. "Look at that," she said and pointed. "Open them."

There was a page like a children's flip book but the flaps to open were things like a picture of a person's ear and eye and other parts. When I pulled the flap back on the eye it opened to show the muscles around the eye and across the nose and on the opposite side it was the eyeball and the blood vessels and the duct through which tears escaped. This particularly fascinated me, to be able to see inside of what I only knew from the outside.

"Too much for me," Ava said and closed it.

While Ava and Mattie pushed the books to the center of the table so they could place their teacups, I reopened the inside cover of the Bilz's book. The whole cover was another fold-out. It was the whole body and all its systems apparently. The top flap opened to a rosy-cheeked man with an upturned mustache. He seemed quite at peace with the fact that you could open him up and see everything that was inside.

"Put that dreadful thing away," Mattie said, making a dour face.

I closed it and picked up another right away. A thick book with a dark cover and the word *Vitalogy* written in gold letters in a fancy and flourishing script. On opening that one it too was filled with glorious drawings of the workings of the human body, more flaps to open and wonderful pages of how to do various things like wrap a wound or set a break. Flipping quickly through it there was also a section on medicinal plants. I was so excited; I could barely contain myself. I turned back to the front inside pages, and it read "Adapted for Home and Family Use." And it was in English! This book and I were going to be new best friends. I held it out to Ava and Mattie showing them how wonderful this one was too.

"It's fascinating," I said, pointing to a picture of human lungs and intestines. "Don't you think? To be able to see all the ways that things work."

"I rather think it takes the poetry out of the human form," Ava said. "I'd prefer to imagine something far more magical working inside us."

I couldn't have disagreed more which I showed by shaking my head. "On the contrary, this is poetry and magic and meaning all at once."

"Sounds like you should be a doctor then," Mattie said and winked.

I drew in a quick breath like someone who'd been found out. But hearing it said out loud that I might be a medical professional and it not be said like a joke was strangely intoxicating. I closed the book and held it to my chest like it was a most beloved book from my childhood.

Ava and Mattie looked at me with raised eyebrows as if they were waiting for me to tell them when I was going to open my practice. I was getting a little heady, so I changed the subject.

"Tell me more about the reporter," I said and set the book on the table, reluctantly letting it out of my arms. "What story is he covering in Certain of all places? Twenty ways to use flour and water to make a meal?"

"Daniel said he met him at the grocery the day that Pop came into town," Mattie said. "Maybe he was buying flour to test his list."

"That's been a while ago," I said.

Ava elbowed me and winked at Mattie. "Was he young and single and looking for a wife who likes books and reading French medical texts and may or may not know what to do with flour and water?"

I blushed. "Stop it," I said. "I'm no more looking for a man than a wasp's nest."

"Daniel said he looked familiar," Mattie said. "And apparently, he's injured or something. He had something wrong with his arm or hand. I forget." Mattie said and then took in a deep breath as if all the talking had worn her out.

My head was buzzing. Certainly, it wasn't true. Could I have been right?

"Are you OK?" Ava asked and reached her hand across the table to touch Mattie's.

"I'm just tired," Mattie said and smiled weakly.

Amid my ridiculous growing hope about the man along the creek, I made a note to myself to look in the medical books for information about fatigue.

"Anything else?" Ava asked. "We haven't had a new face in town since you."

"And Mr. Mobley," I said.

"Daniel said he had a bit of a curious story," Mattie said, sipping her tea and taking forever to tell it. If she weren't my best friend, I would have been very irritated. Instead, it was only irritatingly endearing. "Something about ending up here after having been robbed and lost his transportation and belongings and was just now arriving in town."

"So he's been here for several weeks then?" I asked.

My heart thudded in my chest suddenly. Stranger in town. Young. Injured hand. Now that I thought seriously, I had the sinking suspicion that I knew who this reporter was, or at least where he was.

"Where is he staying?" Ava asked as if she could read my thoughts.

"I don't know," Mattie answered. "Daniel said that the conversation was interrupted when Claire came in and he didn't catch the rest of the story."

"Claire," I said and rolled my eyes. "She's like a bad penny. What is this man's name by the way?" I asked.

"Henry Hall," Mattie said.

My breath caught in my throat and my heart banged around so hard in my chest I thought it would rattle its way down into my stomach. The mystery of who he was was solved. A new mystery of what on earth he was doing had begun.

Oh Cole, I thought, at least come up with a new alias from time to time.

Chapter 8
Cole

I loved May in Certain. If nothing else in the world was certain at all, I could count on green leaves, singing birds, and little wildflowers along the creek bank. I could count on new beginnings. I had thought this would be one, but the other thing I could count on was me to mess it up. Of that I really was certain.

I was out of supplies and had needed to go back into town something fierce, but I'd put not only my foot in my mouth the last time I went, I had put my whole shoe and shoe shining kit with it. Henry Hall newspaper reporter. What on earth? I could have at least come up with a new name. If word got out that Henry Hall was in town my cover was blown for sure. Ruby would recognize that name anywhere. It was my alias in our club The Hell for Certainers. Our motto of Adventure First; Reason Never had caused us to make up fake names in case, well, in case of in case. Hers was Daphne Dandelion. A smile spread across my face just thinking about the name.

"Daphne Dandelion?" I had asked, trying very hard not to laugh. Mostly because she would think I was laughing at her, but really, I thought it was the cutest name I'd ever heard and I was trying very hard not to let her know that I thought she was the cutest everything I'd ever seen.

"I'll have you know," she said as we sat along the creek just two weeks after my family had come into town and she'd been the only kid at school to talk to me, "that the dandelion is one of the most under-appreciated plants. And," she said standing up so that I had to shade my eyes to still see her against the sun, "Did you know that the dandelion is also rather delicious? I bet you didn't know that, did you, city boy?"

I was not a city boy and no, I did not know that people ate dandelions. I didn't know much of anything about dandelions for that matter other than they were a weed.

"Where did you learn that?" I asked. Ruby was clearly the smartest and the prettiest girl in all of Certain.

"Teacher told me," she said and cocked her head at me as if I should know that that alone made her special. I didn't need convincing though. "If you decide to come to school, she might teach you a thing or two as well."

I was only twelve then and hadn't had the chance to go to school for long enough in any one place to learn much of anything. School seemed pointless to me. I could read thanks to my momma and that's pretty much all I thought I needed to know.

I stood up then and walked closer to the creek. "Tell me more about dandelions," I said and tossed a rock into the water. I didn't want to talk about school anyway. School was where people got to know you and you got to know them and knowing people had never done me a lick of good. The less people knew me, the better, and I them.

While I tossed rocks into the water, she launched into a list of things that made dandelions special. "People say they're a weed, but they're very versatile. You can eat them. You can roast the roots and make coffee, and they're used in home remedies for all sorts of health benefits," she said, clearly happy to be telling someone all about her namesake and I was happy to hear her talk about anything at all. "Now, most of that I learned from my gramma."

I nodded at her happily, eager for more plant facts, but her face got solemn then and she said, "I live with my gramma. She's not really my grandmother. My parents are dead, so she says." The sad look left her eyes, but not before I'd seen it. "I know I'm loved though, so it's not all bad."

I knew right then and there that my purpose in this world was to make Ruby happy. I didn't ever want to see that look on her face again.

I had failed at my mission all those years ago. Remembering it made me feel like a fool, but it also strengthened my resolve to do better this time.

"So, what's your club nickname going to be?" she asked me back then.

"Henry Hall," I said and stood up proudly. I liked the way it sounded, the letters rolling off my tongue like warm water.

"That's boring," she said and smiled at me.

The insult and the endearing gesture together confused me. "Pardon me, Miss Dandelion, I guess you'll leave me here by the creek to die of dullness." I had said feigning my ridiculous demise. I knew how to put on an act from watching and listening to my father.

"I didn't say you were dull," she said. "I said your fake name was boring."

"I don't understand you."

"Good."

We were twelve and finding our voices then, figuring out who we were, what our humor and heart and heads were all about. Like parrots, we were trying on the big words and sophisticated adult talk we heard at home and around town. Figuring out what everything meant.

In just a couple of years, I would leave Ruby waiting for me in that very spot the night my family fled town. Just before we'd been run off, my mother had been reading me *Frankenstein* by Mary Shelley. Mom had said she liked that it was written by a woman, but in hindsight I wonder if she thought me and her to be like Frankenstein's creation, Dr. Cooper's monsters who just wanted to live peaceful lives but were caught up in the terrible game of it all. Maybe she knew we'd soon be run out of town by angry people with pitchforks or something like it.

Why she put up with my father all those years, I don't know. Why she went back to him after we got away some years later, I especially don't know. I didn't understand her any more than I did him. Somehow her betrayal, at least that's how I saw it, was more hurtful and demoralizing and if I was being honest, I don't think I ever got over it. I think I was afraid of things that most people aren't afraid of because of the way she chose him over me. Maybe that's dramatic, maybe not, but as a child that's the way it felt. I put that out of my heart. I'd have to ponder over that later.

My whole life had been a game we were playing at it seemed. I didn't know much about grown-ups when I was twelve, but I could spot pretending. But with Ruby, our interactions didn't feel like lying or pretending. It felt like being seen. Like I could say any silly or boring–for that matter–thing and I didn't have to convince her or impress her. She was showing me how to imagine another life, another name, another me. One I created, not one that was pressed upon me.

I had a sudden revelation there on the edge of the Hell for Certain Creek. There was imagination for good and there was imagination for evil. It came from the same creative ability, but one was dark and one was light. And it was all a choice. I didn't have to be Cole Cooper, maybe I could be Henry Hall. Maybe I was still pretending technically, but I was pretending in that way you do when you're trying to figure out who you really are, not who someone else says you are.

There was a chance I was still trying to figure that out and as usual, I'd flubbed it up. It would probably be for the best if I just gave up the idea that I might make things right in Certain and just head on out of town. Coming clean and finding forgiveness was about as much a pipedream as anything. There was no way I could go back into town after my tall tale about being a big city reporter. The best I could do was sneak in, drop off the deeds on the church steps and hope someone found them. Hopefully I'd be long gone by the time they did.

"You've fouled it up from the get-go as usual," I said to myself.

I dragged my rucksack up from the ground and pulled it up. I reached up to the makeshift clothesline I'd strung between two trees and yanked down my extra set of trousers and jammed them, still a little damp from where I'd washed them in the creek, into the bag.

Still talking to myself I said, "You really shouldn't pack wet clothes into your bag."

"No, you really shouldn't," another voice that was not mine said and I jumped sky high like a scared cat.

Once I righted myself, my injured hand very dramatically over my heart which was the kind of exaggeration I'd picked up from my father and truly disliked, I saw Ruby standing amid my campsite with her hands on her hips.

"Ruby, what are you doing here?" Was my clever response.

"I believe that's my question to you," she said, using the toe of her booted foot to nudge my rucksack where I'd tossed it in surprise. "Welcome to town, Mr. Hall."

She tilted her head at me, gave a crooked smile, and stuck out her hand for me to shake. I couldn't read her at all. Had the years been that long that I couldn't tell if this person who had once been my one and only true friend knew me or not.

"It's me, Cole," I said, leaving her hand outstretched. I wanted very badly to take hold of it but didn't trust myself not to pull her closer.

She lowered her hand and put it back on her hip. "I know it's you, silly," she said and rushed forward to grab me in a hug.

I don't mind admitting that that hug just about broke me. In all the best ways, I mean. I knew with my head and even with half my heart that it had been a while since someone's arms had been around me. And I don't mean in a romantic way. I mean at all. But when I felt the warmth of Ruby's arms squeezing me like she'd been right here waiting for me all these years, like hugging me was the thing she'd most wanted to do in all her life, I knew that really it was me who had been waiting all these years and it was me who needed to be held more than I needed anything else in the world. I leaned in and pressed my face into her hair and breathed in the smell of rosemary and lye and clean crisp air and Ruby and home and if she felt a couple of tears roll across her collar bone, she didn't call me out on it.

After we let each other go, she just looked at me and smiled and shook her head and smiled and shook her head some more. It was a moment before she spoke again.

"I don't know where you think you're going, Cole Cooper, but it best not be away again," she said looking at my bag packed haphazardly with my things.

I stammered, mostly to make sure my voice worked and then tried to answer with some cover story but all that came out was the truth or part of it at least. "I don't have anywhere else to be."

"Well," she said with a sigh, "I must admit I was coming here to let Henry have it. But then I got here and well," she stammered a little too and reached out for my good hand. "I found my Cole."

My Cole.

If she was trying to knock me on my knees it was about to work. Here I thought I had built walls up around my heart, that I was tough as steel, and whatever other nonsense I convinced myself of. Turns out those walls were made of feathers and that steel was soft sand.

"It's just me," I said and shrugged my bad arm, careful not to give her any reason to let me go. "Guess you heard about Henry Hall, big time reporter?"

She twisted her mouth and raised her eyebrow at me. "I always told you that was a boring name. Guess your little story in town spiced it up a bit."

I wanted to ask her so many things. What happened after we left? How long did she wait for me before she gave up and went home? How much did she know about what my father had done? How could she smile at me now as if nothing had happened?

But I didn't really want the answers to those things. At least not right then. I just wanted to be in that moment where everything was good and easy. But it didn't last long.

Ruby's face grew solemn and she let go of my hand. "Where did you go?"

I was about to answer, but she put her hand up to stop me.

"No," she said. "Don't tell me that now. You're back and let's just go from there. Unpack your stuff. You're not going anywhere."

I looked at my bag and then back at her.

"Now?"

"Of course, now," she said. "Hang those things back up to dry. They'll get all stinky and moldy if you leave them in there wet."

I just stood there looking at her. She lifted her hands up at me as if to tell me to get a move on. I did. Once the clothes were hung back up, she looked around at my campsite.

"Well, this won't really do," she said. "I know you've been here going on a couple of months now."

I was shocked. "You do?"

"You can't leave again, but you can't stay here," she said looking around as if an answer to my dilemma was just through the trees somewhere. "Especially in the summer. It's much too hot. As you well know. It really will be Hell for certain."

I opened my mouth to say something, although I didn't know what. She just kept talking.

"And with your hand hurt like that, you really need some medical assistance."

"Is there a doctor here?"

"No, but we did just get a shipment of medical books and one of them has several pages about wrapping an injured arm. We have to get it set so that it can heal properly." She held out her hand to me. "Give it here," she said, and I lifted my hurt hand out to her. She took it gently in her hand. "Can you move your fingers?"

She touched my fingers with hers and I all but shivered.

"All of them but my thumb, but it hurts to move any of them really."

She sighed heavily as if she was considering what the trouble may be. "I'll have to read about this."

I nodded for lack of anything better to do. I just watched her looking at my hand and the terrible dirty wrap I had on it. I couldn't believe that she was standing there with me. She was different, but still so much the same.

"Ruby?"

"Yes," she said without looking away from my hand.

"I'm sorry."

I wanted to launch into everything that had happened that night once I told her I'd be right back and everything that had happened in the fifteen years since, but I couldn't get anything else to come out.

She looked up at me, still cradling my hand. Her eyes were at the same time forgiving and full of hurt. My heart almost broke over it.

"I imagine so," she said matter-of-factly. "I waited for you here a long time."

I closed my eyes and blew out a hard breath.

"First things first," she said, apparently closing the topic of way back when. "We need to take care of that hand. And we need to find you somewhere to stay that has walls and a roof."

She let go of my hand slowly so it wouldn't drop suddenly. I wanted to reach back out for her, but she stepped back from me and I knew she was about to leave.

"It's good to see you again, Ruby," I said, trying to keep her there and trying to see if she thought the same of me.

She put her hand on her hips as if she was mad, but her eyes welled up with hurt tears which was far worse.

"I'll be back tomorrow with a fresh wrap and a few books, and we'll see if we can get your hand back in shape."

"OK," I said. I supposed that was better than nothing.

She pointed her finger at me and spoke like she was scolding a child. "You better be here, Cole Cooper. Do you hear me?"

"I'll be here, Ruby," I said softly. "I promise."

I had promised her the last time, but I had broken that promise. I hadn't meant to, but it was a bust all the same.

Just to make sure that she knew I knew all of that, I added, "Come hell or high water. I will be right here."

She nodded back at me and I could see the hope and fear in her eyes. She turned and went back through the brambles and bushes. I heard a horse whinny and neigh somewhere in the distance. I was going to be right here when she came back. I just hoped she did.

Chapter 9
Ruby

I wanted to run right back to the creek as soon as I got out of bed the next morning, but I told myself that I was not going to be that girl. And on the practical side, I did want to look at a few of the books Mr. Mobley had sent and see if I could get an idea of at least how to bandage up Cole's hand. He'd need to tell me more about what happened and what his mobility and pain were before I could really know how to move forward, but a good wrap was a good start.

At the library I hunted for *Vitalogy*, the book with the page on how to properly wrap an injury. I needed to make a special section for all the medical books instead of leaving them piled in the kitchen like I did. Mattie said they gave her the creeps and made her sick to her stomach to see all the insides of everything. She very politely hinted, in her very polite Mattie way, that they might up and disappear if they didn't find a home out of the kitchen soon. I figured there was no time like the present. Of course, I knew I was stalling a bit because I wanted to get my heart and head straight before I went out to the creek. Cole was back. Cole was home again.

I was just gathering an armload full of books to take upstairs when Ella, Mattie's oldest stepchild came running into the kitchen yelling.

"Aunt Ava? Ruby?" She was breathless. She even looked right at me but didn't seem to see me. "Is anyone here?"

"Ella?" I called out, suddenly as hurried and obviously frantic as she was. I put the book down and rushed out into the main room where she'd gone. "What's wrong?"

She bumped right into me like she didn't even see I was there. "Momma Mattie fainted," she said. "Right in the middle of class."

"What happened?" I shouted a little too loud. "Never mind, let's go."

We raced out the door and straight to the church where the school met on weekdays. Ella ran fast enough that she passed by me and opened the door so we could both burst through.

I could see Mattie laying on the floor by the blackboard that Daniel had built her. He'd bartered his carpenter time over in Hazard in exchange for an old blackboard that he shored up with a new frame. My heart fell right out of my chest. I was in such a rush to get to her that I just left it right there on the floor.

"Mattie," I shouted and the kids that had circled near her moved away like Moses was parting the waters. I all but slid in beside her. "Mattie," I called again but she didn't rouse up. I could tell right away she was breathing and all, but she didn't seem to hear me.

"Ella," I said firmly but not harshly. "Find me a pillow."

She took off running back to the library. I lifted Mattie's head and put it in my lap. I looked around at the scared faces of the children in her class. Marie, her other stepdaughter was there, Ava's kids and a few others from here in town and up farther into the hills. Mattie had about twelve kids in total and they all looked scared to death.

"Everything will be alright," I said to them hoping that my words sounded more confident in their ears than they did in mine. "Why don't you all go outside for a moment. Adeline," I said to Ava's daughter, "can you go across the street and tell Mr. Gibbons that Mattie needs Daniel right away."

"Yes, ma'am," she said and darted out the door.

A few moments later Ava came rushing in as well. "I've already sent

Liam out to Daniel's," she said. "I just saw Adeline."

I sighed a little bit of relief knowing that Liam would ride like the wind itself and be back with Daniel before we knew it. Ella came in with two pillows.

"For good measure," she said and held them out to me.

"Thank you," I said and pointed to Mattie's legs. "Put them under her feet. We want to raise them up higher than her heart." I scooted out from under her head and placed it gently on the floor to lower the front half of her body down.

"Will that help?" Ava asked, nervousness making her voice so quiet I almost couldn't hear her.

"It will," I said, feeling more confident. "I read it in one of the books and it feels like the right thing to do."

Ava nodded her head at me and it felt like a vote of confidence. "Yes, that seems good. Smart thinking."

Ella stood there with her hand over her mouth looking terrified and just as I was about to ask her to go check on the children, Mattie asked her for me.

"Sweetheart, go make sure the other children are OK," Mattie said in a voice so tired you would have thought it took all she had to get the words out. Perhaps it did. "Tell them I'm fine."

Ella burst into tears and instead of going out she practically fell beside Mattie and hugged her around the waist as best she could. My heart ached for her knowing what she must be feeling, the fear of losing another mother that she had just started to really know. Mattie stirred around enough to put her own arms around Ella.

"I'm OK, baby," she said and rubbed the back of Ella's head. "You're not rid of me so easily."

Ella's muffled voice answered from against Mattie's dress, "I don't ever want to be rid of you, Ma."

I heard a little gasp escape Mattie and my heart leapt for her. She had told me how she longed for the children to call her Mother instead of Mattie or Mamma Mattie and this was the first time one of them had. And Ma, no less. Just like they called Daniel, Da.

I touched the top of Mattie's head to let her know I had heard it, too.

71

"I think I can sit up now," Mattie said, already pulling herself up before anyone could tell her otherwise.

"Go slow," Ava said and looked at Mattie quizzically. "Mattie, have you eaten today?"

"No," she said, pulling herself up to a fully seated position. "I just feel so nauseated lately. Nothing looks good. I'm so tired. I think I might have the flu."

Ava and I looked at each other knowingly. She more than I, because mine was all book knowledge, but nonetheless. We both squealed and Mattie startled so hard we were afraid we'd make her faint again.

"You're pregnant!" We both shouted as the doors to the church flew open and Daniel rushed in with Liam hot on his heels.

Daniel stopped short. "What?"

"It's probably the flu or some bug or something," Mattie said, but she looked around at me and bit her lip. "I mean, we've only been married two months and it would take longer to show right."

Daniel sat down on the floor beside her. His smile was so big it almost went off the side of his face.

"I always knew right away," Ava said, smiling too. "And I was sick as a dog by two months in."

Mattie reached for my hand and squeezed it. "Ruby, what do you think? You've read all those books cover to cover."

I grinned bigger than the Cheshire cat. "You're tired, woozy, sick to your stomach. You probably fainted because your blood pressure dropped too low. That's something you'll need to watch. You don't want to go falling down when you're out to here." I said and held my hand in front of my stomach at about the six-month size.

Mattie breathed in deeply through her nose and blew it out through her mouth. "I don't want to get ahead of myself."

I knew how much she hoped for a baby. "And right away if God is willing," she had said. I knew Daniel was building on to the cabin to accommodate his growing family. Of course, now Mattie's dad was living in the new room. Oh well, that could be sorted out later. For now, I was ecstatic for her.

"You're pregnant sure as shooting, I bet all my books on it," I said.

I didn't realize it, but the kids had come back in and now they were all jumping up and down and carrying on.

"I have got to get off this floor," Mattie said, and Daniel jumped up to be of assistance. He reached out to her and gently helped her to her feet. She tottered just a little and he held on tighter.

"Let's get you to a proper chair and take a rest," he said looking around. "Where is a chair?"

She pointed to her desk chair and started to head that way.

"That won't do," he said and looked at Liam. "We need one that's comfortable."

Liam snapped his fingers and looked around, smiling. "Didn't work. Zachary and I will bring one from the homestead. I'm sure someone has a spare."

"There's a lovely chair in my living room that she can have here," Ava said. "You'll need a better chair in here going forward."

"You all are making too much fuss," Mattie said. "We don't even know for sure yet." She looked at Daniel. "How did you get here so fast? Was I out that long?"

"I was already mostly here when Liam ran into me," Daniel said and looked at me worried. "Was she out long, Ruby?"

I shook my head. "Not long."

Mr. Mobley came running in at that moment, calling for Mattie.

"I'm over here, Pop," she said from her desk.

"I was over at Gib's store and I heard you fainted," he said, rushing to her.

"Pop, slow down or you'll be on the floor too."

"Where's a doctor?" Mr. Mobley said, looking around like one was hiding behind the desk. "Does Certain have one?"

"We can call the frontier nursing service over," I said. "They have an outpost not far from here."

"Frontier what?" Mr. Mobley asked, still looking around as if a medical professional was just out of his line of sight and would materialize soon.

"They're like us," I said touching Mattie's arm. "Horseback but they're nurses. They come right to your house. Mostly for women and children."

I knew all about them of course. I had seen them come to town on plenty of occasions to tend to pregnant women and see after sick children. I had to admit, I had a bit of a hero crush on them. What a glamorous job. Or at least it seemed so to me. I touched the pin on my chest, still imagining it to be an FNS badge.

Mr. Gibbons suddenly came in apologizing. "I'm so sorry it took me so long to get here. I had to cash two customers out and get the door locked and sign up. I'm here now."

Mattie and I looked at each other smiling. She and I had a fondness for Mr. Gibbons and I knew she was getting a kick out of his feeling that he needed to apologize for being "late."

"I'm just glad you came," Mattie said. "Thank you for checking up on me. I suppose I'm the talk of the town by now it seems."

"Well, catch me up," he said. "What did I miss?"

We all looked around at each other and Ava and I shouted again. "She's pregnant!"

"What?" Mr. Mobley looked shocked and we realized he'd missed that part of the story.

Mattie sighed good-naturedly. "Here we go again. Perhaps we could take a notice out in the paper."

Everyone chuckled. Mr. Gibbons' eyes lit up. "We should get that young reporter back in town. He could write it up for us and print it out."

"Yes," Ava said and winked. "Ruby and I could take the notice around to all our patrons."

Everyone was giggling and making suggestions for headlines and suddenly I had a fantastic idea. The newspaper building had a living quarters, of course. It had been Cole's home as well as the newspaper office. The building no doubt needed a serious cleaning as it had only been opened up on a few occasions when we needed extra space for a meeting, or someone needed to store something. Mostly people didn't care to be in there because of what the building stood for to them, lies and loss. But nonetheless, it was a place with walls and a roof and Cole needed a place to stay.

I didn't know if I could convince him to come back, but I was going to try. I could help him with his hand that would probably need some physiotherapy as I had seen detailed in one of the medical books. I could help him get well and he'd have a place to live. Win-win. And he'd stay. Hopefully.

Daniel spoke up then. "Wonder where that reporter fella went to anyway? Anyone seen him lately?"

Daniel looked right at me and I swear I saw recognition in his eyes.

Hesitantly I offered, "I did see someone out by the creek the other day while I was foraging for medicinals. Do you think that might have been him?"

"I'm sure he's long gone back to Lexington or wherever he came from," Mattie said and one of the kids started jumping up and down raising his hand like he had an important question.

The child said something and everyone started laughing, their attention turned to what he and Mattie were talking about. But Daniel kept looking at me.

"Wouldn't be the worst thing if someone opened up the newspaper again," he said. "Maybe did something good with it this time."

"I suppose," I answered with a non-answer.

"Seemed like that fella was in need of a place to be," he said, his eyes trained on mine like they were searching inside my soul. "He seemed a little lost."

"We all get a little lost," I said, my heart starting to race.

Before he had a chance to say anything more, Ella and Marie were jumping all over him talking about new babies and what they were going to name their new siblings and Daniel's attention was taken elsewhere. He gave me one last long look before letting himself get enveloped in the group excitement of new beginnings.

⚜ ⚜ ⚜

Once everyone went home, all the kids, all the old men, all the soon to be aunts and uncles again and everyone in between, I rode Patty out to the creek.

"We're not going foraging today," I told her, "We're going to get an old friend and bring him home. You must be nice to him."

Patty shook her mane and swished her head back and forth.

75

"I know," I said and patted her neck. "You're always nice."

The closer I got to Cole's campsite the more nervous I grew about whether or not he'd be there. I took my foraging route that would put me on the opposite side of the creek from him, so I'd be able to see if he was there from a distance. I guess it wouldn't matter one way or the next what side I rode in on if he was gone. Gone was gone. But it would put space between where I was and where he should be if it happened that way.

As I got closer, I could hear music. Or something like it. It was dreadful harmonica playing but it was heaven to my ears. He was still there. He had been a bad harmonica player when he was a kid, and he still was. A smile lit my face and relief nestled in my heart.

I clicked the reins to speed Patty up a bit and we stomped through the low water of the creek and straight into Cole's camp. I pulled Patty to a stop beside where he sat in his lean-to.

"You're not very good at sneaking up," he said, standing up to greet me.

"You're still here," I said, sliding out of the saddle and landing firmly on the ground.

"I told you I would be," he said. He put the harmonica in his pocket as if he was hoping I hadn't heard him playing.

I opened the saddlebag and took out a book and a clean bandage and clips.

"Let's see that hand," I said to him, "and then I have some news."

"News?" He held his hand out to me. His trust warmed my heart.

"I found you a place to live," I said, motioning for him to sit back. "The old newspaper building. You can come back home."

Chapter 10
Cole

Home? The newspaper building. The most haunted place in all of Certain. Well, for me anyway. What was Ruby thinking?

"Don't you remember?" I asked. "That's where we used to live. Me and my parents. My actual home when we were in Certain." I kept explaining it just in case she was missing the point.

We sat in my lean-to with my injured right hand rested across my haversack that she had in her lap. She had her medical book open beside her, saved from the dirty ground by one of my shirts.

"That's right," she said and looked up and out into the distance across the creek. "Your dad ran the newspaper." She looked back down at the wrap she folded across my wrist and then wound around my thumb and palm.

"The fake newspaper, you mean," I corrected. It had all been part of the scam.

"There was some real news," she said and glanced at me quickly, "right?"

"Some of it," I said and shrugged.

I had written part of the paper myself. The true parts that were supposed to make it more believable. That's why I didn't go to school some days. I was home being my father's partner in crime.

"I wrote the parts that were supposed to make the lies seem true," I said. "Don't you remember everything that happened? You know what he did, right? Writing all those fake articles about how the government was going to assume everyone's land and then tricking people into signing over their deeds to him?"

Ruby breathed in deeply and looked at me fully in the face. "I remember," she said. Her dark eyes seeing into the past. "You don't have to keep asking me."

Ouch.

"Sorry," I said.

"You also don't have to keep telling me you're sorry."

This was certainly the complicated Ruby I recalled. I sat in silence so as not to put my other foot in my mouth. Ruby wrapped my hand and unwrapped my hand, read more in the book, mumbled to herself and then wrapped the hand again. It hurt, but the good feeling of being taken care of outweighed the pain.

"There," she said, lifting my hand off the bag and nudging it back toward me. "I think that will do."

I twisted my wrist around as much as the bandage would allow and bent my arm back and forth at the elbow, not that it was wrapped that high, it just seemed like the way to test things out.

"It feels good," I said. Much better than the way I had done it. "It feels more secure." I reached and picked up my fishing pole and made like I was going to cast off. "I can hold things." I was pleasantly surprised.

"Go easy on it still," she said.

I was afraid she was going to take her leave now that she was finished with her doctoring, but she didn't make a move to go. She moved my bag aside, picked up the medical book she had been referencing and closed it. She set it in her lap and rested her hands on it.

"Thank you," I said, realizing that I hadn't said it.

"You're welcome," she replied, shaking her head as if it was nothing.

I looked around for something to talk about to make sure that she stayed. I didn't want that something to be me moving into the newspaper building though.

"It sure is lovely here in May, don't you think?" I asked, shaking my head internally at the lame comment.

She turned her head slowly to look at me. "The weather?" she asked and chuckled. "That's all you've got."

I decided to run with it. I waved my left, unbandaged hand, out in front of me indicating the scene in front of us. "I mean, sure," I said. "Look at it. There are leaves on the trees quite suddenly it seems. Don't you love how that happens. It's just brown sticks for months and then one day you notice that there are little green buds all along the branches that surely weren't there the day before and then boom," I said a little loudly, causing the horse to whinny where she was tied loosely to a tree up the way, "leaves everywhere, green and supple like they're the first leaves to ever be on a tree."

She bit her lip to keep from smiling. I knew this expression well. I kept going.

"The creek even looks warmer, don't you think?" It probably wasn't much but it really did look it. "The way the sun glints off the water as it rolls over the rocks, just looks clean and clear and warm like when we were little, and we'd take off our shoes and walk right down the middle of it as far as we dared one way and then back." Sure, that had been in the summers, but still. "Can't you see us out there right now?" I pointed like the memory of us was visible to the open eye. "Remember that one time that a storm came up all of a sudden and we were way up the creek near Devil's Jump and things got a bit hairy all of a sudden? The water was rushing and the rain was coming down making everything so slick." I stopped because that particular memory was an important one and I had almost forgotten until I started telling it.

I looked over at Ruby and she was looking at me with eyes that I remembered from all those years ago. She nodded but didn't speak. I knew I had to keep telling it because that was not something you could just bring up and then drop. That was the day that changed everything.

"You almost tripped over one of the bigger rocks that was all but submerged as the creek was rising and I grabbed hold of your hand and pulled you out of the water." I was telling it now as a man remembering, a man who understood the significance even more than the fourteen-year-old boy who thought he understood back then, but was only at the tip of knowledge about such things. "You almost wrapped your whole self around me trying to jump from danger even as I was trying to pull you to safety. I could feel near about every nerve in my body light up. I didn't have a clue what to do with that feeling. I just knew I liked it and I didn't want to let you go. Everything about how I felt about you, or at least how I realized I felt about you changed in that one moment."

I had never told her how that moment changed things for me. It seemed like it had for her as well, but when you're fourteen, you don't even know what you don't know. All I did know was that something shifted. Not long after that, my father's scheme was discovered and we were gone before whatever it was with Ruby even got started.

"Everything changed for me in that moment too," Ruby said, her voice wistful enough that I couldn't quite read her.

I held my breath as she stood up. Afraid she was about to leave, I stood up as well.

"Sit back down, silly," she said. "I'm just moving to the other side so I can hold your good hand."

I sat back down but over a bit and just like she said, she sat on my left and took hold of my unbandaged hand.

We sat in silence save for the warbling of the creek and the sound of the horse swishing her mane and whinnying from time to time.

Finally, Ruby spoke quietly. "What happened?"

I squeezed her hand just a little and breathed in.

"You said something right after I kissed you," I said, my heart thudding against the story I had kept inside all this time, "remember?"

"There you go again, asking me if I remember," she said, but her voice was warm. "Are you talking about the kiss, because, yes, I remember that."

"Not that," I said and sighed. "What you said after it."

She looked over at me and shook her head. "I have no idea what nonsense might have come out of my mouth at that point. I was so lightheaded I couldn't think straight." She tilted her head and furrowed her brow. "Did you leave because of something I said?"

I looked out over the creek, wishing I had a rock to throw in for the sheer distraction of it.

"Yes," I said, "but you wouldn't have known why."

"What on earth did I say?" She looked completely confused.

I didn't want to make her think anything about that night was her fault, but I had left because of what she said. "You said, 'That was much better than a ride in your dad's car.'"

She shook her head but then she opened her mouth into a little O. "That's right," she said. "I'd seen your dad's car parked beside the grocery store like it was hidden and I thought you were sneaking it out to take us for a ride."

I shook my head. Would that that was it. "I knew he was getting ready to leave as soon as you said that."

I'd been down that road before. He almost never took the car out. Where was there to go? He had everything for the paper sent in and if he did go somewhere, it was mostly just for show to make it seem like he was covering a story and it was always, always, during the day. The fact that Ruby had seen the car, which was almost always covered with a canvas tarp, especially in the evening, told me he had the car out and ready to leave.

Ruby didn't let go of my hand, but she turned herself to face me better. Mid-afternoon had settled in in that way that makes you think it will be mid-afternoon all day long. The sun held its place and the creek was content with its flowing and sparkling and there was just me and Ruby and the story that sat between us.

"Why did you tell me to wait for you?" she asked. "I would have come with you to help if you thought something was wrong."

I looked at the ground and shoved the dirt with my shoe. "I didn't want you to know," I said. "I knew it meant that people had found out what he'd done. Otherwise, he wouldn't have been making an escape at night when there was still a paper being put together on the press."

"Cole," she said and slid closer to me. "What he did wasn't your fault."

I pulled away from her and stood up. This was the part I didn't want her to know. It was my fault. I helped him. And I knew all about the scam by then. And I didn't tell anyone.

"What happened after that?" she asked when I didn't say anything more. She stood up beside me. "After you all left."

"We drove for a couple of days," I said, skipping over the part where I almost got left behind and shrugged. "Ended up somewhere in Tennessee. Much bigger and more bustling town. Dad settled us in for another con. Same old same old."

The "what happened after that" was hard to talk about, so I shook my head like I knew to do when I wanted it to be obvious it was all too much to talk about.

I hoped she'd let me off the hook because not one good thing had happened after that. Things had just gotten worse and worse. I hoped I would never be a con man like my father, but I was good at pretending. I could pretend my heart hadn't been broken and that it still wasn't.

Then she asked the question I feared. "What happened to the deeds your dad stole? Did he sell them?"

"That was the plan," I said, shoving my hands in my pockets. "Step two was to con someone else into buying them thinking they were hot commodities to the government."

Ruby shook her head like it was too full of information. "Wow, that really was a long game he was playing."

I shrugged.

"Did it work?" she asked. "Did he sell them?"

"No," I said. I could almost see them glowing inside the bag just feet from where we stood.

She sighed. "I guess it's all the same. No one ever came to collect the land, so people have moved on."

"Have they?" I asked. "They don't care to get the deeds back?" If they didn't, I had no cards to play at all. I would just be the son of the swindler and no one would want me around.

Mack, that's how I thought of Dad now as he didn't deserve the term, had conned a dozen families out of the rights to their homesteads. He'd fabricated news stories and scared everyone into signing their deeds over to him because he had a plan to save Certain. They'd fallen for it. Well, the deeds had been signed over to me. That's right. He had told them his legal name was Cole, that Mack was a nickname, and he'd had them all signed over to Cole Cooper. I supposed it was to keep his name off the record if things went to the bad. The joke was on him. I had the deeds now in my name.

Except now, I thought the joke was on me. What did I have to bargain with if no one even cared about the deeds? I was just part of a bad memory with nothing to show for it.

"What do you think happened to the deeds?" she asked.

And out came a big fat lie. "I don't know what happened to them."

Ruby nodded her head as if that was that. I shook mine but it wasn't in confirmation like it might have seemed. It was in disbelief that I'd said it. Too many years of playing my cards close to my chest and distrusting everyone was catching up to me.

Just tell her the truth. She'll ask you why you lied and you can tell her the truth again. You're scared. Let her in.

But all that seemed to come out of my mouth was lies, so I pressed my lips together to make sure nothing worse came out.

Chapter 11
Ruby

People probably did want their deeds back, but it had been so long and since nothing had come of it, people had tried to forget. People were embarrassed and that made them "forget" faster.

Mackenzie Cooper, who went by Mack and later told everyone his legal first name was Cole, had opened a newspaper in town. He even bought a printing press and had it delivered to Certain. What grift money he'd used to do that; we would never know. It was a monster of a thing and even though it was already old fashioned everyone thought it was the bee's knees. And they thought Mack was too. He was printing a news round-up of sorts, he said. He was getting all the papers from far and wide and printing a report of all the important items as well as things of local interest in Certain. Mr. Gibbons' grocery specials, who won the pie contest and a list of birthdays for the week so that everyone could tell each other Happy Birthday. Cole even had a nature column of sorts. Everyone loved the energy and sense of community that Mack had created.

Never had a brought-in person ingratiated himself so thoroughly so quickly. Looking back, we figured he must have been "brought-in" by the Devil. I wouldn't really understand the whole story for years. After it happened and it was apparent that there was no way to undo it, it became the topic that no one spoke of. Dared even whisper about. Gramma finally told me everything years later.

It had been a con that took years to accomplish. Mack started printing "reports" little by little that made it look like the government was out to seize all the land between Lexington and Asheville for military use. People were fresh off the horrors of the war and were scared. It had only been a couple of years and the wounds were not healed. Some of our men had been sent to train over near Louisville at Camp Zachary Taylor alongside men from throughout the Midwest. Several of the Certain men never came home. Alive or dead. The war, training grounds, and anything to do with the government were spots raw and red.

So, after enough "reports" on the matter came out in the paper, people started getting worried and wondering what to do. No one wanted to lose their land and it sounded like the government might be able to just take it and send us all packing.

Gramma had told me how people gathered in the church to talk about the problem at hand. She recalled the story to me.

"They can't just turn us out of our homes," Mr. Elders had said. I barely even remembered him as his family did leave not long after. "Can they?"

"They most certainly can," Mr. Thomas, Claire's father, had retorted. "The government can do what it pleases."

Apparently, according to Gramma's story, cries and gasps from all the men and women ensued. Mr. Cooper had piped up then with his answer to it all. Gramma had a good amount of disdain for him after what he did and when she said "Mr. Cooper" the words dripped with sour grapes.

"They will surely place you elsewhere," he had said, trying to sound like it wouldn't be so bad. "Or offer you enough money to at least move away."

"To where?" Someone had asked.

Mr. Cooper shook his head and raised his hands up. "I'm just the messenger, folks. I sure wish I knew how to fix this. I'm as scared as you are. I had hoped to make a life here in Certain. My family is happy here and I've finally got friends and a purpose that means something."

The men nearby him had clapped him on the shoulder and nodded their heads.

"Will they take the whole town?" Someone asked.

"What if we refuse to go?"

"Let's see them try."

Gramma said it got right ugly from there. Fear got the best of them all. It had been Mr. Cooper who calmed the crowd.

"Look," he had said, apparently coming to stand at the front of the church, putting on like he was God's gift to us all—like I said, by the time I heard this story the Cooper name was mud—"Let me keep my eyes on the papers from around the area. I'll go up to Lexington as a reporter and see what I can sniff out. We're not the only town in danger and I bet someone somewhere is coming up with a plan."

People started to quiet down and listen. Heads nodded and eyes grew calm and sure.

"If you trust me to wait before we all do something rash, I promise to figure this out."

By then everyone was fool enough to believe him, Gramma had said. He even got people to voice their oath and that meant something around here.

"Do you trust me?" Mr. Cooper had asked.

Mr. Thomas stood up and looked at the crowd. "I trust him. I think he can sort this out for us."

Everyone agreed.

The Coopers had been in town almost two years by then and had done nothing but come across as people settling into a new town and doing what they could to make it better.

"It was the grift of a lifetime," Gramma had said, shaking her head. "They all stood up that day, me included I hate to say, and pledged their trust to the slickest charlatan we never saw coming."

According to Gramma, Mr. Cooper got started calling town meetings left and right and continuing to run scary articles in the paper.

"Every time one of those things came out people were lining up at the newspaper office to get theirs," she had said. "They were even paying for it as Mr. Cooper was apparently running through his savings purchasing the paper and ink at his own expense. Mr. Gibbons had just taken over the grocery and was buying ads left and right to support the paper. Others were too. People stopped caring about the birthday lists and the latest recipe. All anyone could talk about was keeping their land and keeping Certain safe."

Then one day Mr. Cooper called a meeting with the exciting news that he had discovered a solution. Gramma said people about knocked each other down trying to get into the church and hear what it was.

She had told it all with so much spit and fire in her voice that I thought the cabin was going to go up in flames.

"That man stood up there with this nervous look about him," she had said, "pretending, we know now, to be worried that people would think his solution was crazy, or fear that he was just playing them all for the fool." She shook her head. "Ain't that something? He actually told the truth of what he was doing and didn't nobody see it."

Apparently, this plan was to have people sign their deeds over to him and then he would move out of town for a month or so with all the paperwork. That way when the government came, no one actually owned the land and they'd have to go back to their offices and find out who owned it before they could move forward and that that would take a while. He said he would close the paper and collect up all the old issues so there was no trace of how they'd found out the government was coming for their land. The government would never know they were running them around. Meanwhile, Mr. Thomas, if he was up to it, would start to put them onto another piece of land much better suited for a training ground. Mr. Thomas, as mayor, had been excited to be part of the plan and agreed right away. He was supposed to take the officials who came, and Mr. Cooper said their coming was imminent, over toward Hazard and get them interested in land out that way.

"We can't do that to Hazard, though," Mr. Thomas had said. "They're good neighbors and we need them from time to time."

"We're just sending them out that way because from there they can catch a train onto something better," Mr. Cooper said. "I've already talked to the mayor of Hazard and he's on board with it. It's a runaround like the bigwigs in Washington won't see coming. They think they can fool us; they've got another think coming."

Mr. Thomas had nodded emphatically and said, "When do we get started?"

"Right now," Mr. Cooper said. "Go home and get whatever deeds or paperwork you have for your land, and if you don't have anything but family word passing it down, we can write something up and sign it. Bring me all the issues you have left of the paper and we'll get rid of them. I'll get my family ready to go and we'll start this plan today."

Gramma said it didn't take no time at all for about a dozen of the men to come back with their deeds ready to sign over and old issues of the paper to throw on the growing fire. Some folks were still working on digging up what they might have to show proof of ownership, which sometimes wasn't much of nothing around here except their word. Mr. Cooper had said it was a good start and for anyone else who could find papers or would be willing to draw some up to meet him at the church again tomorrow and they'd finish it all off.

"That was the last time any of us ever saw that man," Gramma said. "He must have been satisfied with what he had and hit the ground running. He got out in the nick of time, unfortunately, because someone figured out he was lying and they came hunting him that night, but he was long gone."

I had asked how they figured it out, but Gramma had shrugged.

"I guess someone took it upon themselves to read another newspaper and since there weren't no mention of any of the things Mack wrote in our paper it started to look suspicious."

"Didn't anyone suspect something sooner?" I wondered.

Gramma shook her head. "He spent so long on things that were mostly real and he measured out the lies just so, that even if someone was reading another paper it all added up. Until it didn't. But by that time, he had enough of what he wanted."

That was the story Gramma told. I had wished, before I knew the whole story, that the Coopers could have somehow stayed, but once I knew what Mack had done, I knew that was never a possibility. I don't know what would have happened that night if the townsfolk had found him. I supposed they would have at least gotten their deeds back but the Coopers would still be gone. Cole would still never have come back that night. Maybe I could have at least gotten to say goodbye. Then again, if it had happened that way, he might not be here now. That all depended on why he'd come back.

No matter, he was indeed here now and I wanted him to stay.

"I know it's not your favorite place, Cole," I said about the newspaper building. "But it's walls and a roof and a real bed to sleep in. And you can heal up your hand and start over."

Cole started pacing back and forth along his little stretch of campsite. "I don't know, Ruby," he said. "I don't think I'm ready to show my face in town."

I walked to him where he had stopped to look out over the creek. I nestled in beside him and took hold of his hand again.

"No one knows it's you," I said. "They think you're Henry Hall."

He shook his head. "I can't, Ruby. I'll be a liar just like my father."

"We'll tell them in good time," I said. "They'll understand."

Surely that was true. No one faulted Cole. Maybe they would even take pity on him. Except that the first thing he had done was lie to them, and about being a reporter for a paper no less. This might be a hard sell, but surely we could sell it.

I sighed heavily.

"I already made a mess of things just by saying I was someone I wasn't," he said as if reading my mind. His grip on my hand tightened.

"This isn't a plan to turn you into your father," I said. "We just have a little clean-up to do. It's a small mess, that's all. This is a plan to get you clear of his name forever and bring you back home again."

He looked at me then and I knew I had, albeit accidentally, hit on a need that I hadn't realized was so deep.

"This is your home, Cole," I said. "I'll see to it." I meant that.

"What will people do when I tell them who I am? Hey, it's me, Cole Cooper, come back to Certain."

"We'll figure that out together," I said. "I'm right here with you."

"I don't deserve your help," he said.

"You're a good man, Cole. So, you have a little propensity for telling a tall tale when you're on the spot. Give it some time. We'll figure out how to fix this. You don't happen to actually be a newspaper reporter, do you?"

He shook his head. "Not a real one."

We needed to work on what was real and what was fake. Cole needed to know the difference for himself.

Chapter 12
Cole

I stalled about coming into town for a couple more days. I couldn't bring myself to face everyone. I knew Ruby wanted me to stay, but this was a bad plan at the very best. The only way out of this was to return the deeds and hit the ground running. But I still wanted a home and another chance with Ruby too much to do that.

So when she and Patty popped up at my campsite again, I didn't wait for her to launch into more convincing. "I'll go," I said, as she slid from the saddle already looking like she had a mouthful to say.

She all but jumped up and down, rushing to get Patty cared for and hurrying over to me. "You will?" she asked, hopeful but as if I might now say no. "This is great!" she exclaimed before I had a chance to change my mind, not that I was going to.

"I don't love it," I said.

I knew I was going to have to face everyone eventually. Those deeds were burning a hole so hot in my haversack that I could almost see it smoking. Truth be told, I was putting it off because as soon as I came clean as to who I was and what I had, I'd be lucky to toss the papers in the air and run before the people of Certain realized they could hold the son accountable for the sins of the father and who knows what price there was to pay. Run out of town again at least.

And I really wanted to stay. Things had gone downhill fast when we left Certain. There was a bright shining moment when I thought Mom was going to leave Mack and she and I could make a new life together, but in the end, she stayed with him and I left. I was tired of moving around, living in alleys or along some creek or hiding out in an empty building. Eating from the trash or getting scraps from a compassionate cafe owner from time to time. Every now and then I had enough money to get a room and a hot meal, but ever since the market crashed in '29 things had gone from bad to worse. Worse enough for me to come back to Certain on a last-ditch effort to find a home.

I should have come back years ago. It's a crime in and of itself that I didn't. That right there would be enough for them not to forgive me. Who knows what heartache and hardship had befallen any of them since we left. Maybe Ruby was right, and no one cared anymore, which didn't leave me with any bargaining chips unfortunately, but that didn't mean they weren't angry about it still.

"Everything will be alright," Ruby answered my unspoken but obvious fear. "Let's get you packed up and head on over."

"Now?" I asked incredulously.

"Now," she answered matter-of-factly. "Best to get there before you chicken out."

She eyed me in challenge.

"You know," I said, stalling. "Chickens have a lot of fight in them."

She put her hands on her hips. "Perhaps, but they scare pretty easily," she said and made a knowing face. She had my number. "You must be really careful and tender with them in the early stages of your relationship. They have to learn to trust you."

"Is that so?" I asked and put my finger to my lip like I was considering something perplexing. "How do you get them to trust you?"

She pursed her lips at me, and I knew she knew I was playing.

"You make them a nice home," she said, "preferably a nicely constructed but well- ventilated solid structure. You make sure they have enough to eat and somewhere soft to sleep."

I nodded along.

"You talk to them softly and often so that they learn the sound of your voice," she said. "You come around and give them treats so they remember your face and look forward to your visits." She was starting to smile now. She was getting silly and it reminded me so much of younger Ruby.

"So you'll come around and give me treats?" I asked. "I like treats."

She smiled full on and bit her lip. That was a new quirk and I liked it.

I sighed. "I would never forget your face," I stepped closer to her, wanting to reach out and pull her to me, but too chicken indeed to try, "or the sound of your voice, and I will always look forward to your visits."

Sunlight licked through the branches and shone in her eyes, but she didn't look away from me.

"Let's go chicken," she said and pushed at me playfully.

I clucked and bawked in my best chicken impersonation.

She rolled her eyes and smiled.

❧❧❧

We packed my meager belongings and headed to town. Everything I had fit in my sack. Ruby rode Patty and I walked alongside them. We went slow and steady, and long before I was ready, we made it into town. I was suddenly glad that I had already ventured in once—even if that visit did go horribly wrong. I think coming back into town and heading straight to the newspaper building, my old home, would have given me the shivers I wouldn't have been able to hide. Talk about chicken.

Ruby pulled Patty to a stop and jumped down. We had talked about how to proceed when we got to town. I would go along with the notion that I had gone back to Louisville to hammer out a last story on the flood recovery and she had run into me as I was passing back this way with some uncertainty about my next steps. What a happy coincidence it would be.

The main street was empty late on a Tuesday. School was out so no one was at the church—over the weeks Ruby had told me all about the library and Mattie and Daniel and just about every other thing that had happened since I was gone. I could see Mr. Gibbons through the window of the grocery but he looked preoccupied which was fine by me.

We went past the store up to the front door of the old newspaper building. My heart beat so hard it was about to come loose in my chest and fall right down into my stomach. Ruby took out a key and held it to the door.

"We got the lock changed," she said as if I might be worried about Mack coming back. "You ready?"

"No."

She opened the door anyway. She moved back to let me step in first. I made it about two feet in and stopped. It's strange to see a room as an adult that you last saw as a child. I don't know what the building had been before we moved in and my dad had the press sent, but the whole downstairs was just one big room with the printing press in the very middle, my father's old desk off to the side, a chair or two along the front window, and a dining table and chairs in the middle just behind the press and a wood stove in the way back. It felt so cliché, which was an old printing term, to say that the room seemed smaller. Really it might have seemed bigger and more ominous than it had the last time I was there. It was also cleaner.

"Did someone clean?" I asked, distracting myself so maybe the old ghosts of memory couldn't get in. "When I left that night there were papers everywhere and I kicked over an ink bottle on the way out." I went deeper into the room then and spun slowly around looking at every inch. I pointed at the wood burning stove in the back corner. "I forgot about that. Mom used to cook there."

I felt Ruby come up behind me. "It's been a long time. I hoped you would say yes, so I've been in here cleaning and trying to get things fixed up a bit. Mr. Gibbons gave me the key."

I spun around to face her. "Does he know?"

He wasn't one of the folks who had given over his deed, but he had put too much of his money into Mack's pocket buying ads to support the paper. I remember that Mack didn't seem to care for him. Mr. Gibbons was always friendly to me, talking to me about my day and asking questions about what it was like to live somewhere other than Certain.

"I can't imagine a better place in the world," Mr. Gibbons had said to me once. "We don't have much of anything around here, but I wouldn't trade it for life anywhere else."

Mack had never liked the questions. He would always tell me to run on off and play when someone asked anything about our life before Certain. I realized now that he was afraid someone would catch a rip in the story. More afraid that I might tear one.

"Don't offer people information they didn't ask for," Mack always said, "and when they ask for it, give them as little as you can."

Ruby took hold of my hand, not answering me about Mr. Gibbons. "Let's go upstairs," she said. "I have a room for you all set. I still need to make the bed though."

"I'll be there in a minute," I said, those ghosts closing in after all.

"OK," she said happily and headed up the stairs that led to a loft style area where the bedrooms were.

I closed my eyes and let the ghosts come. Might as well get it over with. That night had haunted me all this while anyway.

That night out at the creek, when I walked away from Ruby all those years ago, I had tried to casually saunter away like everything would be fine. But as soon as I was out of her eyesight, I broke out into a run. I knew she'd seen Mack's car and thought we were going for a ride. I'd promised to try and sneak it out one night. But it wasn't me who had it ready to go.

When I got into town there were people surrounding the building where we lived, shouting for my father to come out. They didn't see me coming up behind them. I didn't even know if he was home because there was no light coming through the windows. The car was nowhere to be seen. Someone banged on the front door, shouting for him, but the place was quiet.

I had gone around to the back door and let myself in. The lamps were off and the place was eerily still. I ran up to my room to see if my things were there. I wasn't sure if I hoped they were or not. If not, then my parents had packed for me and were expecting me. If my things were there, then I'd been left.

A few things were still there, on the floor, as if someone had been in a hurry and dropped them. My mother, I'm sure. I picked up my remaining belongings and raced back downstairs and out the back door. I could still hear the people yelling for Mack.

"Mack Cooper," Mr. Thomas called out harshly to my father who wasn't there. "Open this door or I'll bust it in." Mr. Thomas seemed to be the leader of the mob, taking it on himself to step out in front and call the commands.

I had come back around to the front of the building then, but I was behind the group of ten or so men standing outside my front door. I went unnoticed. Close to my chest, I cradled the few things of mine that had been left so as not to drop them and ran down the road that led out of town. That was surely the way my parents had gone. My nervous legs were like jelly and I wasn't sure if I was running, slipping, or dreaming the whole thing and I was actually still back in my room hearing the angry mob outside, too scared to move at all.

I could smell gasoline in the air and I knew my father's car had been down that way not too long ago. They must have left just before the mob showed up. My father usually did have good timing. He knew when to hold them and when to fold them. I ran until I got a stitch in my side and I stopped for just a moment. I was about to give up, fall down in the road and just cry. What else was there to do?

I thought about Ruby waiting for me at the creek. I could just go back, I said to myself. Pretend like nothing ever happened. But I knew there was no way to do that. I knew what my father had done. And I felt guilty for not having told anyone. Guilty and ashamed. My time in Certain was over. I couldn't even go back to face Ruby. I didn't want her to know the part I had played.

I was about to sit down and figure out what to do when I heard my mother calling my name.

"Cole," her voice came across the wind in the growing darkness.

"Shut up, woman," my father's angry voice spat. "They're probably following us on somebody's old nag already."

They were just around the bend; I could hear the engine on the car sputtering. I didn't say anything, I just walked toward them. Fast enough to make time, but not fast enough to make noise. I still wasn't sure I wanted to go with them. If it had just been my father, I wouldn't have. But I heard my mother start to cry.

"Mack," she said around a breaking voice, "he's my baby. I can't leave him here. I won't leave him."

"Get out and stay with him, then," my father said and from the sound of the engine purring a little better and the closing of the hood over it, I knew he was about to drive off.

"Please, Mack, we have to go get him. How can we leave him? He's just a boy."

"He's fourteen, that's man enough."

I heard a smack then and my father grunted. I stopped short knowing that my mother had slapped him. My heart turned cold with fear. *That's man enough.* My father's words were still rattling in my head and I ran the last steps around the corner that led me to the car.

"Mom," I shouted just as my father's hand reached out to grab her by the neck.

She turned toward the sound of my voice just then and I wondered if she had seen what he was about to do. He dropped his hand at the sight of me and put on a fake face of concern and relief.

"There you are, son," he said and put his hand to his heart. "We were waiting for you. You gave us a scare."

Still clutching my things, I looked at my mother, wanting her to tell the truth that I already knew, but she didn't say a thing. She just ran to me and pulled me into a hug.

"Where are we going?" I asked, wriggling loose. I didn't say anything about the mob of people. It was my turn to play my cards and I was keeping them close to my chest. "Why is all our stuff packed?" I still held onto my journal, the left of my church shoes, and an old bear I used to sleep with when I was little.

"No time to talk now, son," my father said and got in the car. "Whoever is going with me better come on."

I knew this scam. It was the scam he ran on his own family that he was a loving dad just trying to make do for his wife and son. Times were tough and it was time for the tough to move on. I barely believed it before and I surely didn't now.

I remember glancing one more time in the direction of Certain, even though I couldn't see it anymore. It was over and everything was lost to me.

Now here I was, standing in the room looking around a haunted house.

The upstairs of the building was something like a closed in loft. It didn't span the whole area of the room downstairs. Only about half of it so that the downstairs area where the printing press was had a high ceiling and you could sit along the hallway of the upstairs like it was a balcony. The bathroom was downstairs underneath the bedrooms that were upstairs. There were just the two rooms upstairs. One had been mine and the other had been my parents'. I hoped that the room Ruby had set for me was not theirs.

She came out onto the landing and startled.

"You OK?" she asked. I just nodded and she kept talking. "I know I was only here a time or two," she said, pointing to the bedroom door that had been mine, "but I remember this was yours. I hope it's OK."

I just stood there, waiting for the ghosts to dissipate.

"You coming up?" she said.

I nodded again and pried my feet from where they were stuck to the floor. One step at a time led me up to my old room.

I don't know what became of the furniture that had been in there. Probably rotted and eaten by mice after all this time. Inside the small room now was a bigger bed than I'd had, a chest of drawers and a desk with a chair that sat beside the bed.

"Where did these things come from?"

"I told people you were coming and they all wanted to make you a place to stay." She bit her lip again. "A little presumptuous I know, but I figured I would wear you down."

"So they think that Henry Hall, newspaper reporter, is coming to stay in Certain for the summer?"

She nodded.

"And I bet they hope that I'll fall in love with the town and stay forever," I added.

"Would that be so bad?"

"If it wasn't all a lie, I guess not."

We went back downstairs and I wandered around the room again, taking things in while Ruby fussed with this and that making sure I was set up to stay.

A man's voice sounded behind us walking closer as he talked. "I knew I saw you coming past the store." Mr. Gibbons appeared in front of me then and stuck his hand out to me. "Welcome back, Mr. Hall."

"Thank you," I said. I lifted my right hand to shake. It was still bandaged, but it felt much better. I could still feel a sting and pinch every now and then, but Ruby's care had been wonderful. If she hadn't wrapped it so well which let it heal, I might not even have good use of it anymore.

"Ruby said she was aiming to get you here. I see that she did." He winked at Ruby and looked around and we all stood there in awkward silence for a moment.

He made a little noise and then said. "It's not very homey, is it? Who has a printing press in their living room?" He chuckled and then slapped me on the shoulder. "A newspaper man, like you, I suppose."

I started to protest, but he cut me off. "We don't expect you to start printing anything right away," he said. "Ruby says you're taking a break from work for a while. Tough story or something that got the best of you."

I opened my mouth to say who knows what, but thankfully, he cut me off again. "Don't be surprised when the town gets wind you're here and they show up at your door."

I tried to smile a smile that was not filled with fear and trepidation as I remembered the last time the townsfolk showed up at the door. I swear I could still hear them outside.

"I'll leave you be for the night," he said, tipped an imaginary hat to Ruby and let himself out.

Ruby and I were left standing in the middle of the room, well as much as the old press would give us space for.

"Are you going to be OK?" she asked.

Part of me wanted to be insulted. I was a big boy. But really, it was a fair question. I shrugged.

"Want me to stay for a while?" she asked. "We could play cards. I brought you some in case you got bored you could play solitaire. And of course, I brought you some things to read," she said and gestured to the dining room table where a stack of books and magazines were piled.

"Thank you," I said, suddenly growing nervous. "And yes, it wouldn't be the worst thing if you stayed for a round of cards."

She clapped her hands together and waved me over to the table.

When Ruby left that evening, I wasn't sure I'd be able to stay the night in the newspaper building. I was loath to call it home as this was not the home I was hoping for in Certain. As the day grew dark, those darn ghosts came out of every corner again like they'd just been waiting for Ruby to leave. I didn't know what to do with myself just standing there in the big downstairs room watching them float past me, whispering half remembered words and beckoning me to come with them down lanes of memory best forgotten.

"Go away," I whispered back to them. "Go away."

I ran up the stairs like a scared little chicken boy, flung myself on the bed and crashed headlong into a hard sleep.

I awoke to banging on the front door and all of a sudden, I was a kid again and there was an angry mob outside. I swallowed my heart back out of my throat and into my chest where it belonged. I breathed out heavily twice and got out of bed.

"It's not an angry mob, Cole," I said to myself. "And your father is not here."

Sometimes I had to be very precise and direct with myself. The knocking sounded again and I realized it was not banging at all, just a typical rap on the door to see if anyone was home.

"Ruby?" I called out as I hurried down the stairs, glad I had fallen asleep in my clothes and wasn't about to answer the door in my underthings. I flung the door open to a completely different and unknown face.

"Not Ruby," the man said and shrugged, "and if that's who you were expecting, I'm a sore substitute." He stuck his hand out to shake. "Mr.

Mobley." He glanced at my bandage but I reached out to return the shake.

"Hello," I said and almost introduced myself correctly, but thankfully he broke in talking again.

"Mr. Hall, big city reporter," he said and stooped down beside him to pick up a large and seemingly heavy box the way he struggled just a bit. "I wonder if you might store these in your newsroom here. My daughter tells me you seem to be friendly with Ruby and might keep these so she could read them here instead of leaving them lying all around scaring the little children who come to the library."

I reached out quickly and took the box wondering what on earth it could be. "Come in," I said and stepped back into the room so that he could enter.

He looked all around, eyes landing on the printing press. He whistled. "That's a monster," he said and went over to pat it like he could perhaps tame the beast. "I bet it looks ancient to you. I have a friend in the news business up in Lexington and I know the printing machines there are far more modern than this."

"You know someone at the Lexington paper?" I asked. I hadn't said that was where Henry Hall worked exactly but it was supposedly where he'd been last. Something about coming from Lexington and doing a story about Louisville. I was never going to be able to keep this story straight.

"I doubt you ran into him on the news floor," Mr. Mobley said. "You know how it is, the bigger the boss the less anyone sees them. Of course that's not really true with Charles."

"Charles," I repeated.

"You did meet him," he exclaimed. "Fine fella."

"Indeed," I said, answering something that wasn't really an answer, just a parrot of what Mr. Mobley had said. Another of my father's tricks.

I shuffled with the box both to change the subject and because it was heavy.

Mr. Mobley's face lit up and he lifted his hands out in the air in excitement. "Open it up."

I set it down on the floor and pulled the two chairs from the window over to it so we could look together. Mr. Mobley sat and nodded at me to go ahead. On opening it, the first thing I saw was the book that Ruby had brought to the creek when we wrapped my hand and wrist. Underneath that book, I could see another of the books Ruby had brought on one of her visits to the campsite.

"They're medical books," I said, confused.

"They're old, I know," he said as if apologizing, "but they're still of use."

"I'll make sure to tell Ruby they're here," I said, nodding. "Does she know you're bringing them? I thought she told me they were in a special section of the library."

Perhaps I wasn't supposed to know that.

"So, you and Ruby have been in touch?" he asked and my heart thudded, but then he said. "Mattie said Ruby told her about you."

"She did?"

"Mattie's pregnant, you know," he said and I nodded. Ruby had told me that.

"Ruby and Mattie are good friends," I added. I knew that too. I was only a little, well a lot, jealous.

"Mattie was going to help her clean the other day, but Ruby wouldn't let her," he said, reaching down to pull one of the books out of the box. "Mattie said she got the impression that you and Ruby knew each other well."

Keep your mouth shut, Cole. Another thing I learned from my father was just to let the other person talk and say as little as possible if it seemed like they were hunting for information or were just accidentally running amok too close to blowing your cover.

Mr. Mobley pointed at the books. "I had them sent from my home in Asheville a while back. Ruby seems to be enjoying them. They give Mattie the willies."

My ear caught on an important piece of information. "You live in Asheville? Not here?"

He blew a hard breath through his mouth making his cheeks puff out. "That's a good question, son." He shook his head. "I guess I should own up to it and say that I used to live in Asheville and that my home there is for sale. I've been cleaning it out little by little. I'm especially glad

I kept these books. They're very important to me."

I just had to make sure. "So, you've never lived in Certain until now?"

"No," he said. "You and I have something in common."

This conversation was making me feel faint. "We do?" He looked at me like I was supposed to say what that was. I made a guess. "We're both new to town?"

"That's right," he said. "You and I are the newest citizens of Certain. My daughter, Mattie is the teacher here. She recently got married."

"Yes, to Daniel," I said.

"You know them?"

"I've heard about them," I said and changed the subject. "You know, if these books are important to you, you should have them."

He shook his head and waved off the offer. "They didn't work anyway."

"They don't work?"

He laughed and shook his head again. "I'm sure they work well in the way a doctor would need them to. They just didn't work in the way a brokenhearted widower needed them to, so I donated them."

I furrowed my brow. "I don't understand."

"You don't have time for the ramblings of an old man, and besides that was ages ago now," he said, but sat back in the chair like he was settling in.

"Of course I do," I said, putting the books back in the box and scooting my chair around to face him.

He looked first at the floor for some long moments and then back up at me. I could see old memories glistening in his eyes.

"When Mattie was a young girl her mother was killed in an automobile accident."

I sucked in a breath. "I'm sorry."

"Me too," he said and breathed in deeply through his nose. "My wife was a wonderful woman, a loving wife and a tireless mother."

"What happened, if you don't mind me asking."

"I did offer to tell it, didn't I," he smiled. "She had gone over to the bakery to get a treat for Mattie and some fool who didn't know how to drive very well ran up onto the sidewalk and ran her right into the brick building she was walking past."

My mouth fell open. "That's awful."

"It was," he said. "And I was flummoxed by it. I just couldn't make it be true. I kept thinking even after the funeral that it was all some mistake. That there was some way I could fix it even. If I could just figure out how to undo it, I could make it right." He reached forward and patted me on the leg and chuckled at himself. "Doesn't that sound like the naivest thing?"

I shook my head. "I understand."

"Have you lost someone like that?"

"Not like that, but lost nonetheless," I said. I did understand the notion of thinking the clock could be turned back and wrongs would be righted. "I know your loss is all the harder because of its permanence."

"That's a good word, son," he said. "I think that word was part of the reason I bought all these books." He waved his hand at the box at our feet. "I thought if I could just figure out exactly how and why she died, that I could fix it. I had a very precarious relationship with the word permanent in those days. My own parents were still alive at the time and the loss of Mattie's mother was the first permanent loss, other than a puppy here and there, that I had experienced."

"So you bought these books to study the human body?"

"I bought them to figure out how life worked," he said. "I bought them to study what made someone die and what would have made them live."

I nodded again. I thought I understood. "Like a doctor, so you could get a grasp of how the injury killed her."

He shook his head. "Like a heartbroken widower looking for magic."

I did understand then. "And you didn't find it in the books."

"I did not." He sighed noisily. "In hindsight I know how silly such a notion was. Of course, no medical understanding would change what happened and there was no magic in those books or anywhere else that would have either. It's funny the things you think are true when you're lost in despair."

"I do understand that," I said.

In different ways, but I understood thinking, heck needing, there to be a magical fix. Something to change things for the better. I understood not finding it. I wanted to understand why my mother chose to stay with Mack when he was so awful to her. I wondered if there was a book somewhere that would tell me that. Mr. Mobley started talking about Mattie and the new baby and another ghost caught my eye in the far corner of memory.

A couple of years after we left Certain, Dad fouled up another scam and we'd moved to Boston. While we were unpacking, I found the deeds he'd stolen from the people of Certain and I stole them back.

"Cole," my father's voice rumbled so hard the house all but shook. "Where are they?"

I knew exactly what he meant, but there was no way I was giving them back. He came barreling into my room. It wasn't much more than a glorified closet, but it had a door that shut and that was all I needed. He banged the door open so hard it came off one of its hinges. It wasn't that well-made and he was pretty darn mad.

I just sat there on my bed daring him to come after me with my defiant glare. He wasn't getting those papers back no matter what. It was the least I could do for Certain and I felt like even though Ruby's family wasn't really involved, it was the least I could do for her.

"Boy, you better hand those over now or I'll beat them out of you."

"Come on and try," I said and stood up from the bed ready to defend Certain.

I was sixteen by then and even though I still had one growth spurt left in me I had filled out a bit. I thought I could stand my ground with a grown man. I was wrong. But I had tried.

"I ain't gonna ask again," he said, the devil's own fire glowing in his eyes.

"Wouldn't do you no good anyways," I said and shrugged like it was no never mind to me.

That turned him all sorts of sideways and he flew at me hard enough we both crashed into the bed and then up against the wall and after some tussling, we landed down on the floor. I punched and missed a couple of times. He punched and hit. He turned loose of me then and started tearing up the room.

"Where are they?" he screamed so that spit flew from his mouth.

I scooted up against the bed. Wiping my hand over my mouth, I felt and tasted the blood there. I was hurting from being flung into the wall and onto the floor and punched squarely in the face, but I got up anyway.

"You're wasting your time," I said, trying to sound casual. "They ain't here."

He stopped cold. "Did you sell them?"

He asked because he knew I could have if I wanted to. I just shrugged. He lunged forward and backhanded me so hard I stumbled right out the door and into my mother's arms where she had come running up the stairs.

"What's going on?" she asked and then looked at me and gasped. "You're bleeding. Mack, what did you do?"

She looked at him so dangerously that I thought, finally, finally she's going to do something. She's going to stand up for me and for herself. And maybe she wanted to, but Mack—I stopped calling him Dad right that moment—pushed on out of the room and grabbed her by the neck like he'd aimed to the night we left.

"You have always been in the way," he said with his hand clutching her throat so that she croaked and gagged for air. "You and that boy are going to be my downfall. I'll regret bringing you along. I know it. I already do."

If he was so set on regret, I was about to give it to him. I wanted to punch him square in the face like he'd done me, but he was a head taller and turned with his back to me then, so I punched him hard in the back, right in the kidneys just like he'd taught me to do back when he might have liked me and was trying to teach me how to "be a man" he said. He was not the kind of man I wanted to be, but right then I had to save my mother and at any cost. He grunted and his knees gave a bit, but he didn't let her go. He just laughed.

He laughed and squeezed her neck harder so that she made no noise at all. My heart stopped. I turned back into my room looking for anything that I could use as a weapon. There it was, a soda bottle I had picked up alongside the road the day before. I didn't know why at the time. It was empty and really of no use, but sometimes things happen for a reason and now that soda bottle was about to see its purpose. I held the neck and smashed the bottom end hard on the dresser. Nothing happened. I drew back with everything in me and smashed it again. That time the bottom broke out and without another thought I pushed back out into the hall and slammed shoulder first into Mack full force so that it turned him around just enough that his hand came loose from Mom's neck. I lunged at him with the jagged edge of the bottle. I cut him good. I didn't see exactly where my strike landed, but I did see blood. He put his hands to his neck and face and yelled out.

"Get out," his voice was a mix of anger and fear. "Get out."

I didn't need to hear more; I grabbed Mom's hand and yanked her down the stairs. For just a second, she pulled against me like she was going to stay, but then she looked me in the eyes and we just ran. Out of the old house we were staying in and into the street. I didn't know if Mack would come after us or if I'd slit his throat and he was bleeding to death on the floor.

"We have to go back, Cole," Mom said when we'd slowed down to rest.

"We can't go back, Mom," I said. She looked so scared. "We'll be fine. We don't need him. You don't deserve that."

"You don't either," she said and just for a second, I thought I saw the mother she meant to be, the courage she meant to have. But then it was gone.

I knew she would go back to him. And she did. Not right then. We found out that he'd stumbled out into the street and got someone to help him. I had cut him bad but nowhere near fatal. He got stitched up and then sort of went off the rails. He ended up in jail for a couple of years. Those were good years, but then he got out.

"I'm not going back, Mom." I told her when she came home one day to tell me the news.

"He's sorry, Cole," she told me, her eyes bright with hope. "I've talked to him and he wants us back."

I harrumphed. "He's got some scam he needs us for at best."

"We can't keep living like this, Cole," she said and I could see how tired she was. "I'm working all day and night and we still can't make ends meet. You should be in college and not working in the mines. It's too dangerous."

"And Mack isn't too dangerous?" I said, pleading with her. "Mom, stay with me. We'll make it work. It's not safe with him. He's either going to land you both in jail or in the ground."

I didn't want to say "it's me or him" because I already knew the answer. When I woke up the next morning, she was gone. It was him. It had always been him. I had just turned eighteen. I was man enough to be left all alone.

"Well," Mr. Mobley said. "That's enough of that sad tale."

I thought for a second he was talking about my tale and I wondered if he was able to see my ghosts as clearly as I could.

"Mattie didn't have her mother as long as she should have," he said and I realized that he was wrapping up his own sad tale after all. "I hope these books will now be used in the manner they were intended. Medical care, not magical thinking." He smiled and I knew that even though the memories were still painful that he had made his peace with them.

I asked what seemed a simple question until he answered it. "How long ago did your wife pass?"

"Been just almost twenty years now," he said. "Beautiful Asheville day, not a cloud in the sky. Idiot in a brand-new Overland that I later found out he had stolen. The actual owner was beside himself. Never caught the man who stole the car, whoever he was."

Every ounce of my blood stopped flowing in that instant. My breath caught in my chest and I couldn't seem to let it out. I became stone and then immediately turned to jelly so that I thought I would slip right out of the chair and into a puddle on the floor. The shifting states of being as I processed what he was telling me were too much to handle.

"Are you OK, son," he said, getting up quickly and coming to my side.

I managed to start breathing again, but there was no way I could stand on my jelly legs. "I'm OK," I lied. "Just such a sad story, so unnecessary to have lost her." I was rambling. "In that way, I mean. It shouldn't have happened. I'm so sorry, so very sorry."

"Son, it wasn't your fault." He patted me on the back. "You weren't even there."

I closed my eyes. No, I was blocks up the street sitting on the corner waiting for the Overland and its idiot driver to return.

Thankfully Mr. Mobley had walked back over to the printing press and was talking at length without needing me to interject about how amazing such a machine was and how he'd once had dreams of being a reporter and who knows what else as his voice seemed to get farther and farther away and my breath grew thicker and thicker in my chest causing it to heave so much it was almost painful.

If I had only convinced Mack not to go. If I had maybe gone with him, he might have driven more carefully. If only.

Suddenly more voices sounded in the room behind me and before I had time to turn around a little tow-headed boy that I recognized as Daniel's son, Hugh, ran around in front of me and handed me a toy block with a C on it.

"I'm Hugh," he said, perhaps not remembering we had already met. "My name starts with H just like yours. I was gonna give you my H block, but that's when Miss Ruby said you like the letter C." Or maybe he did remember me. "What's C stand for?"

"Curious," I said and tried to gather my wits. "What all good reporters should be."

He pushed the block into my hand and ran off. I stood up slowly, careful not to dissolve into the floorboard and turned around to see that the room was filled with people. I would have gotten nervous but the first face I made out clearly was Ruby's. She was walking toward me with a huge smile across her face.

"They all brought you things," she said and gestured toward the people. "Word got out yesterday that you were here and everyone wanted to come say hello." She shrugged.

Before I knew what to make of it a parade of people introduced themselves and gave me something they thought I would need. People were coming so fast and talking so much that I didn't have time to really look at them all. Everyone was just a big familiar blur. I tried to keep my head tilted or my hand close to my face, anything to keep people from getting a clear and direct look up close. The only hope I had of no one remembering me was that fifteen years was a long time not to see a person and back then if they were much shorter, scrawnier and more baby faced, it might be just hard enough to make the connection if the mind didn't spend that much time on it.

I hoped.

"I'm Ava," a dark-haired woman said. "Ruby seems to have some explaining to do. She never mentioned to us before that she'd met you. Anyway, here's a quilt you may have need for sooner or later."

"I sewed you some curtains," a young teenage girl said and handed me a set of pink frilly window coverings. "My name is Ella Barrett. Sorry they're pink. I used an old dress of mine and one of Marie's. She didn't make anything."

"I did too," said a younger girl who was certainly Marie if her indignation had anything to say about it. "I made up my mind to let you have my dress."

I laughed. I liked that kid. "Thank you both," I said even as the next person was coming to say hello.

I was handed a set of sheets, a set of dishes, a wash basin, a hat, some suspenders which made me check to see that my pants were in place, a rocking chair, and a coffee percolator and some coffee, and a baseball glove, a pair of pajamas and so many things I lost count. I wondered if they'd be so giving if they knew who I really was.

Mr. Gibbons found me once the line of people dwindled and most everyone was lingering around the press or poking their nose toward the rooms upstairs like everything was a great curiosity.

"I knew people would show up. Now," he said, looking over his shoulder as if he was checking to see that no one was listening. "Never you mind it if someone comes through here with a scowl or any unkind words to say. This place has a ghost or two in it and some of these folks might be here to catch a glimpse." He put his hands on my shoulders. "Most of the people here have long ago assumed that those ghosts have moved on unto the hereafter, but a folk or two might still have hard feelings. It's nothing to do with you."

He clapped his hands on my shoulders then and walked off.

Little did he know, it was to do with me, and the ghosts here had not gone on to the hereafter.

A happy couple approached me and I recognized Daniel from the day in the grocery store. My eyes went to the woman's face and my legs got jiggly again.

"I'm Mattie," she said and put her arm around Daniel's waist. "Mattie Barrett. Nice to meet you and welcome back."

Daniel nodded to me and although he looked concerned, he didn't say anything. Mattie kept talking.

"I can't believe that Ruby didn't tell us she was keeping in touch with you. Heck, she didn't even tell me she'd met you." Mattie looked me up and down and winked. "I'll get the story out of her sooner or later. She is my best friend after all. You must have met her that day that Daniel said you were at the grocery store." She smiled and winked at me again and I knew she was just being playful and that nothing she said was meant to be anything other than lighthearted but my mind was circling itself so that I was getting dizzy. "I do love a good story," she said. "Is that when you met Ruby?"

Daniel cleared his throat and smiled at Mattie. "I'm sure Henry here is getting a bit overwhelmed with all these people in his face."

Mattie agreed. "I'm sure you are. You're the talk of the town already, you know."

"Already?"

A man in his seventies, who I didn't recognize at all, sidled up and said, "That's true. People are already starting to talk about you doing an investigative story on what happened here in '22."

"Pardon," I said and my voice cracked.

Mattie's eyes lit up, but Daniel's closed.

Someone else came over, pushing up beside Daniel. "That's right. Now that we have a reporter right here where it all happened, we can finally find Mack Cooper and get our justice."

Justice.

"Will you do it," the first man said, his eyes eager. "Do your reportering and find out what happened to our land deeds? Maybe even find that scoundrel and bring him back to pay for what he's done."

A third man appeared and the small crowd that was growing in front of me parted.

"That will do folks," he said, his voice firm, but loving. "Let's give the man some air."

"Sorry, Pastor Collins," someone else who had gathered said. "We just want justice and Mr. Hall might be our chance to get it. He knows how to hunt down a story, right, Mr. Hall?"

I opened my mouth to speak, but Daniel spoke instead. "This is supposed to be a housewarming, fellas. We're making Henry feel like he's on trial or something. Which he isn't." Daniel put his hand on my shoulder briefly and then put his arm around his wife. "We'll talk more later, Henry."

After receiving a curt nod from Daniel, the rest of the crowd dissipated into the room leaving me there with just Pastor Collins. I remembered him so very clearly. He had aged more, it seemed, than the other men who were probably his contemporaries. Life had been harder on him it seemed, but his eyes were peaceful and he smiled at me.

"Welcome to Certain, son," he said and looked at me with sharp focus. "Not everyone here holds a grudge. Don't let them make you think you have to right the wrongs of the past." He clapped me on the shoulder and wandered away.

My eyes searched the room for Ruby. I saw her by the stove in the small kitchen area, sipping a cup of tea and talking to Mattie. Mattie seemed happy. Ruby glanced over and caught me looking at her. She smiled and waved. Mattie smiled and waved as well. I think I returned the gesture but I was too shaken to know.

I sat down hard in the chair closest to me and closed my eyes. It was no use; I couldn't get Mattie's face and her kind smile out of my mind. I wondered if she looked like her mother. I thought of Mr. Mobley searching the medical books for a way to bring his wife, Mattie's mother, back to them.

Bad was indeed going to worse. People wanted me to uncover the mystery of what Mack did and where he went. They wanted me to find out what happened and where their deeds were. I guess the good news was that they did still care about the deeds. I had a bargaining chip after all, but there was no way I would be able to come clean and settle in here. I was not the long-lost son I wished I was. I was the devil's boy come back to set things on fire.

Chapter 13
Ruby

I got my saddlebags packed for the day's book delivery route a little faster than I expected to, probably because I was rushing around like a madwoman, so I decided to let Patty drink a little extra water and eat a snack while I dashed across the street to check on Cole.

Practically the whole town had come out to see him when he moved in the other day and he'd seemed a bit overwhelmed by it. I had been so set on getting him to stay and to come in from the creek that I hadn't really stopped to think about what came next. He'd tried to tell me that he was worried about deepening the lie, but I'd been so sure that it wouldn't be a problem I hadn't really stopped to consider what if it was.

I burst into the newspaper office front door without knocking. Across the room, standing beside the printing press, Cole startled like a man on edge.

"It's just me," I called, striding over to him. I wanted to throw my arms around him in a hug, but I didn't really know what our relationship allowed exactly, so I just patted him on the shoulder awkwardly.

He breathed out deeply and offered a weak smile. I stepped back and looked at him. He was disheveled as if he hadn't slept well, shaved, or eaten anything in the last couple of days. He pushed his good hand through his thick dark hair.

"Cole, what's wrong," I asked.

He shook his head and walked to the other side of the room and then back to the press and back again.

"You're officially pacing," I said, my stomach growing nervous. "What's the matter?"

"They want me to find Mack and the deeds," he said, pointing toward the door as if to indicate who "they" were, but no one was there.

"What do you mean?"

He sighed heavily and raised his hands in the air. "They want me to put my reporting skills to use and find out what Mack did with their land deeds. They want me to enact some kind of justice."

Suddenly things seemed brighter to me, if not, obviously, to Cole.

"That's great," I said and clapped my hands together.

"Did you hear what I said?"

"Cole," I said, following him across the room as he was pacing again. When I caught up to him, I took his hand in mine and pulled him to a stop. "This is a great plan." I pointed to a chair at the dining table. "And sit down. I can't run around after you all day."

He sat and I took a seat across the table from him, ready to strategize.

"Look," I said. "Maybe you're not a reporter, but you know everything about what your dad did and where he went after you all left here. You know the towns he scammed in and how long he was there. At least for a while. You can retrace his steps and see if anyone knows anything."

He just sat there looking at me like a madwoman had sat down at his dinner table and was demanding high tea.

I continued. "Maybe you really can find the deeds," I said. "Wouldn't that be exciting? You could return them and be a hero. The town will be so happy they won't mind that you lied at first. They'll understand and you'll be a hero."

I expected him to respond with excitement too, but he just sat there looking at me. His mouth was slightly open as if words were working their way out but had gotten lost on the way.

Finally, he said, "What if I don't find the deeds?"

I shook my head as if that was an unlikely outcome, but I said, "Then you would have at least tried. That will count for something, I'm sure."

He put his elbows on the table and rested his face in his hands. He seemed so dejected. My heart sank.

"Cole," I said softly. "It's worth a shot, isn't it. What do you have to lose?"

He took his head from his hands and looked at me intently. He spoke without much inflection. "Nothing. I have nothing to lose."

I decided that even if he wasn't excited about the plan, I would be excited for him. This might just be the thing we were hoping for with the town. And if he did find the deeds, how wonderful would that be? He could give them back and make everything right. Not that it was his job to, but he might be able to.

I reached out across the table toward his hand and he reached out a little ways toward mine enough that I was able to reach him.

"Here's what we'll do," I said. "You start by going to the first place you got to when you left here. Ask around about Mack. I bet there will be people who remember him considering he tends to leave a memorable impression on people."

Cole let go of my hand and sat back. "I suppose."

"If that's a bust, go to the next place and talk to the next person, until you find something. Do you know where he and your mother might be now? You could start there."

He shook his head. "I don't know where they are." His voice was cold. We sat a few minutes in silence and then he asked me as if he was pleading for the answer, "Do you think this is the only chance I have of staying? Do you think it might work?"

"It just might," I said, trying to sound hopeful. "I could go with you if you want."

He spoke more urgently then. "No, no," he said. "I'll go by myself. It would be strange for me to take the local librarian with me to try and crack the story. You should stay out of it."

I paused, not sure what he meant by that.

He must have been able to read me because his eyes softened when he spoke. "I mean, I don't want you to get caught up in my lie. I'll handle things." He sighed and looked off into the distance. "Maybe I will find the deeds after all."

"You just might," I said. This was going to work. I knew it. I pressed my hands together like I was about to make a grand plan. "We'll start tomorrow. I'll see if you can borrow a car or a horse and you can set out to search. I'll make you a meal to take with you. We'll have to see about places for you to stay along the way."

"Sounds like I'm going on a long journey." He smiled, but there was no joy in his face.

"You'll be home in no time and I can't wait to hear all about what you find out."

He nodded and pressed his lips together before he spoke. "Sure. I'll tell you all about it."

Suddenly I grew nervous. "You'll come back, right?"

"Of course," he said. "I have nowhere else to go."

Chapter 14
Cole

At first, Ruby's plan seemed like a shovel spading the ground deeper and deeper, but as she talked, I began to realize that perhaps it wasn't the worst plan ever. There really was no good way out of this Henry Hall hole, but this plan at least bought me some time. It would be impossible, after the parade of townsfolk came through the other day for me to simply say, "Oh, what a misunderstanding this all is. It's me, Cole Cooper. Let me run upstairs and grab your land deeds."

I could picture their confused faces. Everyone looking around at each other, shrugging, whispering. "What was this all about?" They'd ask. Then as I called the first name and handed back the deed, they'd all look at each other wondering if this was true. "Is that your land deed?" They'd ask the first man. He would be bewildered as he nodded his head. Cries of "where's mine?" would come racing toward me, knocking me back as I tried to call the next name. Then, assuredly I'd be mobbed, hands reaching, angry faces lurching forward, the deeds snatched back by their rightful owners and then what of me?

No, that wouldn't work at all. This plan of Ruby's, as crazy as it may be, was my only option. Of course I'd be able to find the deeds. I knew exactly where they were. All I had to do was keep lying to Ruby, pretend to go out on investigation, stall as long as I could, eventually find the deeds, give them back and… then, again, what of me?

I sighed. Perhaps there would be less angry faces as Henry Hall handed back the paperwork that proved the people owned their land, but as soon as Cole surfaced, there would come the confusion, the whispering, the anger. I could remain Henry Hall, hero. Or I could come clean as Cole and be ushered out of town.

Talk about a losing situation no matter what. I supposed the upside was that people would have their deeds and therefore their pride back. I did want that. That would be worth it. And in the meantime, perhaps some other better plan would arise.

"Cole," Ruby said, waving her hand in front of my face as I had assuredly drifted off from paying attention. "So, what do you think? Let's give it a try?"

I nodded and let the possibility of possibility inch its way into my mind. "Sure," I said with more passion than before. "It's worth a try. And who knows, I might be able to find the deeds."

"And if you find Mack?"

"Let's not think about that," I said and shrugged. Yes, I could dredge up hope for this plan. And as I said, I had nowhere else to go anyway, so why not buy as much time here as I could.

❧❧❧

"OK," Ruby said, handing me a sack lunch on the bright and sunny day of my first fake investigative trip. "There's a sandwich, some carrots, and a hunk of cake that is probably dry but nonetheless."

"Thank you," I said earnestly, both of us standing beside Mr. Mobley's car. "I'm sure it will all be delicious." It was a heaping of food that I knew was a sacrifice for her. "I hope it wasn't a burden to part with this much food. And thank you for arranging with Mr. Mobley to use his car. I appreciate it."

"You'll really look the part coming into town in this fine vehicle," she said, patting the hood. "Isn't this thing fancy?"

I nodded but bunched my brows. "Ruby," I said, "you know that I'm not really a reporter, right? And that as of this moment, I also have no actual idea where I'm going."

"You could be a reporter," she said and patted my arm. "And you're going wherever the story leads you."

I wasn't sure who was more delusional about this whole charade, me or Ruby.

I blew out a breath and opened the driver side door. I ducked in to put my lunch on the seat. My bag was already in the trunk. I was sort of surprised that the whole town hadn't turned out to see me off.

"I better get going," I said, standing there awkwardly.

"See you when you get back," she said, seeming about as awkward as I was. She bit her lip and looked up at me. "You're coming back, aren't you?"

I had no idea where Ruby and I stood regarding our feelings, but I hoped that if nothing else we were still friends and friends could hold each other's hand. I reached out and closed my fingers around hers. "I will come back. I promise."

She nodded purposefully, but I knew it was in that way a person does when the gesture is less about believing the other person and more about convincing themselves the thing is true.

If I did anything at all in regard to this pretend attempt to find the deeds, it would certainly be to come back. I would not break that promise again.

Ruby stood up on tiptoe and kissed my cheek. Yeah, I'd do just about any fake thing she wanted me to right then. I touched the place her kiss had warmed on my face and slid into the driver's seat.

I started the car, waved good-bye and headed into the wherever.

And so began the next four months of my life. Spending the better part of the week in Certain, helping around the grocery store and aiding Daniel with carpentry work thus allowing me to earn my keep in the newspaper office by being a service to the town and the people. Then spending the weekend, or a day or two in the middle of the week if the plan was to speak to a business that ran only on workdays, getting the scoop on Mack and hunting down the deeds.

I'd come back to town and hold court at the grocery store telling my tall tales about what I'd found or if I was lucky, slip back in and only have to tell a lie or two to Ruby before I managed to change the subject to medicinal plants or a medical book that would see her forgetting all about my ruse and get her talking for hours about something else.

Of course, I never did any of the things I claimed. I didn't go to Hyden or Hazard or Lexington, I didn't talk to the mayors and the newspapers, I didn't go all the way over to Tennessee on a whispered hint Mack was there, and I didn't think I'd found the deeds only to determine they were old farmers' records on plots bought and sold.

I did eat up the praise from Ruby and the look in her eyes when I came back to town reporting that even though I hadn't found them, I really thought I was getting close.

"I knew you'd be a natural at this, Cole," she said when I got home one mid-October evening. "You know so much about Mack and how he runs his scams, it's only going to be a matter of time before you find the deeds." She hugged me tightly and lifted on her toes to kiss my cheek like she had come to do every time I came home.

I would get so wrapped up in the game that sometimes I actually believed myself. "I was so close, this time," I said, still feeling the warmth of her kiss on my cheek. "Maybe in the next town, I'll uncover something."

We sat on the front steps of the newspaper building that night looking up at the stars. She slipped her hand in mine and I closed my fingers around hers.

"Who would have thought," she said, "that this crazy idea would actually work."

Not me. "It hasn't worked yet," I said.

She laid her head on my shoulder. "It will, Cole. You'll see."

In the meantime, fall came into Certain and Cole and Henry began to fade together and I began to think that maybe there was some way to keep this up forever.

Chapter 15
Ruby

Cole had been working hard on uncovering the whereabouts of the deeds. He seemed determined and I hoped this mission gave him purpose, but time was passing without much success. Henry had ingratiated himself into the community quite well. Everyone loved him and why wouldn't they? But he wasn't Henry. He was Cole and I wanted him to be able to be Cole. Besides, Henry was a little stiff and nervous and somewhat like a stage prop version of a real person. And the two were blending in a way I didn't love. Lately when I was with Cole, I wasn't sure it really was Cole.

The previous night as we sat again on the steps of the newspaper building enjoying the cool October evening, I almost called him Henry and it had scared me. Today he was riding over to Hyden one more time to talk to a woman who had said she'd remembered his mother and might have some insight on how to find her. I wished he'd let me come with him sometimes because I knew how raw his wounds were still when it came to his parents. And selfishly, I really wanted to go to the Hyden Hospital. I was enamored with the nursing service and longed to see the likes of a real hospital in action.

To keep occupied, I decided to spruce up Cole's place while he was gone. He was a decent housekeeper, but things got a bit dusty and disheveled pretty quickly. I didn't usually go over to the newspaper office if he wasn't there, but we'd gotten close over the months and I was feeling pretty at home there. I cleaned the downstairs with just some light dusting and sweeping. I ran a cloth over the old printing press. It looked like it belonged in a museum somewhere, but the thing was so heavy how would we get it to one. Cole said he was sure it still worked and perhaps one day he would use it again. I tried to remember if I'd ever seen his father at work on it, but I didn't recall. Cole and I had always been shooed outside to play which we preferred anyway. I honestly had a hard time conjuring up the exact faces of his mother and father and I couldn't really imagine any given thing they had done or said. Instead, I had an image of them that was static like in a picture.

The kitchen area was the biggest mess and took the longest to clean up, but something about working around Cole's things, helping to get his house back in order made me smile. I made myself a cup of tea when I was finished and took it upstairs to see if there was work to do there. His room was tidy for the most part, but the bed wasn't well made. I set the mug of tea on the desk and went around the backside of the bed to straighten the cover. The bed was pulled out from the wall enough that you could scoot in, but not comfortably. I nudged the bed frame a bit to be able to get closer to the headboard. My foot shifted a loose board, startling me. The last thing we needed was for the floor to be coming loose. I pushed the bed a little harder, bumping it into the desk which sloshed my tea.

"So much for cleaning up," I said aloud to myself. I hadn't taken a rag or anything to wipe the spilled liquid. One of Cole's undershirts had fallen behind the bed and was lying at my foot. I bent down to pick it up and my shifting feet hit the loose floorboard again. With the bed mostly moved and the tea practically already dried into the wood of the desk I abandoned that task and reached to check the board. It was indeed totally loose. I pulled it up to see if the wood was rotted but it seemed fine. That was when I noticed a small leather folding satchel in the hole. I retrieved it and sat on the cattywampus bed to investigate.

I unwound the leather strings that held it closed and opened it across the bed. There were papers inside. Some so old I was afraid to touch them. Some much newer. All of them were detailing plots of land and who owned them. As I sorted through them carefully, I recognized each one. It was the land deeds that Mack had scammed. Right here in the floorboards. For just one delusional and hopeful second, I thought I had made a miraculous discovery. The deeds had been right here all along! What were the odds of that?

Then my heart thudded the answer; pretty slim.

I didn't want to believe it, but what else could be the truth. Mack wouldn't have left without them. That would make no sense. The only explanation was that Cole had hidden them here.

He'd had them all along.

He'd been lying to everyone all along.

He'd been lying to me.

I stacked the papers back together and wrapped them back into the leather folder. Placing them back under the floorboard and putting the bed back where it had been, I left the bed half made, retrieved my mug and slipped out of the room in hopes he'd be none the wiser I was up there. My mind numb, I sat at the table and drank what was left of my tea hoping some brilliant thought or other explanation would come to me.

It didn't.

I washed the mug and ambled outside, closing the door behind me.

The next morning, I was determined to discover the truth. Cole had already said that he'd be late getting home so we had had no plans to share his adventures like we usually did once he got home. That was good, because last night I was not in a frame of mind to hear all about how his search was going. This morning, I was ready to try and understand his reasons for lying to me.

I was so lost in my thoughts that I didn't even see Claire come out the front door of Cole's place until I ran smack into her on my way up the steps. She and I both stumbled back from each other and took a moment to right ourselves.

"Good Heavens, Ruby," she said, making a show of brushing herself off as if I'd knocked her clean into the dirt, which I hadn't.

"Are you lost?" I asked, pointedly, wondering what on earth she'd be doing at the newspaper office just after the sun itself woke up.

"Not at all," she said, a coy smile spreading across her face. "Found is more like it." She raised her eyebrows and flapped her hand back and forth like a fan in front of her face.

My mouth fell open. What was happening here?

"Better close that mouth, Ruby, before the flies get in," Claire said. She wiggled her shoulders and stood up straight so that she towered over me by at least four inches. "You might want to give Henry a moment or two to collect himself."

My mouth gaped open even more. I huffed and pressed my lips together then and pushed past her slamming the door behind me as I went in.

Now he sauntered down the stairs, slipping his suspenders over his shoulders and walked right up to me like nothing was amiss.

"Ruby?" he asked, a look of assuredly fake concern on his face. "What's wrong?"

"Was that Claire?" I asked, knowing of course that it was.

He smiled and looked toward the door as if he could still see her there. "She sure grew up fancy, didn't she? For someone living in Certain anyway."

I wanted to ask what she was doing there, but that stupid grin he had on his face told me enough. Besides, I felt like if I said anything at that moment I would burst into tears and I was not about to give him the satisfaction of that, so I let him prattle on, digging another sort of hole.

"I have to admit," he said, brushing his hand over his disheveled hair, "I was about to slip off into the night that first evening I was here. It was all too much with everyone coming around asking me if I could sleuth out the whereabouts of the deeds and bring Mack Cooper to justice. I was beside myself. But I have to believe there's a way to make this work."

I found my voice and asked, "So you found the deeds, then?"

He shook his head. "Not yet, but as soon as I do, I think I'll be able to put everything right. I know I was against your idea of me moving into town, but I think it's going to be a good thing."

My heart burned so much my whole chest felt like it was on fire. I wasn't sure if it was pain or anger, likely both.

"You do, do you?" I asked, my voice tight.

If he picked up that I was upset, he just put it right back down and went on. "Running off again isn't the answer," he said. "I see that now. I'm not entirely certain how I'll pull this off, but I'm going to make it right. I like it here. I want to stay." He looked back at the door; the door Claire had just left through.

"I'll bet you do," I challenged.

He reached out and put his hands on my arms at the elbows. He wasn't wearing the brace anymore and his hand looked fine. He gave me a squeeze. "I woke up this morning feeling like things were going to work out."

I wanted to yank free of him but his hands were so warm and strong on mine that I didn't want him to let go. I hated that he had that effect on me still. Was this whole thing just a grift that I was playing into? It had been fifteen years since I'd seen him. He was his father's son after all.

"What was different about this morning?" I dared ask.

"I had a good conversation last night," he said and smiled widely at me before turning me loose. "And I woke up this morning feeling all warm inside."

A "conversation" no doubt. I wanted to cry or slap him. Or both. But he turned away from me and headed for the wood stove at the back of the room as if nothing out of sorts was happening at all.

"Coffee?" he called out over his shoulder. "I made enough for two. Not everyone is a coffee drinker though. Do you like coffee? It's real!"

My shoulders slumped. How could he do this? I couldn't move. I watched him pour two mugs full and head back my way. I hadn't moved an inch. He stopped at the table and put the mugs down.

"Ruby?"

I thought it was the same Cole who left fifteen years ago that had come back now, but it wasn't. That boy I'd been waiting for never came back. I didn't know who this man was at all.

"I was waiting on that creek bank just like you told me to and you never came back to kiss me again like you said you would." My heart was beating slowly again. I had gone numb. "I must have been mistaken. I thought you liked me. But you didn't come back."

He stepped closer and his eyes burned into mine. "Yes, I did," he said and pulled me to him before I could think twice about what he was doing. "And I didn't say I was coming back to kiss you. Is that what you thought? Did you want me to?"

Before I could speak, he pressed his lips to mine and heat shot through me just like I knew it would have if we kissed, but now with Claire just leaving and doubt eating me alive, that heat reawakened my anger. I kissed him back like I was enacting some sort of revenge or rather like I might be able to turn him back into the Cole I knew and wanted. He must have misconstrued my intention because when I pulled away from him, he looked rather pleased with the whole thing.

"It just took me a while," he said. "That's all."

"That's all?" I asked, still mad but now totally discombobulated and completely uncertain about how I should feel. "Did you really think that was going to work?"

"What?"

"Ambling over here after fifteen years, after Claire just walked out the door, after I know now that I can't trust you and kissing me?" I asked. "That's what."

"Well, yeah," he said and raked his hands through his hair. "Or at least I hoped it would work better than it did apparently and what's Claire got to do with anything?"

I folded my arms across my chest and glared at him, waiting for him to ask me why I couldn't trust him, but he didn't. I could still feel the sensation of him kissing me and I bit down on my bottom lip to try and stop it.

"So it didn't work at all?" he asked, trying to be cute.

"No, it did not," I said, pushing him away from me as he was standing much too close and he smelled much too good thanks to the fancy soap I'd given him when he moved in. Wasted my money on that frivolity.

I wasn't even sure what I meant by that.

"What's happening?" Cole asked. "I thought we were going to…"

I cut him off before he could finish. "You thought wrong. I don't even really know who you are."

"I am the same me I have always been too afraid to be," he said, his eyes blazing. "Maybe it's time to change that. I don't know, but I'm going to find out. I'm tired of running and scraping by. I want a place to call home."

"What does that mean?" I asked him. "You're talking in circles just like your dad."

His eyes went cold and he stepped back from me even further. That was over the line and I knew it, but wasn't he just here to run a scam? If I put two and two together, something didn't add up. He was hiding along the creek for weeks probably and never once came into town looking for me. When he did come into town, he claimed to be someone he wasn't. He played the victim and I ate it up. I invited him into town and set him up in his old stomping ground. He had played me for the fool with all this nonsense about searching for the deeds—to what end I had no idea—and now he was taking up with Claire and kissing me at the same time. It was obvious that he just wanted to keep stringing me along.

"Don't you have books to deliver this morning," he said and nodded toward the door. "Better get to it."

"Don't you have a scam to finish running?" I asked.

He looked sick to his stomach and angry all at the same time.

"Don't worry yourself," he said. "Once I do what I came here for, I probably won't be around that much longer."

"Good," I said. "Then I'll get on with my life and forget you were ever here."

"Is that what you want?" Cole asked, his eyes trained on mine.

I knew well enough that I was about to draw a line in the sand, but I couldn't stop myself. I was too scared of being hurt by him again and it seemed like that was already happening.

"Yes," I said. "This whole thing was a bad idea."

He looked confused and dejected. "This isn't going the way I thought it would," he said. "I don't understand what's happening."

He didn't expect I'd call his bluff was what was happening. I harrumphed and put my hands on my hips. "A Cooper is a Cooper it looks like."

He furrowed his brow at me. "I guess so," he said, his voice breaking just a bit.

Either he was a very good actor or there was a chance I was mistaken about things. Either way, I couldn't take any more of it and rushed out the door before the tears threatening my eyes broke free.

Chapter 16
Cole

Most of the time that I was supposed to be hunting up the deeds and sifting out the story, I was really hiding out along the creek in my old lean-to that was still leaning-to. Sometimes I went further into the middle of nowhere and sometimes I was tempted just to keep driving, but I always went back. This time I wasn't so sure I had anything to go back for.

Disappearing was my forte when things got stressful and what had gone down between me and Ruby the other day was confusing and hard on the heart. This whole thing was out of hand.

I hung on Ruby's last words the other day, *a Cooper is a Cooper it looks like*. That stung and my worst fear was that it was true. I didn't understand what had set her off but even Ruby's kiss felt like she was scolding me. Whatever I'd done, it was clear she just wanted me to go. And my pride was hurt so I let my own anger feed the whole situation. Had I misread things between us that badly?

I'd meant what I said to her that day. I really felt like everything was going to be OK. I had a new plan: I had decided to slowly stop looking. I would say that I had tried, really, I had, but wasn't it always a longshot that Henry Hall would ever find out what happened to the land deeds from Certain that were stolen fifteen years ago by a masterful con artist. What if I just ran out of leads and eventually stopped looking. Already people asked me about it less and less. More and more they just talked to me, well Henry, about whatever you might talk to a person about. I figured I was in the clear from getting recognized after all this time and what was so bad about being called Henry anyway. It was a nice name. And Henry was a better person than Cole anyway.

I laid back on the bank and soaked up the sun. October was cool, but very orange and the sun and the sounds of the water rippling against the rocks in the creek lulled me to sleep. I don't know how long I was out, but I was awakened by the giggles of children and the sound of a deep voice calling them back in line.

"Children," the voice scolded, "You leave Mr. Hall alone."

I shot awake fully then and sat upright. I was face to face with Hugh, Daniel's son. The boy's blonde curls blew up and out in the cool breeze along the creek.

"Hugh," Daniel's voice rang clear then, confirming me. "Get on back over here."

I looked around and saw the two older girls, Ella and Marie, wrangling little Hugh back toward a couple of horses just up the creek. I stood and brushed myself off. Daniel's tall form approached me and I grew nervous. He was always friendly to me and on more than one occasion had ended a conversation I'd gotten trapped in right as things were getting dicey. He tended to magically appear like he was my guardian angel or something. Although I wasn't sure what danger I was in at the moment.

"Good to see you, Henry," he said, his grip was firm. "Working on that story still?"

"No," I stumbled, wishing so much that I could get out of this hole I'd dug. "I'm not reporting on anything."

"I know," Daniel said and nodded, causing alarms to sound in my ears. "Just taking a break out here. I understand."

Daniel turned and waved for the girls and Hugh, to come over. "We were on the way to town," he said looking at my makeshift campsite. "Are you staying out here? Something wrong with the newspaper office?"

It was probably obvious that I had been hanging around here a day or two what with the lopsided lean-to sporting a pile of red and gold leaves bunched together to form a bed and my rolled-up jacket making a pillow.

"I was just taking a nap," I said, waving it off like nothing. "Nice to be out of the office for a bit. Enjoying the weather before it turns cold." We just looked at each other for a moment. The longer he looked at me without speaking the more nervous I became. "So, how's Mattie doing?" I stammered. "She's getting closer to the date, right?"

"She's hanging in there," Daniel said, eyeing me like he was deciding whether to say something. I knew that look. It was the look someone had when they were putting two and two together. "We figure she's got a couple of months yet. Mid December. She's getting tired. It's been a while, but I remember how things were with Emily around this time."

"Emily, I remember," I said. She was Ava's sister. "Your first wife," I said and immediately knew I'd put my foot in my mouth. And even though I'd been in town a while, why would I remember some other lady he'd been married to."

Daniel's brow furrowed. "Yes. Did Ruby tell you about Emily?"

Think fast. What did I remember? "I remember Ruby telling me that you'd been married before," I said and pointed to the children, "And clearly you have experience with a pregnant wife."

He nodded. Daniel and I had run into each other from time to time, but he seemed to keep a low profile. Mostly he appeared in church and at the grocery store. Ruby had dragged me to church a time or two, but sitting there I felt like my spot on the pew was going to catch fire any second. With Daniel looking at me like he was waiting for me to come clean, I sort of felt like that now.

For a long moment neither of us said anything and then Daniel asked, "Did you ever find your car?"

I knew he didn't mean Mr. Mobley's car that I had poorly hidden and was probably scratching up. I had watched my father be caught off guard enough to know that the first thing you did was stall. He wasn't much for fatherly advice unless it came to running a scam and on that I had been told all the tricks of the trade. *Give your brain a second to catch up.*

Speaking fast is speaking stupid. So I stalled. I honestly couldn't remember what I'd told him and Mr. Gibbons that day. I had been so nervous.

"It wasn't my car, actually," I finally said. "Just borrowing it from a buddy."

"I'm sure he'd want it back." Daniel slipped his hands into his pockets and looked at me sideways.

"I saw him not that long ago and it had turned up in working order," I said and nodded affirmatively. "All's well. What a crazy ordeal that was."

Daniel nodded, but his eyebrow raised up and stayed there. "So, how's the search for deeds going?" He glanced around the campsite again. "Seems to keep you on the road."

"The life of a reporter," I said and chuckled, shaking my head in the "it's all too much to talk about move." I wanted to kick myself, I sounded so superficial and stupid.

"Sounds like you spend too much time on the road," he said. "I was like that myself a long time ago. Not for such noble reasons as reporting the news however."

I wanted to blurt out everything right there and beg him to forgive my lies. Instead, I just slipped my hands into my pockets as well and we stood there considering each other while the children tossed rocks into the creek beside us.

I looked closely at the man Daniel had become. It was strange to see him all these years later, grown. He was enough older than I was that we didn't run in the same circles as kids, even in a town as small as Certain. He was courting Emily by the time my family moved here. I heard the tales of how he'd been rescued as a young orphan by Pastor Collins and how his family was bad seeds. Or at least his father had been. Daniel and I had more in common than he realized, if he had known who I was anyway.

I got the impression that the town now viewed him as a good man. I didn't know what all transpired between the time I left and now, other than Emily had died and he'd remarried to Mattie who wasn't from here. Somehow, he'd gotten out from under his past. I wanted to do the same thing. I opened my mouth to confess everything when one of the children spoke instead.

"Da," the oldest girl called out to him, "Are we going?"

He looked at her and then back at me. "Just a few minutes, Ella," he said over his shoulder, having turned back to look at me. He had terribly green eyes that seemed to be able to see right through me. I didn't know whether to look away or meet his stare.

"Can Hugh and me play in the water?" the other girl called out.

"It's I," Ella corrected her. "Can Hugh and I play in the water?"

Daniel's eyes left my face and he chuckled to himself.

"Shut up, Miss Know It All," the younger girl said, dragging her brother down with her toward the creek even though she didn't yet have permission to play in it.

"Girls," Daniel said, looking back at them, "be nice."

Ella came running up to Daniel to plead her case. "But I'm right, Da, it's Hugh and I, Ma says so and she's the teacher."

Daniel put his hand on the top of the girl's head and smiled at her. "Yes, you are correct, but perhaps be correct without making Marie feel poorly about her own grammar skills."

"How do I do that?" Ella asked.

"Ask your teacher," Daniel said and winked at her.

She huffed and walked away.

"Don't get in the water," Daniel called after them. "It's getting too cold for playing in the creek."

"What's the fun in that," the little girl, Marie, called back and then immediately reached down into the creek, scooped up some water and splashed her little brother.

I pointed toward her, but Daniel shook his head.

"It's fine," he said. "Worth a try to keep them from getting a mess, but it usually doesn't pan out."

"Kids," I said and nodded as if I knew about them.

"So," Daniel said as if he was about to launch into a conversation we'd been waiting to have, "how are things working out for you at the old newspaper office? It seemed a bit unfair for the town to hold you accountable for the lost deeds. That was quite a hard time back then. Not your fault or job to fix."

"I don't know," I said, my heart rate picking up as I sensed a turn in the conversation. "It's OK," I said, trying to sound like it was all in a day's work and that the town hadn't hit the nail on the head expecting me to fix it. It was my job.

"The family that used to live there left a bad taste in everyone's mouth," he said, picking up a stone and tossing it across the water. "Cooper. The man everyone is forcing you to use your fancy reporting skills to find?"

"They're not forcing me," I stammered. I looked out across the creek like I was looking for something. The creek was wide here, but not deep and people used it as a place to cross from one side of the Hell for Certain to the next. I wished someone would come passing through and save me. I hoped it would be Ruby, but I doubted it.

"It did seem like everyone was pretty put out with him," I said. "Seems like he's disappeared. Maybe for the best."

"They had a son," Daniel said and put his hands in his pockets. I started to sweat. "He was a few years younger than me. He was friends with little Ruby."

I nodded, but kept my mouth closed.

"I felt bad for him," Daniel said.

I perked up just a little. "You did?"

"I knew what it was like to have a father that was no good. I knew what it was like for people to assume that I was no good because I was his son."

I nodded again, blinking more often than I should.

"When did you get into reporting?" Daniel asked, taking his hands back out of his pockets and putting them on his hips. "Did you write as a kid?"

"Write?" I asked, stalling. "Like stories and such?"

"Or newspaper articles?" Daniel said. "About fishing and camping out?"

I closed my eyes. I'd been had after all.

Along with the birthday lists and other trivial items that Mack had me write to make things look legitimate and because he couldn't be bothered with such things, he'd let me write a little column about my adventures along the Hell for Certain. He thought having words from a kid, his own son, would give people the idea that he was a solid family man, supportive of his son, making room in the paper for his little articles. Surely a man like that could be trusted.

"I suppose," I answered carefully and noncommittally. My heart hammered against my chest.

"I always enjoyed those," he said, pressing his lips together and raising his eyebrows.

The jig was up, there was no use pretending. It was a terror and a relief at the same time.

"You read them?"

He nodded. "I felt bad once you left. I was too wrapped up in Emily and being young to get involved in all the town stuff back then. I heard Pastor Collins talking here and there as things were heating up and then when everything boiled over. You were gone by then."

I felt so weak and shaky I feared I was going to fall down right there in front of him.

"Dad didn't take his land." There was no Collins on any of the deeds I had. I bet he sure wished he could have gotten it though. Between the pastor's homestead, the rectory and the church, Dad would have been in hog heaven. Or headed for Hell.

Daniel shook his head more in confirmation than accusation, but he asked, "You knew about it all?"

I closed my eyes and breathed in slowly trying to calm my heart and slow the rolling of my stomach. This was the worst of it. "Not when it all first started, but over time Mack dragged me into it with little jobs here and there that helped his cover story. He'd tell me things. I think he was so proud of himself he had to tell someone what he was doing."

"He made you an accomplice," Daniel said, scoffing and shaking his head. He sighed and ran his hands through his hair. "I'm sorry, Cole." He reached out and clapped me on the shoulder. "That's your name, right? I didn't remember it at first, but it came to me a while back."

I nodded. The sound of my name, spoken so freely, almost bowled me over.

"How long have you known it was me?" I asked, feeling a bit foolish that I'd spoken to Daniel on numerous occasions now in full pretend of being Henry.

"You looked familiar right away," he said, looking at me intently as if trying to call up those first notions. "But I couldn't place it and the name you gave wasn't familiar at all."

I winced but he waved it off.

"It was seeing you with Ruby," Daniel said, continuing, "that made the connection. All the talk of newspaper reporting and the deeds drove it home."

"Do you think everyone knows?"

He shook his head slowly. "If anyone does, they've not said anything to me about it."

"Why did you just let me go on and on with my," I hesitated, but it was time to call it what it was, "lies?"

"Listen," Daniel said and bent down to retrieve another rock which he tossed in the creek, "I take it you're trying to figure things out. Maybe you're even trying to find those deeds. Or maybe you already know they're long gone. Who knows, but I trust that you're not your father's son. I know I'm not. I thought I was for a while and it near about got the best of me. You're getting caught up in tall tales, but I like to think I can spot a good heart. I hope you get things sorted out."

I stammered for a moment before getting a sentence out. "You're not going to tell anybody?"

"That's yours to do," he said. "I really did like those articles. You're a natural reporter. I hope you put it to good use one day." Daniel reached his hand back out to shake, letting me know he was taking his leave. "I know what it's like to want a second chance. I hope you get one."

He didn't say another word, just turned and walked toward his kids. He called them lovingly out of the water and they all mounted the horses, he and Hugh on one and the girls on the other.

"Daniel," I called out and he turned the horse toward me. "I'm not my father's son."

He nodded and called for the horses to head out and they all stepped into the creek, one horse more reluctantly than the other and headed across to the other side toward town.

My legs had turned to jelly and I sank down on the bank of the Hell for Certain.

❦❦❦

When I got my wits back about me and my legs would carry me, I hotfooted it back to Mr. Mobley's car and drove into town. I darted into the newspaper office before anyone could see me, I hoped. Only moments after I closed the door behind me there was a knock on it and I almost jumped out of my skin. I guessed I'd been spotted after all and quickly. I hoped it wasn't someone else asking me to find a deed or track down Mack or ask me if I knew anyone from Louisville and were they getting things sorted out after the flood. I needed a break.

The knock came again and I realized it was soft, like a woman might knock and not the boisterous banging of an insistent man. It had to be Ruby. I flung the door open.

"Ruby," I called out into a face that was not Ruby's at all.

"Nope," Claire said and stuck out her hand for me to kiss, I presumed. "Much better if I do say so myself."

Debatable, except that Ruby wanted nothing to do with me anymore.

"Nice to see you again," I said, taking her hand into mine and lifting it to my lips for a quick peck.

"May I come in?" She asked. "I'd like to finish our conversation from the other day. I didn't mean to cut it short so suddenly."

I looked past her out into the street hoping to see Ruby. Still wanting my conversation with her the other day to have been a bad dream or at least something easily apologized away and forgotten. I sighed, since when had life ever gone my way?

I stepped back so Claire could enter. "Sure, please come in." I looked down at myself, my pants covered in creek dirt after three days. "Pardon me," I apologized. "You caught me just home from a small camping vacation."

She smiled. "Oh, I heard you were over in Hyden following yet another lead," she said and winked at me. "Perhaps you were undercover, using an alias and all that."

This felt oddly like a shake-down.

"What can I do for you, Claire?"

She batted her lashes at me dramatically. "Just when I thought that

137

no one interesting would ever move to Certain, you came to town."

"I'm not that interesting," I said and stepped back a bit. This conversation caused the hair on my arms to stand up.

She stepped forward and put her hand on my chest. "On the contrary, you are the most interesting thing to appear in this little dirt town in just about fifteen years."

"I promise you," I said, hoping she couldn't feel how fast my heart was beating, "I'm not worth your time."

"I'd love to get to know you better, Henry," she said and her eyes trailed me up and down and she moved her hand from my chest to rest it on my cheek. "You're quite an attractive man, Mr. Hall," she said, batting her lashes at me. "You have a very familiar look about you. Do we know each other from somewhere?"

I stammered. "I doubt it. I'm not from around here."

"Where are you from?"

"Here and there," I said and pulled my face from her hand. "I don't usually stick around one place for long. I'll be taking off for somewhere else soon."

"Not too soon," she said, her tone less hopeful that I wouldn't leave and more like a command for me to stay. "I think you and I should get to know each other better."

That seemed like a terrible idea. I was a mouse cornered by the smiling house cat. I employed one of Mack's favorite tactics. Say nothing. *Don't show your hand, son. Let the other person play all their cards first.*

Claire stood silent as well, the both of us looking at each other, no one laying down a card.

Finally, she winked at me. "I think you should take me to the fall festival."

"The what?" I asked.

She chuckled. "Surely you've heard people talking about it," she said and gestured toward the door and the world outside it. "Halloween," she said looking at me as if that should explain it. When I shook my head, she explained. "Certain has started putting on a Fall Festival on Halloween to help keep people entertained and out of trouble. Games, contests, a dance."

I nodded. "Is there much trouble to get into in Certain?"

She smiled at me in what I could tell was her best coy smile. "You'd be surprised."

"I'm not much for parties and festivities and such," I said, trying to move toward the door in hopes that would end the conversation.

"This year you are," she said and winked at me. "I think you'd be smart to get to know me better. Who knows, perhaps we can become friends. It might benefit us both."

"It might?"

She nodded. "In the end."

Chills raced across my arms and up the back of my neck, but I didn't dare say anything. Play your cards close to your chest, Cole. Things are changing. The upper hand might be everything.

"OK," I said to her, trying to sound casual and nonchalant. "Why not. Let's go to the festival together."

She clapped her hands together and pressed closer to me so that she could kiss my cheek.

"I'll see you around until then," she said. "You're making a wise decision."

I smiled weakly, opened the door to see her out, and then slipped down into the nearest chair before I fell out onto the floor.

Chapter 17
Ruby

I hadn't spoken to Cole in weeks. He hadn't spoken to me either. I had gotten good at being in town without looking at the newspaper building and that was saying something as the town was small and Cole's place was right in the middle of it.

I had said the most awful things to him the last time we'd talked. *A Cooper is a Cooper it looks like.* I was sick just thinking about it. But wasn't it true? I wasn't blind or deaf. I'd seen Claire coming out of his front door early in the morning and him coming down the stairs still dressing. I didn't have much experience with love or things like it, but I knew what was what.

I just didn't know why? The only answer to that was that I was being scammed and that he was so good at it, or thought he was, that he was going to keep right on scamming me even after I had found him out. Well, I wouldn't be taken that easily.

Still, I wanted him to stay forever and love me and marry me and be the father of our children and grow old with me and all the other unrealistic things that came along with the idea of being with Cole.

What a fool I was and it made me so mad at myself. I really was better off being alone. Just me and my plants. I didn't need Cole. He wasn't going to stay anyway. He'd said as much. He'd said it like a proclamation. Or at least that was how I took it. I had spent long minutes trying to recall everything we'd said and how it had been said to see if I was misinterpreting something. But mostly all that did was lead me to thinking about that kiss.

It had worked. Just like Cole hoped it would, but I couldn't let him know that.

So never had any librarian been so dedicated to delivery, repairs and report, and sorting out new materials than I was over the weeks following my falling out with Cole. Unfortunately, my patrons were quick to fill me in on the gossip about Henry and Claire and how they must be an item and did I know they were going to the fall festival together and wasn't that great that after all Claire had been through she landed someone like Henry to make her happy.

After all Claire had been through? Claire? Really?

My gramma used to tell me I was a glutton for punishment. I didn't know what in the world that meant as a kid since I was no more punished for things than the man in the moon. But today, I finally understood. I just couldn't keep myself away from something that would hurt my heart, because I just had to know what was happening.

The Fall Festival was today. The name made it sound much more fancy than the gathering it really was. Just a group of folks each bringing the best dish they could muster from their meager pantries to share with the rest of the folks. But there would be music and dancing and crafts and most importantly, there would be happiness. Even if just for a while people could forget all the things they didn't have and enjoy what they did have. Each other. And it kept people out of trouble. Because it was Halloween and on a Sunday no less. I'd been to church and then gone back home to mope. I planned to stay there and let the festival happen without me, but I couldn't bear it. Patty and I walked back into town that afternoon on the back roads trying to see through the trees and between the few buildings to what was happening along the main drag with the festival. It had been Pastor Collins' idea to bring the tradition back. Something happy to build hope and community and it wasn't such a bad by-product if it kept people out of trouble on such a traditionally trouble-making evening. The main event was a dance right out in the street. Daniel and his brothers-in-law on Emily's side, Liam and Zachary, were playing music and Pastor would be calling the dances. The dance of course that Claire would accompany Cole to. The whole idea left me a bit nauseated. Luckily, it was early and the whole terrible event was still in the set-up phase, which meant Cole and Claire were nowhere to be seen yet.

I came into town telling myself that I was making a point. I supposed that point was that I wasn't going to hole up at home while the rest of town celebrated. But I was the one lying. I just wanted to see Cole. Even if he was with Claire. I turned Patty toward the main road and taking a deep breath, I rode past the church and the grocery, not looking at the newspaper building as I went on around to the library.

I looked around for Opal or Daniel's wagon that might indicate Mattie was in town, but I didn't see either. She was busy with her new family and her baby on the way and Cole was busy being someone else with someone else and I was about as lonely as all get out.

The town looked lovely already with paper pumpkins painted orange hanging in every window and tacked to signposts and buildings alike throughout the town. I really did love the fall festival. Usually.

I stabled Patty in the pen beside the library and walked around to the front door. Ava was sitting on the front porch reading. She had a blanket tossed over her lap and looked quite content on this cool Halloween afternoon. She looked up at me and smiled, but then saw my face which must have looked terrible because the smile fell off her face and a frown appeared.

"Do I look that pathetic?" I asked.

She closed the book she was reading, *Murder in the Calais Coach*, by Agatha Christie. I didn't recall that one being on our shelves or that Ava liked mysteries.

"You look sad," Ava said and pointed to the chair beside hers that I might sit down, which I did. "And you tend to go to great lengths not to most of the time."

"I do?" I questioned, wondering what that meant.

"Everyone gets sad, Ruby," Ava said and turned the book over in her lap so that the bright blue back cover faced out, showing a pink diagram of a train car. "Everyone but you. Which of course cannot be true. I don't need to be Hercule Poirot to deduce that."

"I didn't know I worked hard to fake being happy all the time," I said, but I suppose I did once I thought about it.

"Want to tell me about it?" she asked.

Yes, but how.

"No," I said.

"Are you wishing you had a date to the dance?" Ava guessed. "Or that you had a dish to share? Maybe you could set up a booth along the street and talk about medicinal plants."

I scowled at her. "No one wants to hear me talk about medicinal plants."

She smiled at me. "I do. I'd come to listen to you talk about anything."

A lump formed straight away in my throat and tears burned hot in my eyes. She reached across the small space between our rocking chairs and took hold of my hand. She gave it a gentle squeeze and knowing me, changed the subject.

"This book is special," she said, letting go of my hand and giving me the book to see. "Open the front cover."

This copy is one of a limited first edition presented by the publisher to friends in the book business. Not for sale. #126. My mouth fell open. If there was a way to get my mind off something bad it was to present me with something amazing about a book. Numbered and limited. Maybe that didn't mean much to other people but I knew what a prize I held in my hand.

"Did you know," Ava asked, turning to face me better, "that this is the US version of *Murder on the Orient Express?*"

I began looking, very gently, through the pages, turning the book this way and that. One day, this book would be highly sought after. Agatha Christie was a rising star. I just knew it.

"Was this in one of the donation boxes?" I asked incredulously. This sort of book was not the usual thing we got. It was relatively new for one thing and Christie's books were originally published in England. How on earth had it gotten to Certain, Ky?"

Ava shook her head. "Mattie's father brought it over a few days ago. I thought you might want to see it."

"Today you mean," I said, knowing full well that Ava was sitting on this porch on this day with this book because she knew I would be coming to town despite myself and that I'd wish I hadn't and that I'd need a distraction. "Am I that transparent?"

"Not at all," Ava said. "But I am that much your friend, and I know you well."

"Claire's going with him to the festival." I dared not say his name, real or fake.

"I know," she said.

"And you know that I like him?" I grimaced again. I had worked so hard not to let anyone know that I knew him that I hadn't considered that they would still be able to tell that I had feelings for him.

Ava nodded. "Why else would you be avoiding him or any discussion of him at all costs for weeks now when you've spent the last months glued to his side."

"That showed?" Apparently, I was an open book.

"Like Mattie's big baby belly."

I laughed at Ava's unexpected joke. Everyone thought Ava was so serious all the time, but she was quite witty and fun.

"It doesn't matter now," I said and shrugged. "He's made his choice and it wasn't me."

"Did he have a choice?" Ava raised an eyebrow. "Or did you push him away before he had the chance to hurt you. Supposing that he would have."

"Wow," I said, impressed but also a little vulnerable. "I guess you do really know me." I handed the book back to her in case I needed to make a quick escape from the porch where nothing was a secret apparently. "But you're wrong about one thing."

"What's that?"

"He would have hurt me," I said. I wasn't going to tell her why or what I knew, but it was true all the same.

"So you hurt him first?" Ava's only slightly lowered eyebrow raised back up. "Why else would he choose Claire over you?"

"He's not what he seems to be," I said. I wasn't going to rat him out, but I needed to start facing facts.

"Is anyone?"

I didn't answer. I just looked off into the safety of the woods on the other side of the road. The leaves had mostly fallen from the trees and the bare limbs waved around like stick arms trying to distract me from seeing what was just beyond them.

"Choose to be happy, Ruby," Ava said. "But for real, not for show."

I took in a deep breath. "I'm not sure how to do that."

"Head over to the festival in a while and get one of the sticky buns Mattie's bringing in. She might be here by now," she said. "That's a good start. Then maybe stick around this evening and dance with someone. You shouldn't be lonely."

"You either," I said and offered her a small smile.

"Touché," she said. "Maybe I'll see you over there," she said and it was then that I noticed a sadness in her own eyes.

"Are you OK?"

She waved her hand at me as if to brush away my worry. "Just missing Emily today."

I reached down for her hand and she put hers in mine. "Sister of my heart," I said to her.

She smiled at me. "Yes."

We said our goodbyes and I reluctantly headed back toward the growing festivities. More families had set up makeshift booths or were gathered on blankets and the street was filling—as much as Certain could fill—with people choosing to be happy in a time where happiness was sometimes harder to come by than bread.

I placed a smile on my face and headed for Mattie's booth. I could tell it was hers because it was the most beautifully made which meant that Daniel had crafted it.

"Daniel should have a booth about building booths," I said to Mattie when I walked up.

She came around to the front of the stand and gave me a hug. Her belly was pretty big and it made me happy to know the baby would come soon.

"Thank you for coming by," she said as if she didn't think I would. I really was pathetic.

Ella, Marie, and Hugh came from around the back of the booth as well, all hugging me wherever their arms reached. I talked to them all for a few moments. Daniel, Liam, and Zachary arrived not too long after in his wagon. The three of them were lost in laughter and conversation as they pulled up.

"There you are," Daniel said and jumped down to make his way to Mattie. "I thought you were going to ride in with me?"

"Opal couldn't wait and the kids were already here with Ava," Mattie said and received a quite romantic kiss from him without regard for who was watching.

"You rode Opal?" he looked concerned and touched her belly. "Is that safe?" He looked at me then and I was flattered.

"I will not concede to riding in the wagon like a cow," Mattie said.

Daniel smiled widely. "There's no way I could haul a cow in that wagon."

Mattie feigned indignation, "Are you calling me a cow?"

Daniel ran his hand through his thick dark hair and winked at me, "This is a no-win situation here."

Liam and Zachary joined in then slapping Daniel on the shoulders and wishing him luck. It was so lovely to see them all getting along again.

"Good luck, brother," Liam said and held his hands up like he was surrendering a fight. "I've sparred with this one before and she's feisty."

Mattie promptly punched Liam in the arm which made him smile and bow to her.

Zachary looked back and forth between Liam and Daniel and Mattie like he was responsible for keeping the peace between them. It was all in jest. Never had I seen a more loving family between them all. Jealousy sidled up next to me and I could almost feel it put its arm across my shoulder like the old friends we were.

Daniel took hold of Mattie's hand and kissed it. "You're the prettiest," he paused as she eyed him, making him laugh because he never would say such a thing as he pretended was about to come out of his mouth, "woman in all the world and I'm the luckiest man around."

She nodded her approval. "Well done," she said, then looked at me concerned, "do I look like a cow?"

I laughed despite myself. "Not at all. Daniel is correct."

"As usual," he said and patted himself on the shoulder, winking at us.

I had known Daniel many years and he had not laughed, played in jest, or so much as smiled for years after his wife Emily died and the town turned against him. Mattie had changed all that and I loved seeing the Daniel I had known as a child resurface.

Perhaps the real Cole was still somewhere beneath his Mr. Hall costume. Perhaps when Halloween was over, he'd take it off. Mattie was talking to me and I tried to bring my attention back to the present.

"Look at the paper pumpkins the students have made," she was saying to me, holding one out in each hand, wiggling them around. "Don't they look spooky?" She smiled. They were not at all spooky.

She set about showing me one hand-cut and glued-on face pumpkin after the next. They really were adorable and the sticky buns she had brought smelled delicious, but what had caught my eye was Claire and Cole in the near distance. The smile on her face was radiant and although he looked a bit sheepish and nervous his face was just as beautiful as I always thought it to be. His eyes were kind and his strong jaw made him appear solid and dependable. He was more handsome than ever and I hated that I thought so.

Over Mattie's shoulder I watched the two of them play a game of ring toss. Claire hung on every throw he made as if he was the greatest sportsman she'd ever seen. He missed more than he made it, but she cheered him on as if he made them all. The more I watched however, the more I could tell that she only meant it when he was looking or when she thought someone else was. I could see the sincerity fall out of her eyes when she didn't think anyone saw her.

She didn't mean it at all. She didn't really have feelings for him. My heart lurched not knowing what it all meant.

I furrowed my brow and was about to excuse myself from Mattie when Cole tossed his last ring and Mr. Gibbons gave him a small potted plant as a prize that he then gave to Claire. She acted as if it was the greatest gift she'd ever received. Then to my horror, he kissed her on the cheek. The look on her face was triumphant, as if she had just won the game whatever it was.

I was stopped in my tracks. Something was amiss but I didn't know what it was. And I supposed it didn't much matter. He had kissed her. Right out in public. She had won and I had lost. She looked right at me then and smiled even bigger.

I had to get away from everyone and fast. The library was open to the public, as was church and grocery store. Anyone could be anywhere. All that was left was Cole's place. As soon as Claire looked away, I rushed over to his door. I just needed a place to hide for a moment before I started crying and gave myself away.

The door was unlocked and I ducked inside. Once out of sight I burst into tears. Which made me mad. I was not going to let myself cry about Cole. Cole who was not Cole anymore and maybe never had been. Fifteen long years had passed since he was here, and people changed. Or rather they became who they really were and perhaps he had always been Henry. For all I knew he had spent the last years in one con after the next and everything he'd said to me since he got here could have been one big grift. He had even used Henry Hall as a nickname in our club. Maybe Cole had never been his real name. Maybe nothing had ever been real.

But it sure had felt real.

"Stop it, Ruby," I said out loud and brushed the tears off my face. I stomped my foot like I was making a point to someone. "Pull yourself together." I took a few breaths and calmed myself down. I looked out the front window to confirm that Henry, yes, that's what I would call him from now on, and Claire were still outside holding court. I turned from the window and walked toward the printing press in the center of the room. Behind me the front door opened and I jumped.

"There you are," Mr. Gibbons said and closed the door behind him. He walked over to me and I let myself fall into his fatherly arms. "I had a feeling you'd be here and you'd need someone to talk to," he said once I'd pulled myself away from him and wiped away the tears I was trying not to cry.

I looked at him confused. "What gave you the feeling that I'd be here of all places?"

"I saw you run over here," he said and winked at me.

I nodded then started crying again.

Then, I told him everything.

Mr. Gibbons listened to my weepy story about Henry and Cole and all the things I'd hoped all those years ago and then hoped again when he came back to town. Mr. Gibbons didn't seem surprised at all, but instead he placed his hand on my cheek and kissed my forehead and said, "Everything will be alright."

I wanted that to be true, but my heart was heavy despite the levity of the festival outside. The music and dancing and laughter should have been just the medicine that I needed, but it was making me feel quite ill instead.

"Let's go, dear," Mr. Gibbons said, reaching for my hand and leading me to stand.

He led me back outside and over to Mattie and Ava for safekeeping. They enveloped me into their arms and didn't ask me to explain a thing. Friends knew how to wait for a story to be told.

Chapter 18
Cole

This whole charade had gotten so far out of hand I wasn't even sure what I was acting out anymore. I had wanted a second chance with the people of Certain but would have settled for just being forgiven. All that was pie in the sky now. No matter what I did from here, all anyone would think about me was that I was a crumb, a grifter, a chisel and it would all result in the kiss-off no matter what I did. Maybe that was all a bit Hollywood dramatic but with every passing day and every public outing I felt more and more like a man flailing around trying to get his message across but having forgotten what it was. I didn't know if I looked it, but I felt like a madman in a suit that was tailored for someone else. My father had always been able to slip into a role like he was a silver screen actor and maybe he should have been instead. I was never able to assume a part and play it well. How I'd gotten this far in Certain was a mystery.

Today I was acting out *Henry Hall takes Claire to the festival where everyone bombards him about when the story will break on the deeds being found.*

"Mr. Hall," Yet another unfamiliar voice called out to me in a familiar way and I knew what was coming. I turned around and found a man in his late 60s holding his hand out for me to shake. "Mr. Halifax," he said by way of introduction. I knew the name from my stack of deeds. "My uncle's land deed was one that was taken all those years ago. I think he had it recorded with the bank over in Hyden though. Have you checked records for recorded deeds. People lose papers all the time."

I did a sort of half head shake, half nod. No, I hadn't checked with the bank about things being recorded. I didn't even know what he was talking about. Claire was holding onto my hand and staring at me intently. It felt much less like support and much more like she was pinning me to the ground.

Mr. Halifax went on, "I'm sure you've checked the courthouse already and there must have been nothing on those deeds or else this whole mess would be over," he said, his words sounding like someone talking through a thick pane of glass. I watched his lips move and tried to focus on the words. "It's almost as if Mack knew which deeds to seek. Which ones the owners had never recorded anywhere. But I think my uncle might have. He was old, he might have forgotten."

I stammered for a moment and then words came out of my mouth. "I did check," I said, but of course that was not true. I couldn't remember the last true thing I had said. "Dead end there, but I haven't given up." I slapped him on the shoulder in hopes that would signal him to move along.

It didn't. And to make matters worse, we seemed to have drawn a little bit of a crowd. One man after the next was sticking his hand toward mine and calling out a name that I knew. Just like the day everyone had come to "welcome" me to town, bodies and voices pressed in on me asking all the questions I wanted to avoid.

"It's been a few months now. Do you think you're going to find anything?"

"Have you stopped looking? Seems like you don't go off to investigate that much anymore?"

"What happens if you don't find them?"

"What happens if you do? Can you get them back? Do we get them back?"

"What will you do after all this is over?"

My heart raced around in my chest and I felt like I should run after it somehow. I slipped my hand free from Claire's, which I probably only accomplished because my hand was sweating so much that she couldn't keep hold of it.

"Gentlemen," I said, trying to get control of the crowd with my shaky voice. "I know everyone wants some answers and I'm working on it. I've got to head over to the grocery right now to see about a lead."

"At the grocery?" Claire asked with raised eyebrows.

"I'll be right back," I said and pushed through them all like a man running for his life. I wanted to go home, but I knew I'd be alone there and that Claire would follow me. I needed to get out of the pickle I was in, but I still needed a public enough place Claire might not press me like she had the day she'd asked me to take her to the festival.

I didn't look back. I just hoped they'd go on about their day at the festival and leave me be. I didn't look back especially because I didn't want to see whatever face Claire might be making at me. Suspicion at best. I flung the door to the grocery store open and practically launched myself inside, pushing the door closed as if there was a mob of people rushing to get in at me. I exhaled deeply and stepped back from the door, still watching the festival crowd through the glass.

"I know a person trying to escape other people when I see one," Daniel Barrett's voice sounded behind me and I turned quickly to face him, trying not to act as startled as I was.

"Oh," I exclaimed, failing, "I didn't see you in here. I was just. Just."

He stepped closer, put his hand on my shoulder and led me further away from the door. He said, "You're safe here, Cole."

"I really was here to get some … some," I stalled and then my shoulders slumped. "Some place to hide. You're correct."

Daniel nodded his head toward the counter and motioned me to follow him. He opened the entry flap by the cash register and went behind the counter. I hesitated but followed. Beyond that he pushed open a curtain and led us into the storage area. There he pointed at a small table and chairs and we sat down.

We looked at each other for a few very long moments and then he spoke.

"I should have reached back out to you after we talked at the creek," he said and looked frustrated. "I've just been busy in my own world and I didn't really know how to help you other than to be there for you, which I haven't really been. I'm sorry."

I hung my head. "Don't be. I'm a victim of my own stupidity. This whole endeavor."

"I wasn't very friendly along the creek either," Daniel said. "I admit I was pretty suspicious of you and trying to catch you in the lie I already knew you were telling."

I shrugged. "Fair enough. I don't blame you. It was sort of nice to be found out."

"Well," Daniel said, still sounding pretty upset with himself, "I could have been more of a friend. Understanding someone's plight is just part of the picture. I haven't done anything to help you. That's what I want to do now."

"Help me?"

"And be your friend."

I didn't dare say anything for fear it would be the wrong thing and I'd burst this little beautiful bubble I found myself in.

"Didn't you and Ruby have some little club?" Daniel asked. "And this special call for it, or a whistle or something?"

I looked up at him amazed. He was only a few years older than me, but when you're a kid a few is like a million. "You remembered that?"

"My brothers had a mind to give you a hard time about it," he said and then waved away the threat, "just in jest. You were too little to pick on in our book."

"I wasn't that little," I said.

Daniel smiled a sort of cheeky smile and nodded his head. "I was pulling for you with Ruby. You guys were cute." He shook his head and I lowered mine again. "Then all that happened with the land deeds and your father. I felt terrible for you, Cole."

I was getting heady with the sound of my real name falling off his tongue again. Daniel pressed his lips together as if to tell me everything was alright. I wanted to say something, but words were lost to me. Daniel filled in the quiet.

"Listen," he said, "I know all too well what it's like to be a lost child. To grow up under a shadow so big you don't ever see the sun. Then to find a place and a people who make you feel whole. And then to lose it."

I nodded. The truth he spoke trapped me in my chair and freed me at the same time. I needed him to look into my eyes and see me. And he did.

"And I know now what it feels like to get another chance at happiness and wholeness," he said and when I dipped my eyes in shame or embarrassment or whatever it was that made me feel like I couldn't face him or anyone, he tapped the table to get my attention and when I looked up he pointed at my eyes and then his own.

I wasn't naive to my own need for forgiveness and acceptance, but I hadn't realized how much I needed approval. More so, I needed someone I could trust. In those moments Daniel was the big brother I didn't have and the father I had needed.

"I knew God expected me to help you. I just didn't know how," Daniel said. "Then you came in here obviously spooked. Maybe I still don't know exactly what to do, but I want you to know that I've got your back, Cole."

When I spoke, my voice was not as strong and manly as I wished it was sitting across from someone like Daniel.

"I gummed it up, though. It's too late."

He broke into a smile and laughed. "Don't I know that feeling as well," he said. "Good news for you. I've already blazed that trail. This town is better at forgiving than you think."

"I hope so," I said and exhaled hard.

"Is something else bothering you?"

"Ruby," I said, shaking my head. "I don't know what I did there, but she can't stand me. She's so mad she won't even look at me."

Daniel chuckled. "Sounds like just the opposite."

"What do you mean?"

"That she stands you too much," he said and winked. "Show her your heart. The heart you've been holding back."

I wrinkled my brow, about to ask him how he knew such a thing, but he cocked his head and pressed his lips together. I guess us guy types were good at holding things in and good at spotting when another one of us was doing the same thing.

"What can I do right now to help you?" Daniel asked.

"Pretend like I was never in here and show me the back door," I said and shrugged.

"Done." He pointed me to the back exit and I had all confidence that if anyone came looking for me, Daniel would forget he'd seen me.

I headed to the creek again to get my mind right. I could have just left town from there. Easy as anything I'd ever done, just walked off along the creek and into someplace else. It would have been a long walk, but it would have been the easy way out. I stayed along the softly warbling creek until night whispered its coming. I listened to the last of the noises that signaled the end of the day. The quieting of the songbirds gave way to the howling of a hoot owl and the low croaking of frogs. October was still noisy in the South.

I breathed in deeply and instead made the decision to go home. The home I intended to keep if I could.

I slipped back into town under the cover of darkness and with the height of the festival distracting everyone with its lively music courtesy of Daniel, Liam, and Zachary and its luminary lights along the main road and kids running here and there with their little voices raised in the excitement of being out after dark mostly unsupervised and high on life itself. Grown-ups danced and carried on and no one seemed to notice me skulking back home.

I opened the door slowly and crept inside as if I was afraid someone else was there. Or perhaps hopeful. No one was. The moonlight from the window on the back wall threw a purposeful beam across the open room lighting up the corner of the printing press like a dare. Could I do it? Could I write a letter to the town and name the names of the deeds I held and the time and place I'd give them back and still be allowed to stay, even accepted? Could I tell them who I really was? Those might be two different levels of courage and I wasn't sure if I had both in me.

First things first, I needed to draft a new letter. I had brought one with me when I feared I would only have the courage to drop the deeds and run. But after all this time in Certain, and all the lies I'd told, that letter was no longer enough. I went upstairs to my desk, opened my journal and started to write. Everything. All of it. If I was going to show Ruby my whole heart, I might as well show it to everyone.

I had put things off long enough. Fifteen years. Come what may I had to face the music and it wouldn't be the lively fiddle music I could hear Daniel and his brothers playing in the street outside the office. I wrote a letter to Ruby first because she mattered most, then I took the deeds from their hiding place under the floorboard and tore some blank pages from my journal.

I needed to make a list of names. Then I needed to make an escape plan. But first I needed to make an apology to the town. I knew exactly what I wanted to say, I just hadn't been brave enough to say it. I took one of the blank pages and began to write a letter to the town. I wouldn't be around to read it, but I knew someone would find it and the deeds and that they would make sure that everyone got their land back. I hoped whoever it was would also share the letter, but if not, I'd never know. I had hoped that there would be a way for me to stay. For me to stay as Cole. But there just wasn't. All my nonsense about Henry Hall reporter looking for the deeds was just me stalling, hoping that people would like me enough to overlook my past. Heck, I even had daydreams that people forgot about the deeds. Forgot about Henry looking for them. I imagined people asking less and less and then none at all. But the downside was, I would still be Henry. I didn't want to be Henry. I wanted to be me. But Cole had no place here and I didn't know how to find him one.

Downstairs the door opened and I jumped up from the desk and hurried out onto the landing. I didn't understand what it was I was hoping for until the name came out of my mouth.

"Ruby?" I called already skidding down the stairs before I caught sight of who had entered.

"I'm afraid not, Cole Cooper," Claire said, her voice steely and cold as she stood by the front door which she'd closed behind her.

I froze about two thirds of the way down the stairs. First Daniel and now Claire. I had been a fool to think I was going unnoticed. The forces of good had called me out, but I feared now that I was face to face with the force of evil.

As if in confirmation, Claire smiled and winked at me, but it was not a pleasant gesture. I wanted to run back up the stairs, but what would that accomplish? I edged down the remaining steps slowly while she stood her ground with her hands innocently clasped in front of her. Music and laughter from the festival outside slipped in through the old cracks and seams of the building.

Claire took in a deep breath and exhaled slowly before saying, "So here's what's going to happen," she said, folding her arms over her chest. "You're going to fire up that printing press and write a story that says you've discovered that my father actually found the deeds years ago and was planning to return them before he died suddenly of a heart attack."

"What?" I looked around as if everything I had missed between the last time I saw her and now was somewhere pushed off into the corner of the room.

She put her hands on her hips then. "You'll say that you discovered that the deeds were in a lockbox in Lexington and that my father had arranged to retrieve them, but died before he could get there. You'll give the deeds to me and I will return them to their owners, thus making my father the hero."

Mr. Thomas had been the one who convinced the others to sign their land over to Mack. He'd been the voice of reason they listened to. I could only imagine that he felt awful when the scam was uncovered.

"I'm sorry your father felt bad about the deeds, but it really wasn't his fault. Mack is very good at what he does."

She wrinkled her brow at me. "Are you trying to be sympathetic? I have no use for that. My father never got over the guilt of what he'd done. His health was ruined over it. This is how you're going to fix it." She held her hand out as if I was about to give her something. "The deeds," she said.

"What if I don't have them?" I said, trying hard not to look up towards my bedroom where they were hidden under a floorboard.

"Then you best find them," she said. "You've been looking long enough, haven't you? Especially since I'm pretty sure you know where they are."

"What makes you think that?"

"Why else would you be here?"

I looked around like a cat cornered by a dog. Claire laughed.

"Cole," she said and reached out to me like I was going to let her touch me. She shook her head and stepped closer when I tried to get even farther away. "I'm a reasonable person."

"Are you?" I asked, cutting her off.

She continued. "I know I'm springing this on you, so I'll give you a few weeks yet to find them," she said, rolling her eyes as if she knew I already had them. Which I did. "December 1st."

"It won't bring your father back," I said, suddenly feeling a pang of sympathy for her. "It wasn't his fault."

"Of course it wasn't," she said, rolling her eyes at me. "It was your father's fault and now you're going to make it right."

I shook my head at her, not to tell her no, but just to express the timing of it all. I don't think she got that.

"Don't shake your head at me," she said sharply. "I can go ahead now and tell everyone who you are." She pointed toward the door as if she might go there now during the festival and rat me out. "I'm sure they're going to find this very funny, don't you?" She asked. "That all this time you were really Mack Cooper's son. That you've been pretending to crack the mystery of where the deeds were. And all along you had them."

She looked toward the door again and the thought of facing the whole town at once scared me so hard I could barely breathe. This wasn't my plan. I was going to leave the letters and the deeds and run. Not be outed with the whole town outside my door. I backed further into the room away from Claire, away from the door.

She put her hands on her hips and pretended to think hard about something. "I bet they'll wonder why you didn't just give them back when you first got here. That will be a real head scratcher, don't you think?" She turned her face up like she was trying to figure something out. "You must be up to something," she said, pointing at me. "Wonder what it is."

"So, you're hijacking my scam?" I asked, even though I didn't have one, other than making people like me even though they really should hate me.

She smiled and nodded. "And isn't my story so much better than whatever it was you planned to tell."

"I didn't have a story," I said, stepping further away.

"All the better then, you're going to need one."

"What about me?" I asked and suddenly, I was back in the newspaper office all those months ago talking to Ruby about the exact same thing. I hadn't come up with a plan that allowed me to stay here as Cole back then and I still hadn't. This didn't seem like one.

I'd sealed my fate on that first lie. There was no way out of it now.

"What about you?" she asked. "Do you mean can you come clean and tell them who you are and that you were afraid to say it because you thought people would be mad, but you hoped that once you found the deeds everyone might forgive you?"

I was an open book apparently.

"Yes," I answered honestly.

She sighed and looked at me like I was a little lost puppy. "I tell you what. I'll agree for the next few weeks to act as though we're still courting and perhaps when everything comes out, if you do it correctly, I'll plead with the town to be understanding of the man I love."

Nothing about this spoke of love. I kept quiet for a moment trying to figure out a counter move.

"What if I just tell everyone now and give back the deeds?" I asked. That's what I was about to do anyway.

She cocked her head. "The deeds you don't have?" she asked. "I suppose you could, Henry, but like you said, what happens to poor Cole?"

Ruby knew it was me. Daniel did too. With Claire having figured it out as well, who else might know? And what side would they be on?

"Perhaps I should just take a chance and come clean," I said, laying my cards on the table.

"It's not advisable," she said, pretending to ponder it. "Either Ruby doesn't know you have the deeds or she does and she's in on it. Which thing do you want to have happen? The town hate Ruby, or Ruby hate you for lying to her?"

The joke was on Claire because Ruby already hated me.

"What makes you think Ruby knows it's me?" I asked, but Claire just tilted her head and smirked at me. Then I tried to play my hand. "Claire, your big discovery that I'm really Cole Cooper has already been scooped. Daniel knows it's me, as well."

I stood up straighter thinking I'd won the round, but Claire smiled and clapped her hands together.

"This just gets better and better," she said. "You just handed me your best bargaining chips, silly. I can tell you don't take after your father at all."

I was glad someone thought that at least. "I'm confused."

"Of course, you are," she said and waved her hand at me as if I was a peasant and she was the queen. "If you don't give me the deeds, I simply tell everyone that both Ruby and their beloved Daniel have known all along that you were Mack's son here to finish us off, lording the deeds over our heads. What did you want from this poor town now, Cole?" She wore a pitiful look on her face and put her hand over her heart as if she was injured. "I can only hope that people will forgive them, but it's not looking good for you. And when you leave town, Ruby and Daniel will have to stay and take the brunt of everyone's anger."

"Claire, I really don't care if your father gets the credit for returning the deeds," I said. "Sure, I'll write the article and say I found out he was in the process of retrieving them. I'm not here for the glory of handing them back."

"That might have worked if we'd come to this plan sooner," she said. "Or if you'd simply given them back when you first got here. But instead, you've lied to everyone for months. Making friends with people under the name Henry Hall. Borrowing cars to make trips all over the area, lying right to people's faces and telling them all sorts of tall tales, making them believe you were someone you're not." She put her finger to her lips, thinking. "I was wrong. You are just like your father. A liar and a conman. And people in these hills don't take kindly to being tricked. Especially by an outsider. And especially by the same man twice."

That last part stung. I was not my father. I tried to call her bluff. Tried to imply that worrying over how the town would treat Ruby and Daniel didn't bother me as much as it did. I was already going to go along with whatever she said, just for their sakes.

"You know, Claire," I said and folded my arms in front of my chest, "in order for a blackmail to work, you have to have something that I want for myself in exchange."

I thought I had her, but she just stood there smirking at me.

"I do," she said, her eyes holding mine. "I have two things that you want."

"What's that?" I dared.

"Forgiveness and love."

Chapter 19
Ruby

Finally, night had fallen and the festival was winding down. The last notes of the last song Daniel and his brothers were playing hung in the air. Little children allowed up past their bedtime twirled and danced in the street, reaching up like they might catch those notes and take them home to play them in their dreams.

I hadn't seen Cole or Claire since Mr. Gibbons brought me back outside. Ava and Mattie and their kids had done a fine job of keeping their poor "Aunt" Ruby busy and entertained, but it was time to slink home and put my broken heart to bed.

"I think I'm about done here," I said to Mattie and offered a weak smile.

She looked over her shoulder like she was making sure the coast was clear. "Is this about Cole?" She said and waved her hand up and down indicating me in general.

I drew in a hard breath. "You know?"

"Daniel told me," she said sheepishly. "But don't tell him that I told you. It's supposed to be a secret."

"Don't I know it," I said. Meeting her compassionate gaze, I continued. "And yes, it is about Cole."

"You could have told me," she said, her voice filled with love but also a little sadness. "That's what friends are for you know."

My heart fluttered in my chest. "I wish I had," I said. "Everything has gotten so jumbled and I don't know how to fix it."

"Sounds like it's not yours to fix," Mattie said.

I shook my head. "Maybe at first, but I've played a role in this mess that I need to clean up."

"Then do it," she said. "Putting off a hard task never makes it any easier."

"I was sort of hoping it would," I said and offered a pathetic smile which elicited a huge smile back from her. "No?"

"Whatever you're afraid of," Mattie said, "I'm here to help you through. You know that right?" She looked concerned as if I might not. Perhaps I hadn't really been sure.

I nodded and looked in the near distance. Luminaries lined the street—the candles inside the bags flicked like there were fairies hiding out in each one. The world looked magical despite the lingering depression of the times. Which of course, was the whole point of this night's festivities.

I needed a little magic of my own if I was going to fix things. I stood up straight calling on the only magic I had at the moment, courage.

"I'm going to talk to him," I said with determination, although I don't know if I was talking to Mattie, to myself, or to God above.

I didn't wait for a response from anyone, even myself, I just marched across the street toward the newspaper building. My magic courage faltered when I saw none other than Claire coming out the door with an enormous smile on her annoyingly porcelain-complexioned face. Again.

How did she manage to look so regal when the rest of us looked like we'd been rolling around in the dirt in comparison. And the stupid moonlight and twinkling stars just added to her beauty. Well, I was not going to be driven off by Claire. Again.

I continued my march, stepping over the firelit bags on the other side of the street and stomped right up to the landing where she still stood as if she was about to wave to her subjects and deliver a speech.

"May I help you, Ruby?" she said, nodding at me curtly.

"You just had to make sure I saw you leaving Henry's office," I said, having barely caught myself from saying Cole's name. "Didn't you?"

"Do you know Mr. Hall?" Claire asked, raising an eyebrow as if she didn't know good and well that I did. "And on a first name basis?"

"I do," I said, and put my hands on my hips. "Better than you probably know him."

She cocked her head and took her time replying. "How is that exactly?"

I stared back at her and took my time too.

"None of your business."

She fluffed her hair as if anyone around here had hair worth fluffing what with shampoo being a long-lost memory to most of us and baking soda and water doing the trick well enough. In fact, that was all my gramma had ever used. Me too for that matter until Mattie had brought me some of her shampoo. It had been fun while it lasted, but even she didn't spend the time or money to get bottled shampoo sent in. All you had to do to feel fancy was add some lavender or rose water if you had it. Mattie and I had talked about opening our own business. Soaps, shampoos, and other things. We talked about growing a flower garden the following year come spring again, but now that she'd have another little one around, she might be too busy.

But I digressed. The problem at hand was Claire.

"I'd say matters regarding Henry are definitely my business," she said and looked at me like the cat who just ate the canary.

I hated cats who ate canaries. Not that I hated cats, mind you. I just meant that I hated Claire. The Claire who just ate the canary. Better. I joked to myself to try and put out of my mind what she might mean.

I failed. "What do you mean?"

"My Henry and I have become quite close these last few weeks, nearly a month now we've been together," she said and although she kept on talking, my head started to buzz so that I couldn't hear anything else.

My Henry? My Henry?

That was not her Henry. That was my Cole. Or at least he had been. Although I didn't really know who he was now. It was all very confusing, but I wanted to believe that somewhere inside this new man was the boy I had known.

I tried very hard not to show any emotion at her words as they came back into focus in my ears.

"Just now we've made things official," she said, holding her left hand out to me where a modest but lovely ring caught the stupid moonlight and jabbed its sparkles out at me like a threat.

I wanted to grab her hand and rip the ring off, but I was stunned immobile.

"I'm sorry, Ruby," she said and pursed her lips together for a moment. "I know you had your eyes on Henry and I'm trying not to flaunt our relationship, especially since come December I imagine things will be all the more serious between us if all goes as planned."

I couldn't tell which emotion was strongest: anger, fear, or despair. All I knew was that I was either going to pass out or punch her. Just then the door opened and Cole came out.

"Oh," he said, looking from Claire to me and back to Claire. "You're still here?"

"I ran into sweet little Ruby," she said and batted her lashes at him. "We were just talking."

He looked at me nervously. "About what?"

I piped up, my eyes trained on his. "About how you asked Claire to marry you."

For a moment the color drained from his face and all but dripped down onto his shoes, but then he stood up straight and his eyes grew hard. "That's right," he said.

I don't know what I expected him to say, but his words hit me like I'd been the one punched. I was aware that I was standing there with my mouth hanging open.

Claire slipped her hand into his and for just a flash of hopeful moment, he seemed to ask me with his gaze to not give him away, to just wait until she was gone so that he could explain. But that flash was over and then he leaned in and kissed her cheek.

I took a step back and almost stepped right off the landing. His hand jerked from hers and he reached out to me, grabbing my hand and steadying me back on my feet. He looked at me in a pitiful panic that caused me to see his face from all those years ago along the creek bank. I saw the scared kid afraid that everything was crashing down.

My memory shot back to that night long ago.

It hadn't been unusual for Cole and me to meet at the creek long after the sun had set. Especially on warm nights when his parents and my grandparents were busy being busy adults or sitting on their own porches enjoying the starlit sky. Summers were times of freedom and magic. Anything could happen under a full moon. And that night, I just knew that Cole was going to kiss me. And he had.

"Ruby," he had said and stepped closer to me there on the creek bank. "I was going to kiss you tonight if that's OK."

My heart had thudded so hard I thought it was going to break. I guess it did after all.

"That would be OK," I said nervously.

Our faces came together slowly in the fourteen-year-old's way of wanting the kiss, but not really knowing how to do it even though we'd seen it done. All nerves and tingles. It was just a peck on the lips that first time, but it had set my whole body ablaze.

In the awkward giddiness that followed, I'd filled the silence by mentioning that I had seen Cole's father's car behind the grocery store.

"Are we taking a ride in your dad's car?"

"What?" he asked.

"I saw it behind the grocery store," I had said or something to that effect. "You said we'd ride in it one day."

Cole's face had clouded over like a sudden storm rising up.

"I have to go back into town," Cole had said, his voice breaking. He took hold of my hand. "Wait here?"

"Sure," I said nervously. "What's wrong?"

"I hate living like this," he said, but I didn't know what he meant. "I just want to fit in some place and have people think I'm a good person. This always happens. I hate my dad sometimes." He kicked the ground but didn't let go of my hand.

"You are a good person, Cole." I was getting scared.

Cole had closed his eyes and squeezed my hand. He didn't tell me anything else about his dad, instead he just sighed.

"You're the best friend I've ever had, Ruby."

"What's going on?" I gripped his hand tightly.

"Wait for me," he said, looking over his shoulder back toward the town. "I'll come back and I'll kiss you for real."

He pulled his hand from mine and I felt the absence of it grip me instead.

"I'll be back, I promise," he said.

"I'll wait."

"Ruby?" he asked and I nodded. "Will you promise me that if people think bad of me one day, that you'll tell them I was a good person?"

My heart thudded hard again. "I'll tell them," I had said, heartsick that I was confirming what I already knew. He wasn't coming back.

And he didn't. Not for fifteen years. What was I supposed to tell people now? I wanted to believe he was a good person, but I knew those deeds were hidden in his room and he had lied to me about them. Now here, again, was Claire and wearing an engagement ring this time. I felt like a fool.

Claire spoke then, dragging me back to the present. "You caught her just in time. What a gentleman, Henry," she said, batting her eyes at him and then leveling me with her cold stare. "I think Ruby can see herself off now."

He smiled sheepishly at me. "Was there something you were coming to see me about, Ruby?"

I opened my mouth, but Claire spoke. "If there was, she's thought better of it now that she knows about us."

Cole's head jerked sharply toward Claire. She wiggled her ring at him and her eyebrows lifted.

"Right," he said slowly and stepped closer to Claire.

She kissed his cheek and I thought I might die. His eyes left mine when her lips touched his skin. My eyes darted to his, but his flickered away so that our glances never quite met. If he would just look at me I could tell what he was thinking, but he wouldn't. Which told me enough.

Chapter 20
Cole

The kiss Claire planted on my cheek burned. I wanted to scream out to Ruby that I was being held hostage—save me, save me from myself—I wanted to scream, but the devil herself had just claimed me for her own and I knew I was where I deserved to be, so I just stood there letting the fire rise around me.

I had to appease Claire. Of that there was no way out. What happened to me afterward would depend solely on what Claire chose as my fate. Who else got hurt in the process was up to me as well depending on how I played along. I couldn't take the risk that Ruby and Daniel would take the fall. I had four weeks left in Certain and then I knew I'd be sent packing. I knew Claire's promises to speak on my behalf were made of mist, but I had to hold onto hope somewhere.

"It's getting late, ladies," I said and nodded to them both. "Can I see you home, Claire?"

Ruby winced and I felt sick to my stomach.

"No dear," she said and touched my arm. "I'll ride home with my aunt. It looks like everyone is heading home."

I glanced over Ruby's shoulder at the remains of the fall festival. "And you," I said to Ruby, but she was already turned away and headed down the steps.

Claire clicked her tongue and turned to me. "Be careful, Cole," she said and took hold of my hand. "I hold all the cards and we both know it."

I yanked free from her. "Do you?" I asked. "We'll see." I pushed the door open and went inside, slamming it once I was on the other side.

I thought about locking it. I probably should have. I made it halfway up the steps toward my bedroom when the door opened.

"How dare you kiss me and then ask Claire to the festival," Ruby's angry voice said behind me. "And how dare you ask her to marry you."

I came back down the stairs but didn't move toward her.

"I didn't ask Claire to marry me." I put my hands on my hips hoping that would end things.

"She's wearing a ring that says otherwise," Ruby said. Her face was mad, but her voice shook.

"Listen," I said. "Things aren't like you think."

She scoffed. "I already know that."

"You do?"

"I know you lied to me," she said. "You're not who you're pretending to be. The real Cole was brave and real and I've been waiting for him all these years to come back."

I pressed my hands to my chest to indicate my own self. "I'm right here."

She shook her head slowly. "No, you're not him. You're a liar. I don't know who you are." Her words were like an arrow in my chest.

"This was your idea, Ruby," I said, stepping closer and pointing at her. "You made me come here," I said, gesturing around at the old, haunted house I inhabited once again. I yanked the arrow out of my chest and threw it on the floor, blood splattering everywhere. She was mad, but I was getting mad too. "I would have just stayed on the creek until—"

She cut me off. "Until what?" she said, her face flushed with anger or hurt, I wasn't sure. "Until you do what you're here to do and sneak off again? That was your plan, right? You never expected me to find you. You have something you need from this town and then you're on your way. I heard you say it."

"I can explain all that," I said, stepping closer still.

"I don't want to hear it," she said. "You and Claire deserve each other. Maybe you can take her with you when you leave."

She pushed me away from her and stormed toward the door.

"Ruby," I called. "This is all torn up."

She stopped for just a moment, giving me the chance to say more, but my chest hurt too bad from the arrow strike and the coward living in my heart got the best of me. Ruby opened the door and walked out. I thought she might slam it behind her, but she closed it quietly instead. The small click as the door shut was the loudest noise I'd ever heard.

Silence and stillness surrounded me like ghosts closing in. I shut my eyes against them, but they were still there, following me around like they always did. Making themselves at home. Heating some water in the kettle to make tea. Opening the blinds to see if anyone was still out on the street. I just stood there in the middle of the room afraid to take a step because if I did it might be out the front door, back toward the creek, and gone for good.

Chapter 21
Ruby

I threw myself into my work over the next few weeks. I mended every book in the repair bin, I created new charts for reports that we didn't even need, and I rearranged the entire layout of the library. Neither Ava nor Mattie questioned my madness; they just pitched in and helped move things around. I created a whole new section for medical and medicinals and grouped new categories of plants and how to find and use them. And mostly, I tried very hard not to think about Cole.

Mattie's pregnancy gave us all enough to talk about that other things needn't come up. Every now and then there was a lull in our talk and I felt Cole's presence creeping in. Mattie always caught things in the nick of time and either had a sudden but "nothing to worry about" cramp or the baby would move, or she'd remember something one of the other kids did and Cole would fade into the distance.

"You'd make a great nurse," Mattie said one day, finding me in my new medical section complete with Mr. Mobley's books that someone had retrieved from the newspaper building and brought back to the library.

"Did you bring these back?" I asked, holding up one of the thickest tomes. "Or did someone else?"

She sat down in the armchair next to where I sat on the floor surrounded by all the books I was reading.

She pressed her lips together knowing who I meant. "Daniel brought them."

I closed my eyes against the conversation I imagined where Cole told Daniel to get rid of the books because he didn't want reminders of me lying around. He'd probably had them all boxed up and sitting on the stoop. Or maybe he'd taken them over to the grocery story and dumped them there.

Mattie reached down and put her hand on my arm. "He asked Daniel to bring them because he knew they were important to you."

I turned my face up to hers trying to catch anything more she might say about Cole like a child trying to catch snowflakes on her tongue.

"Daniel says he keeps to himself." Mattie continued knowing I wanted more. "He says Cole seems sad." I looked away and she scooted back in the chair. "I know you're mad at him and I know I don't have any room to talk because I wasn't here then, but what if you're wrong?"

"About?"

"Everything that's keeping you away from him."

I wanted to tell her about the deeds under the floorboard. I wanted to tell her about how he kissed Claire on the cheek right in front of me. But I'd kept all that hidden. I wanted those little bits of proof to stay pure. If I spoke about them, someone might be able to challenge them—or prove them right. I wasn't sure which one was worse to me.

"Does Daniel see him often?"

Mattie nodded her head. "Is that bad?"

I shook mine. "No," I said, understanding that he needed a friend too. Maybe that understanding meant that I still cared for him. "I guess he needs a friend too. Other than Claire."

"He doesn't love Claire; you know that, right?" she asked.

I shrugged. "Then why did he ask her to marry him?"

"That's a good question," Mattie said as if she was answering mine, not asking a new one. When I didn't reply, she changed the subject. "I'm glad you came to Thanksgiving dinner the other day. The kids loved having you there. I did too."

I nodded. "I had fun. It was nice not to be alone. You were right for making me come."

She feigned indignance. "I didn't make you. I just threatened to send Liam and Zachary after you if you didn't come."

I smiled, but then my face fell a bit. "What do you think Cole did for Thanksgiving?"

"Are you hoping he wasn't alone?" Mattie asked. "Or that he was?"

I shrugged and she held my gaze. I knew she could see right through me.

She tried to get up out of the chair and when she failed, I jumped up to help her. She took my hand in hers and squeezed it. "It's getting late," she said and pulled me as close as her belly would allow, giving me a gentle hug.

Outside the windows of the library, darkness was whispering near. I walked her outside where we met Daniel coming across the street. His face lit up at seeing her—his eyes going straight to her belly and the baby inside it. When he reached us, he put one hand on her stomach and with the other he drew her face in for a kiss.

Mattie turned to me before they left. "See you tomorrow."

I nodded. I watched them walk back to Daniel's buggy where he helped her up into the seat. She was giggling at her clumsiness and he was laughing along with her. Out of the corner of my eye I saw a light flicker in the newspaper building. I imagined it was Cole carrying a lantern up the stairs to his room. I wondered if he was alone and then felt ashamed of myself for thinking it.

"Go home, Ruby," I said out loud to myself, but myself led me somewhere else instead.

I ducked inside the church and was immediately flooded with memories of the library being here. Now the old building was a church again like it should have always been. If a building could shake her shoulders and throw off an old dusty cover and come back to life, this one had. I knew that Pastor Collins was here somewhere because candles lined the windowsills all around the church, lighting up the bottoms of the stained-glass windows enough to see the toes of angels and the hem of Jesus's robe, the hooves of sheep and the green grass of safe pastures.

The light didn't reach the tops of the windows, but I knew the rest of the story told in each glass. They weren't just comforting tales to take away the sorrows of hard times. The stories painted on the windows were a history and future that guided my present, that lit the way, that pointed me home. This place was a thin spot between here and Heaven. Memories of Gramma and Grampa bringing me here as a child lived right alongside grown-up me sorting books and followed present me all the way up to the front pew where I sat down with a heavy sigh.

"Hey there, Miss Ruby," Pastor Collins said, sitting down beside me. I knew he was there, but where he had popped up from was beyond me. "What a treat it was to have you at our family celebration the other day."

"How did you know I was here?" I asked.

"I saw you sneak in." He smiled at me. "I was outside. Although I suppose it's never really sneaking in when it's church you're sneaking into."

"Was it obvious I was hiding out?"

"To anyone paying attention," he said, motioning to the space beside me in a request to join me. I slid over. We both stared up toward the altar for a few moments and then he said, "It's my experience that when a person comes to church on some other day than Sunday and it's already getting dark outside, and they look over their shoulder to see if anyone sees them that they're here for a particular reason."

I looked over at him. "What reason is that?"

"Comfort."

"Isn't that why everyone comes to church?"

He tilted his head and made a little noise with his mouth. "People come to church for all sorts of reasons and many of them don't even have to do with church. Comfort is a particular desire. You look for it when you don't have it. You look here for it when you know that what you need isn't found out there at all. You come here when you want to go back to the beginning and start over. Or when you know that's not an option, but you want it anyway."

My mouth fell open. "That is what I want. You're good."

He waved off the compliment. "I'm just an old preacher who's seen a lot of things." He took in a deep breath and exhaled slowly before saying, "You know that's what he wants too, right?"

"God?" I asked.

Pastor Collins chuckled and then shook his head. Then I knew who he meant.

I took in a short but sharp breath. Pastor Collins patted my hand where it rested on my leg.

He continued. "He just wants to put things back like they were, but the thing is, the way they were isn't what he wants. Not really."

My fingers were tingling and my brain buzzed. He knew. Of course, he knew.

I dared a thought. "He wants Claire?"

Pastor Collins laughed right out loud, startling me. "Gracious no. He wants family. He wants acceptance. He wants a home."

"Cole?" I said his name out loud to see what it sparked in the air.

Pastor Collins folded his hands in his lap. "We've been trying to make sure he didn't run off, you know. Asking him to sort out this and that and could he bring back a whatnot or gig-a-ma-bob from Hyden when he went. Even sent him up to Lexington in Mr. Mobley's car because we knew he needed to get out of town that day and that he was too honest to take the car and run. We're just trying to keep him home."

"A gig-a-ma-bob?"

"Whatever it took," he said. "But he seems particularly flighty now. Like he's about to fly the coop. Something has changed but we don't know what."

"Who exactly is we?" I asked.

"Me, Mobley, Gibs and Daniel," he said. "Daniel calls us the Council."

I smiled at the thought of all these men watching over Cole. "Why didn't you tell him that you knew?"

"He needs to come to it on his own. Being told something and realizing it yourself are not the same. He came back to make it right, not to have it made right for him. He's just stumbling a bit. We're just here to help him back up."

I shifted around in the pew. "What if I told you I knew something that he doesn't know I know."

Pastor Collins was quiet a moment and then asked, "Is it something that you need me to know or just to get off your chest?"

"Oh, it's not gossip," I said, "but it is perplexing and it's made me doubt that he's as honest as you think."

Pastor Collins' eyebrows raised. "Go on, but only tell me what you think is important to Cole's well-being."

I twisted my mouth up. I wasn't sure if it was or not. It would certainly make him look bad. I said it anyway. "I know he has the deeds. They're hidden in his room. I found them by accident one day when I was tidying up for him."

Pastor Collins nodded. "I figured."

"You did?"

"Sure," he said, nodding some more. "They're his currency. He's trying to buy his way home. He wants acceptance," Pastor Collins said and shrugged as if that was obvious. Which it was. "That's what the boy has always wanted. He's wanted to be seen for who he is and not some tall tale."

"Then why does he keep telling them?" I folded my arms across my aching chest.

"Fear, my dear," he said, shaking his head. "We make most of our bad decisions because of fear."

I sighed heavily against the truth of the statement. That did make sense. "But why did he lie to me about having them? Why hasn't he given them back in all this time?"

"Because he knows it might not work," Pastor Collins said and looked back toward the altar. "He knows that no matter what he does some people might still not accept him. He could give them the thing they want most and they will still send him away."

I understood. "It's his way of holding on to hope."

Pastor Collins nodded. "It's not his best plan, but his best plan went out the window when Henry showed up."

I sighed. "I was part of helping Henry stick around."

"We all were."

"I was too busy trying to get what I wanted that I didn't think about what he needed," I said, feeling ashamed. "I just want to help him."

"Then let's help him."

Chapter 22
Cole

Since my whole relationship with Claire was a sham, she hadn't expected, and probably didn't want me, to come to Thanksgiving with her family the other day. So I had spent the day at the creek. It was OK though. The cool air, the gentle warbling of the water over the rocks, the particular quiet of the outdoors in late fall was all I really needed.

OK, that was a lie. But that was all I was going to get. My time was nearly up. In just a few more days Claire would come calling and I'd have to pay up so to speak. It was time to write the letter to the town. I would have loved to give Mr. Thomas the glory for finding the deeds like Claire wanted me to, but writing that article would be getting away with all my lies and that didn't seem right. I had never been on the up and up. I had come to Certain with those deeds and I had wanted something in return for giving them back. I had lied to Ruby and everyone else for that matter. I let them think I was someone else for the better part of a year. I had gained their trust and their friendship. They deserved the truth.

I'd gone along with Claire up until now so that she wouldn't try to drag Ruby and Daniel down in my wake if I was to preempt her by turning the deeds over and leaving. And I still didn't know that she wouldn't try to. All I could do was address that first in the letter. Tell the town I'd acted on my own and no one was at fault but me. I had thought that maybe Claire really would try to sway the town to forgive me, but if I was honest with myself, I knew she'd toss me in the lion's den as soon as the deeds were in her hands. And if she didn't, if she kept my secrets, that was all the worse. I'd get away with it. I didn't know if I'd get away with it as Henry or as Cole, but neither man could stomach that. I really would be my father's son then.

Now, back at the newspaper office with only days left until Claire's December 1st deadline, I took my pen and a piece of paper down into the kitchen area to hunt some tea that might keep me going while I wrote the letter. All of Ruby's little concoctions and mixes lined the shelf under the window. Seeing her handwriting on the labels made my heart ache so hard I thought I might just keel over right there. How had everything gone so terribly wrong? It would have been so easy to do the right thing right away. But as usual, fear stalled me and then walloped the hope right out of me and now, here I was with nothing but these little bottles of tea and the jagged knowledge that my time in Certain was over.

I reached for the jar labeled "When You've Had Enough" because I had. I set about making myself a mug of Ruby at her best. I took the mug out to the kitchen table and sat down to finish the letter to the town. To remind me why I was doing this instead of just fleeing under the cover of darkness again, I took out the letter I'd written to Ruby that day Claire showed up instead. Daniel had encouraged me to show her my heart. And I had. I spilled it all out in that letter. Reading it again after not seeing it for a few weeks just made everything in it more desperately real.

I folded it up and pushed it to the side as I took out the paper to draft my confession to the town. I was going to fire up the press and make it official. For once, my dad's printing machine was going to publish the truth. The warm tea and everything I needed to say must have gotten the best of me because I suddenly woke up in the state of confusion you wake up in when you didn't know you were falling asleep in the first place.

My next sudden revelation was that I was not alone in the room. I scooted the chair back from the table so forcefully that I almost fell over before I managed to stand up and turn around. The lantern that I had lit at the table was now sitting on the edge of the printing press where someone was bent over it clacking one thing and the next like they were pulling it apart and putting it back together.

I was about to yell out to him, but a woman's voice, Ruby's voice, beat me to it.

"I think I have this thing figured out," she said matter-of-factly as if she and I had already been working out how to use it. "It's actually a pretty impressive machine, despite the age on it." She came around from behind it so that I could see her and just kept talking as if nothing was out of the ordinary. "I understand from what I've read that there are much newer versions that do more pages than one and there's a mimeograph out that just lets you copy the page you made over and over without having to press a new one."

I looked around me to see if I could find some clue that might tell me what was going on. I felt like I had woken up to a different reality than had existed when I fell asleep.

"Ruby?" I questioned, starting with the basics in case in this reality she was someone else.

"What?" she answered, unaware of my confusion.

I stammered, "What are you doing?"

She looked at me and laughed lightly. "I'm getting your letter and the list laid out so we can print it."

My letter. I turned around quickly, looking to see if she was talking about the letter I had written to her but it was still folded on the table beside my empty mug. I was so relieved I put my hand to my chest and turned slowly back to face her.

"Are you OK?" she asked, looking concerned.

"Well, no," I said honestly. "I'm not sure what's happening. I," I faltered and then looked around behind me at the table again, pointing at my chair. "I was sitting here writing something and then I woke up and you were here working the press and I'm lost."

"I'll fill you in," she said, wiping her hands on a cloth she was holding and setting it on the press. She stepped closer to me which put her in front of the lantern enough that the room darkened just a tad. "I came over here the night of the festival to tell you I was in love with you despite everything, but then Claire came out and waved a ring at me and you came out and kissed her and I was devastated. I knew you had the deeds even though you told me you didn't, and I created this whole story in my head about you and Claire conning the town together and I felt like a fool. But then I talked to Pastor Collins." She paused then and pointed to me. "He knows it's you by the way and suddenly it was all clear to me. Or at least clear enough. So I came over here to help you and found you passed out at the table." She walked past me, and I turned to track her through the room. She went to the shelf of jars and picked one up and walked back over to me. "This is the one you should have used. "Keep Me Going" is a black tea. "When You've Had Enough" is a green tea with lavender and valerian root."

"What?" I asked. I was trying to follow her, but my mind was still caught on the bit about how she was in love with me. That and Pastor Collins knowing the truth.

She went to the table and picked up the mug and smelled the inside. "As I guessed. You're so literal sometimes, Cole. When I've Had Enough indicates that you need a rest. Get it?"

I nodded. I did, now, understand that part.

She touched the piece of paper that was the letter to her, and my heart fluttered. She didn't pick it up or mention it and I sighed in relief. She walked past me again, and again I turned toward her to keep her in my sight lest I take my eyes off her and she disappeared.

"I wasn't really sure how to help you," she said, "but then I saw the letter you were writing and understood what you were aiming to do, so I thought I'd get started while you napped."

I just stood there looking at her.

She sighed and continued. "I went back over to the library and dug through the machine section and came up with a manual for a press close enough to this one and I read up on how to use it and then I came back here." She ended the sentence as if that was the final one.

"I don't follow you," I said. "And how long was I asleep?"

"I have an idea that might work," she said, not answering my question, but stepping closer to me. She reached out and took my hand

and I thought I might pass out from relief. "But I'm here to help you with whatever your plan is if you'd rather do that."

I nodded but didn't say anything.

She shook her head at me. "Well, what's the plan? We print the letter and then what?"

I was suddenly afraid that I was in some dream and that Ruby wasn't here at all. That if I looked outside, I wouldn't even be in Certain. That if I spoke, the spell would be broken.

She raised her eyebrows at me. "OK, well if you don't have a plan past the letter, which is very good by the way, what about this? My plan is, we print a bunch of copies and Ava and I ride our routes and deliver the first newspaper Certain has had since your dad was here. We get the news to everyone at once and then set a time for them to come here and collect the deeds."

"Come here and collect the deeds?"

She nodded. "Yes, we'll change that part where you have apparently left town before anyone reads this copy at the grocery store and picks up their deeds from Mr. Gibbons. I don't like that."

"You don't?"

"No," she said and squeezed my hand reminding me that she had been holding it all that time. "It means you left and that's not acceptable. So, we'll have to rewrite that part."

I tried very hard not to smile against her scolding. "OK, we'll do it your way. I'll stay." She opened her mouth to say more, but I held up a finger to stop her. "There's just one problem."

"Just one?"

"Claire knows it's me," I said and in her shock, Ruby let go of my hand and stepped back. "And she wants me to tell the town that I, well Henry, discovered that her father found the deeds but died before he could retrieve them and return them to the town. Then I give everyone back their land and that's that."

She shook her head more vigorously. "How is that that?" she said and put her hands on her hips. "What about you? Do you just go on being Henry? Does she tell everyone who you are?"

"Honestly, I don't know. I don't think it matters much to her what happens to me."

Ruby stepped closer again and put her hand on my arm. "Well, it matters to me. It matters greatly that Cole stays here in Certain."

Those were the best words I'd heard in some time. They were the words I needed to hear.

"Because you're in love with him?" I asked, daring to hear more of what my heart craved.

"Yes," she said and moved her hand from my arm to my chest, resting it over my heart. "I'm in love with you. And you better be in love with me too."

I laughed despite myself. "I don't know about Henry, he's sort of a dolt, but Cole, he's head over heels."

"Sounds like we don't need Henry anymore, do we?"

"We never did," I said, and just like that, Henry was gone and it was just me, Cole. Here with just Ruby. Just like I wanted it to be from the start.

I put my hand against her cheek and wanted very much to kiss her, but I wasn't sure just yet if the time was right. Just the feel of her skin against my hand was enough for the moment.

"What if this doesn't work?" I asked. "It's hard enough to tell the truth, but to tell it and then hope for..."

"Forgiveness?"

I stepped back from her and nodded. I didn't have a reason to be forgiven when I got here, other than taking so long to come, but the hole I'd dug once I set foot in town was too deep.

"Do you forgive me?" she asked and I was stunned for a moment.

"For what?"

"For convincing you to come to town and pretend to be Henry for a while," she said and pouted pitifully. "For not helping you to tell the truth once I knew about the deeds, for jumping to conclusions about you and Claire, for saying you were just like your father." She closed her eyes and said, "For reading the letter you wrote to me and then folding it back up so you wouldn't notice." She opened her eyes again and looked at me tentatively.

"That's a long list," I said and looked toward the table, my heart thudding. "You read the letter?"

"That was the intention, right?"

"After I was long gone," I said incredulously.

The letter was rough and rambling as I wound my way around to telling her how I felt, what I really wanted, and how sorry I was that it was never going to happen and could she ever forgive me and I hoped she had a good life, and on and on. She stepped a half step back and I feared she was rethinking everything, but she reached up and touched my face and whispered softly.

"Write me a new letter," she said. "One where you tell me how it *will* all work out and that you'll stay here forever. No goodbye. Write me a letter where you kiss me in the end."

"I don't have another piece of blank paper," I said and before she could say anything else, I put my hands on her hips and pulled her back to me.

She opened her mouth to say something, and I kissed her instead. Deep and long and like I was never going to stop. I pulled her tighter to me and she pulled me tighter to her and I felt like everything in me was exploding and coming back together like a universe being formed.

Finally, when we needed to breathe, we pulled away and I whispered into her hair, "Love, Cole."

She pressed herself against me and I released every bit of fear I had been holding onto all this while. We stood there in the lantern light just holding onto each other for a moment. Then she pulled away, clapped her hands together and pointed to the press.

"Teach me the rest of how to work this thing and let's get started."

"How do you know we can make this work?"

"I don't," she said, but she didn't look concerned about it. "I trust that God will work it out for us."

"What if God has other plans?" I asked. "What then?"

I already knew "what then." Acceptance and that was harder than trust. It meant I didn't get what I wanted and I didn't know how to deal with that.

"Just because His will is different doesn't mean that He's left you," she said. "It doesn't mean that you're alone. And you'll have me. I'm not going anywhere unless you do. We'll get through this, the three of us."

I smiled. "I suppose you're right," I said. I'd only gotten by through His grace so far and even though nothing was like I would have planned it, here I was, with Ruby by my side in the place I wanted to be. I had to trust now.

She nodded purposefully. "Alright then. Let's get this thing printed."

Memory lit my mind up suddenly and I was surrounded by the ghosts of the past again. My father's voice calling out to me, which words came next in an article so that I could pull the correct letters and bring them to him. Sometimes he had written the articles out and I could just read as we went and sometimes he was so eager to get something published that he would just make it up on the fly calling out the next sentence and the next so rapidly I often got things wrong. Sometimes he was angry at me and sometimes not. The unpredictability was the worst. Setting the composite was time-consuming and frustrating as everything was backwards and tedious and small. I tried to focus on the parts of the paper that were true and useful. I enjoyed the times we'd print birthday greetings or a new recipe. I especially liked when my father would let me write a small story "to take up space" he'd say. I pretended like he enjoyed my writing, but I knew that even though he was setting the letters and saw the sentences, that he wasn't really paying attention. He merely accommodated the parts that he had to spend time on to make the latest fraudulent report look more real.

"It's got to look like a real paper and that we're just as interested in all the rest of it as we are about the land."

He'd talk to me as if I was in on it with him. I hated that the most. Sometimes we'd print whole copies that had nothing to do with the land grabbing or the fake government takeovers at all.

"If we overdo the whole story, it won't look legitimate. People will either get suspicious or start to think that it's all overblown and just more government propaganda. You must know how to dole it out just enough to keep everyone scared."

He spoke like he was teaching me how to do it. Like I was his pupil and he was the master. He seemed proud of his instruction and I think he thought I was listening and learning how to follow in his footsteps.

Really, I was dreaming up stories, or singing songs in the silence of my head, anything to drown out his words. Anything to keep from accidentally becoming like him.

Now I looked at the old Washington Press with the faces of George and Ben looking back at me and the thought of inking the plate, of sliding the tin pan under the press, and pulling the toggle to make the print turned my stomach. It was always that last moment that did me in. My father always had me push the toggle, which lowered the heavy press onto the ink and paper and then pull the toggle back to complete the process. He acted as though he was letting me do the fun part, but even I knew that he was putting the blame onto me. Everything before that was just setting the type, putting in paper, inking the plate, lowering the pan, sliding it under the platen. It was me pushing and pulling the toggle that made the lie come to life.

But now I had a chance to make it right. This would be the first time that running this machine would be for someone's benefit. This would be the first time this machine was used to tell the truth. I ran my hand across the curved metal top of the press, just above the letters that spelled out Washington Press and felt like both the machine and I were getting a second chance.

I nodded to Ruby. "Yes, let's get it printed."

We went back over to the table where she was working on the composite. She had gotten almost half of the letter I wrote to the town set. The hard part. The true part. All that was left was the change from me leaving to me staying. The risky part.

"You read how to do this in a book?" I asked, touching the backwards letters hesitantly.

"Of course," she said. "I thought setting the type would be easy," she said and made an exasperated face. "Takes more time and I don't have much finesse with making it look like a real paper. I remember your father's looked real. Mine just looks like a printed letter."

"That's all it needs to look like," I said. "And the less it looks like the *Certain Herald* the better."

She lit up then and clapped her hands. "Speaking of that," she said.

I looked at the top section of the plate and read the bigger backwards type. *The Certain Phoenix*. She had renamed it.

"From the ashes indeed," I said and a new resolve filled me. "Let's get this done."

We spent the next hours setting the rest of the letter and listing out the names of those people whose land deeds I had in my possession. At the bottom of the list, we gave instructions to meet here at the office on Wednesday, December 1st at 10:00 a.m. That was Claire's deadline.

Our eyelids were heavy as we placed the last letter, but our hearts were light. I was giddy. Or maybe sleep-deprived.

"We did it," I said.

Ruby yawned. "That was hard work. I can see why you put it off after all." She laughed.

Her joke was an acceptance. I didn't need to explain myself anymore. She understood me and always had.

"So, what's next?" she said. "I only read the part about how to make the plate."

I looked over at the machine and shook my head. "Next is sleep," I said.

"But we're almost there," she said. "Don't we press it now or something?" She went over to the machine and touched the platen. "Doesn't this do it?"

"It does," I said. "But we have to set the plate and ink it." I joined her at the machine and touched things here and there miming what to do. "Each sheet is printed one at a time. So you have to load the paper, close this flap, roll it under and press for each copy. Then it takes hours for the ink to dry." I yawned as well.

"But we could get it done by morning," she said.

I looked at my watch. "It's three a.m. and we've got some time left."

She started counting on her fingers and made a pouty face. "Well, we could get it done by late morning."

"Let's sleep," I said. "That way we can print out a copy tomorrow and make sure it's correct. We're too tired to see straight tonight. In the light of day, we'll know better if we have it right. Then we'll make the copies."

"But Claire," she started. I took hold of her hands and pulled her to me.

"Claire has given us until Wednesday," I said. "She's playing with me and she won't call the game ahead of time. Let's take the time she's given us and do it right."

Ruby folded herself into my arms and sighed. I tightened my arms around her and didn't want to let go. When I did, it was only so that I could tilt my head to hers and kiss her goodnight.

"You take the bed upstairs and I'll sleep down here."

She looked around. "Where are you going to sleep down here?"

"I've spent nights in more uncomfortable places," I said and kissed her again for good measure. "Toss me down a pillow and blanket and I'll be OK."

She pressed her hand to my cheek again and opened her mouth like she was going to say something, but she closed it without a word. That was OK, we didn't need any more words.

She pulled away from me and walked toward the stairs that led up to the living quarters. At the top of the landing, she turned and waved to me. I laughed.

"Tomorrow, we finish this and make Certain your home again," she said and blew me a kiss.

I made a show of catching it and pressing it to my heart. "Goodnight, Ruby."

"Goodnight, Cole."

She turned and went into my room. I looked around expecting to see my old ghosts slipping out of the shadows once I was alone, but they didn't come. I looked over at the press where the memories of my father had played out just moments ago, but the lingering filmy images of the past dissolved into the air and were gone. Henry was gone. They were gone. It was, finally, just me. The real me.

Chapter 23
Ruby

When the morning light found its way past my eyelids, I had that moment of forgetting where just for a bit, I didn't know where I was or why I was there. Then it quickly came back to me. I sat up from the warmth of Cole's bed and all but fell over myself trying to get up, out the door, and down the stairs to find him.

"Cole," I shouted across the seemingly empty room below me as I hurried down.

"Under here," his voice called out to me.

"Under where?" I called back, down the stairs now and searching for him amid the printing press parts.

He stood up from behind the tall flap where the paper went on the press. I couldn't remember any of the names of things. He told me as we talked last night, but I hadn't gotten that far in the manual and seeing things in writing made them stick for me better than just being told.

"You said underwear," he said with a wink and came around toward me.

I rolled my eyes at his silly joke. "No one will ever think that's funny.

Come up with a new one."

"I bet it takes off," he said and winked again. "There's another joke in there somewhere but we don't have time for that."

"No," I said, smiling at him despite myself. "We don't." I clapped my hands together ready to work. "Let's get the ink on and get this thing printed."

"Two things first," he said and reached for my hand. "I want to make sure I wasn't dreaming last night."

He stepped closer to me, lowered his lips to mine and kissed me softly. My heart raced and I got that weak-in-the knees feeling. I had read about it in romance novels, but it had never happened to me before Cole. His kiss lingered and then he pulled back, closed one eye, and grimaced like he was waiting for me to punch him.

I raised up on my toes and kissed him again instead.

He sighed, opened his eyes and smiled widely. "Good."

"And the second thing?" I asked.

He pointed behind me to the wood stove. "I made coffee," he said, but took hold of my hand when I turned to go get it. "Just so you know," he continued, "that day I kissed you and you got so mad at me, that first day you came over as Claire was leaving," he paused. "Do you remember?"

I deflated. I had let myself forget. "Yes," I swallowed the lump that had suddenly formed in my throat. "You were quite happy that day if I remember correctly."

"Claire spilled coffee on my pants," he said. "That's why I was upstairs when you came in. That's why I was still tucking my shirt in and pulling on my suspenders. I was changing out of the coffee-soaked clothes. I wasn't getting dressed. She didn't stay the night here. Is that what you thought?"

He still held my hand in his and I felt him give it a little squeeze.

"You said you woke up feeling all warm inside because you had a good conversation last night," I said, drawing out the words "last night."

"With God," he said. "I meant I was praying."

OK. "But you said Claire was fancy."

He smiled through a sigh and dipped his head. "Once I thought about it, I knew you'd gotten the wrong impression and I should have told you what really happened, but I was mad. Claire did come over here flirting, but she spilled coffee on me, thank goodness and I had an excuse to send her on her way." He pulled me a little closer to him and I let him. "And yeah, Claire is fancy, but even if she wasn't trying to blackmail me, I don't like her kind of fancy."

"You don't," I said, hoping my voice encouraged him to go on.

He shook his head. "I like Ruby fancy. Overalls with jeweled plants pinned to them. Wild hair and carefree smile. Big medical words coming across soft pink lips that I don't want to stop kissing. I could go on or I could just kiss you again."

I pretended to think about it, pursing my lips to tease him. A low growl sounded from his throat and he bit his lip. I smiled and pulled him the rest of the way to me.

"You can just kiss me," I said and he already was before the last word was out.

After a blissful minute at least, we pulled back from each other. I had forgotten all about coffee, but it might be best that we had some and got to work.

"I'll get us that coffee and you get the ink rolling thing going, let's test it out," I said, not really wanting to let go of him.

I went to the wood stove and poured two mugs. I was just about to take a sip of the coffee and head back over to Cole when I heard him grunt and sigh heavily.

"What's wrong?" I asked, setting the cups down and meeting him at the table that held all the printing supplies.

"I'm trying not to swear," he said.

"Why?"

"The ink is dried up."

I asked the only dumb question that came to mind. "What do you mean it's all dried up?"

He shook his head and laughed, which I thought was a crazy reaction to this plan-stopping problem.

"I don't know why I thought there would still be usable ink here all these years later," he said and ran his hands through his already disheveled hair. "I just got so carried away placing all the furniture and

190

locking it down. It all came back to me so easily once my hands were on everything again. The quoins and toggle and the platen, all the words and the functions rushing back into my mind. It was a little overwhelming to tell you the truth. Working this thing wasn't a good memory, but it felt good to finally be making it into one. I forgot about the ink."

"Furniture is what you call the letter blocks," I said, remembering, trying to catch up. "I read that much and the chase is the frame that holds it." That was about as far as I'd read.

"And the ink is the part that prints it," he said with chagrin.

I tried to make him feel better. "I like hearing you say all the big newspaper words," I said and touched his hand. "If I tell you they sound impressive coming across your kissable lips, will it help?"

I didn't know what newspapers used these days, but I knew that the Washington Press was going out of style even in the small offices. Probably already had. Bigger papers had machines with all sorts of wheels turning and half a dozen people or more manning the parts and places. I liked hearing him talk about the press.

He smiled despite himself. "It doesn't hurt," he said, but he still looked dejected. "We can place the furniture, lock the type in the chase with the quoins, put the paper in and roll the bed under the platen all we want, but without the ink, when we pull that toggle, nothing much happens."

He sighed and sat down hard in one of the chairs he had pulled up to the press. He lifted and lowered his hands in defeat.

I kissed the top of his head. "Well, it did sound sexy, you saying all that."

He chuckled but sighed again. "It's over."

"It most certainly is not." I put my hands on my hips. "We're not giving up now," I said, indignant. "There is still ink in the world somewhere. Surely." I let my hands drop to my sides. "Right?"

Cole looked up at me so disappointed. "I'm sorry, Ruby," he said. "I know you wanted to help make things right, but I think the only thing to do here, if I'm still hoping to stay, is just ride the deeds out to people's homes and tell them I'm sorry. I should have done that right away. Waiting has only made things worse."

"That would have been a terrible plan," I said and pulled up another chair to sit with him. "As soon as the first person gets that deed back, word will spread and without you being able to address everyone at once, rumors turn dangerous. We put smiles on our faces as best we can around here, but some people are still powder kegs waiting to go off. The deeds are great, but for most people it's just a reminder that the land isn't worth the paper that deed is printed on these days."

"I hoped the pride of having the papers back might give people hope," he said.

"If we do it right, it will," I said. "That letter defuses the bomb. Without it, you'll get the same angry mob your father did because people won't know that you're not planning another con. Maybe in other places things have gotten better, but here, we were already in a hole and now it's just deeper. We're last on the list here. Other towns get new roads, new schools, more water and electricity. We're lucky we've got the library. The rest will come one day, I just know it, but this isn't the day for Certain. You've got the only ray of hope anyone has seen here in too many years. If we do this right, you're the prodigal son and they will welcome you home."

"The prodigal son chose to leave," he said. "And someone cared where he went. I don't think they minded that I was gone."

"I minded," I said and gave him a playful punch, "but what I mean is that you coming back here and making amends for what your father did will be like the long lost son coming back to the fold. They know it wasn't your fault. Give them the chance to see that you're here to make it right, not finish the job."

He nodded with determination. "We need this press running to do that," he said. He stood up and rubbed his hands together. "OK where do we get ink?"

An idea surfaced so clearly it made me squeal. "Asheville."

"Well, let's just get Patty out of the stable and ride on over there then," he said sarcastically. "We'll be back next week."

"I have a better idea," I said and got up, pulling him with me.

I opened the door onto a morning much colder than the night before it had been. A stiff wind had picked up and it carried with it a sudden

192

frigid air. I felt like we'd fallen asleep in late fall and woken up to the bitters of mid-winter. I shivered but didn't slow down.

Over at the grocery, "the Council" was meeting just like I thought they would be. Morning coffee, talk about the town, and of course, the weather, were all on the agenda for sure whenever Mr. Gibbons, Pastor Collins, and Mr. Mobley got together. Daniel was present most of those days too as he drove both of his fathers-in-law into town and Mattie and kids to the school. Pastor's homestead was on the way up the creek to Daniel's house. I could see his "taxi" wagon out front and I knew all four men were there. We'd get that ink for sure.

I was already talking as I burst in through the front door dragging Cole with me.

"I need to make a phone call," I said looking at Mr. Gibbons, and then I directed my attention to Mr. Mobley, "and I need a favor if you have some left to call in."

At the sound of my voice and my hurried demeanor, all four men had already stood up.

"What do you need, dear?" Mr. Mobley asked as Mr. Gibbons headed for the phone.

"Ink for the printing press," I said. "We've got to beat Claire to the punch, give back the deeds, and save the day."

OK, I was getting a little dramatic, but the situation called for it.

Cole stepped around me then and spoke softly. "Can you listen to a confession?"

Pastor Collins stepped forward. "We don't really have confession at the Certain Baptist Church, but any time you want to speak to God about something and you'd like some help, I'm here for you."

"I need to speak to God and Mr. Mobley," Cole said.

"Me?" Mr. Mobley said. "I'm not sure you have anything you need to confess to me."

I had no idea what Cole was talking about, but I could tell that whatever it was weighed heavy on him. I had let go of his hand, but now I reached out for it again and stepped in closer to him hoping that he would receive my message of solidarity and compassion even though I didn't know what it was about. Raised eyebrows let me know that the action did not go unnoticed by the other men, but no one said anything.

"Let's take care of the printing first," Cole said.

Daniel stepped forward. "What do you need, Cole?" I noticed no man there flinched at the name. They all knew. "What's the plan?"

I filled them in quickly and when I got to the part about having no ink, Mr. Mobley nodded, recognizing his part.

"Gib," he said to Mr. Gibbons, "ring for *The Asheville Citizen* and ask for Charles. Tell him Mobley is calling."

Mr. Gibbons placed the call and we all stood there, anticipation swirling around us. After a few minutes, Mr. Gibbons held the receiver out to Mr. Mobley and said excitedly, "He's on."

Mr. Mobley hurried to the phone and with a little small talk, a few chuckles and one request, "Charles, old friend, I need some ink over here in Certain, Ky. It's an important news matter of great urgency," I knew ink was on the way.

We all watched Mr. Mobley finish out the call, trying to listen without hearing everything so as not to be nosy. Finally, he handed the receiver back to Mr. Gibbons.

Daniel seemed the most anxious of us all. I knew he knew all too well what it was like to be in Cole's position with the town. "Well, can he do it?" Daniel asked.

"Can and will," Mr. Mobley said. "Ink should arrive sometime today. It could be late depending on where he's able to source it."

"Today," Cole said and his hand squeezed mine. "That's amazing."

"What do we do until it gets here?" I asked.

Pastor Collins said earnestly, "Cole and Mr. Mobley and I apparently have something to talk about."

Cole tensed up again and sucked in a breath.

"Do you want me to leave?" I whispered.

His grip tightened on my hand. "Please don't."

I nodded. "I'm right here."

Mr. Gibbons cleared his throat. "I imagine you don't need me, fellas," he said, heading for the door. "Daniel, walk with me over to the church and let's see what your lovely wife and her students are up to at school today."

194

"I won't pass up a chance to see Mattie and the kids," Daniel said and the two men excused themselves.

Soon everyone was gone except for me and Cole and Pastor Collins and Mr. Mobley.

"What on earth could you need to confess that has anything to do with me, son?" Mr. Mobley asked, confusion and interest alike on his face.

I looked at Cole as well, just as confused. Mr. Mobley had just moved to town this year—if you call coming to visit and never leaving moving here. How could Cole possibly know him and have anything to confess? They'd surely only interacted in the briefest of casual moments.

Cole blew out a hard breath and made a small noise like he was testing this voice out before he began. The four of us stood in a close circle in the middle of the store.

Pastor Collins put his hand on Cole's shoulder. "It's OK, son. Go on."

Cole looked at me and then at Mr. Mobley. "It was my father who killed your wife in that stolen car all those years ago."

Cole's words seemed to hit Mr. Mobley square in the chest because he took a step back against their force.

Cole continued. "I knew it that day everyone brought me all the wonderful things to set up a house so that I could stay in comfort. The day you brought all the medical books over and told me the story of what happened to your wife."

Mr. Mobley closed his eyes and I wasn't sure what that meant. I looked at Pastor Collins willing him to do something that would make this news not as shocking as it seemed to be.

"I couldn't tell you then," Cole said. "I was already wrapped up in one lie upon another and I needed so badly to stay in Certain. I was afraid to tell you."

"Son," Pastor Collins started to say, but Cole put up a hand to stop him.

"I need to get it out," he said. "I'm so sorry, Mr. Mobley and I'm so sorry to Mattie. I could have stopped it. My father wanted me to ride with him. If I had gone, maybe he'd have been more careful. Maybe we would have ridden somewhere else. I don't know, but I didn't go with him. I knew the car was stolen and I didn't want to have any part of it. I was just a little kid, but I should have done something. I'm so sorry."

Mr. Mobley opened his eyes then. I worried that they would be filled with anger, pain, even hate. But they weren't. Mr. Mobley looked at Cole with compassion and pity. He shook his head and pressed his hands together against his lips like he was praying.

After a moment he spoke. "Dear child," he said, taking his hands from his lips, but keeping them folded together in front of him as if the prayer continued. "I'm so glad you were not in that car. My heart would have broken to think that a child witnessed that event from inside the car itself."

"Sir," Cole started to speak, but this time he was put on hold.

"Son, don't say another word. There is nothing to confess or ask forgiveness for here. I've already done the same thing as you," he said and then rattled off a list of what-ifs. "What if I had walked with her to the store? What if I had not gone into work that day? What if we'd gone on the picnic she had planned and were never in town to start with?" He shook his head again. "Those thoughts will eat you alive, son. You must have been a very small child at the time and your father's actions were not yours to control. They never have been." Mr. Mobley went on. "Your father had no right to make you part of his plan," he said, firmly but gently and I knew he was talking now about Cole's father's scam in Certain. "A father is supposed to protect and love his children. He's supposed to give his life to them. Care for them above all else. Keep them from harm's way and teach them to be good men and women in the world. Your father did none of that. And none of what he did is your fault."

Cole's grip was tight on my hand and when I looked at him, I could tell he was working hard to hold his emotion inside. He swallowed hard a couple of times and his eyes were blinking fast.

Pastor Collins patted Cole on the shoulder where his hand was already touching him. "Agreed, Cole. That wasn't your fault."

"Then I need to ask forgiveness for not telling it when I knew it," Cole said, searching for something to hold himself responsible for. "For lying about who I was and what I was doing here. For dragging this out so long. For," he stopped, and I knew him well enough to know that he was shutting his mouth while the tears were still safely at bay in his eyes.

"You're making all that right, now," Pastor said and nodded as if that was that.

"How do I forgive myself then?" Cole asked.

"That's a harder one," Mr. Mobley said and smiled just a bit. "Like I told you that day, I didn't find the magic cure in those books that could make anything any different. But I did find peace in another one."

Pastor Collins put his hand on Mr. Mobley's shoulder and said to Cole, "You're not your mistakes and you're certainly not your father's mistakes."

I could see Cole visibly relax, and just when I thought we might get a moment to settle ourselves down we heard Mattie's voice calling out. The sound was muffled a bit through the glass, but the urgency was not.

Mr. Mobley headed straight for the door as if led by an instinct so strong it practically lifted his feet from the floor. We all turned and through the window we saw Daniel lift Mattie up in his arms, pregnant belly and all, and run toward us. Daniel's kids, the rest of the students and Ava were hot on their heels.

We rushed out into the street to meet them. The suddenly harsh wind gusted my hair out at all sides and I couldn't see anything. Cole pointed to the newspaper office and shouted out to take Mattie there.

"Is she in labor?" I called to Ava, running to keep up. All of us pushing against the wind like it was a steel wall.

"I'd say so," Ava said breathlessly. "And maybe has been for a while but didn't realize it."

"Take her upstairs to the bedroom," Cole said, rushing up to Daniel, reaching out to see if he needed any help up the steps to the office door.

"I've got her," Daniel said, fear fracturing his face. "Get the door. Someone call the nurse."

We all pressed inside Cole's house and Cole pushed the door closed with great effort. The wind howled like it was mad to have been shut out. Daniel lowered Mattie to her feet and he and Cole walked her up the stairs, Cole leading the way and Daniel holding her up from behind.

"Is something wrong?" I asked, pulling Ava aside where the kids wouldn't hear. "Daniel is beside himself."

Ava put her hand on my shoulder. "He's just worried. The last time a baby came, his wife died. I don't think he'll live through it if that happens again."

My knees went weak. "Could it happen again?" I asked, knowing that the last time a baby had come for Daniel Ava had also lost a sister.

I wanted Ava to tell me no, surely not, but I knew better than that. Out here any bad thing could happen for no reason at all and even though the nurse midwives of the FNS almost always made sure babies and mothers came through labor alive and well, it was still a possibility to lose someone.

I leaned over, putting my hands on my knees and tried to get my dizzy head under control.

Ava's hand was warm on my back then, rubbing a small circle that was probably as calming to her as it was to me. I finally stood back up and fell into Ava's arms.

"Nothing bad can happen to her," I said as if my saying it would make it true. "Daniel won't let it. I know he won't. He's too much a grizzly bear for anything to mess with him."

Even death, I hoped.

Ava chuckled, probably despite herself, at my invocation of Daniel's old nickname. "He's a force to be reckoned with. Always has been even when he lost sight of it himself. He'll do whatever he can. I know it."

Mr. Mobley and Pastor Collins had corralled the kids just inside the front door, assuring them that everything would be fine and trying to usher them back out.

"Let's get back to the church," Mr. Mobley said. "Everything will be OK."

"I'm old enough to help deliver a baby," Marie said and stomped her foot on the floor. "And it's my baby just as much, so I'm not going anywhere." She put her hands on her hips and planted her feet in place.

Her older sister, Ella, picked up their little brother, Hugh, in one arm and put the other one around Marie. In a softer voice she pleaded, "Let us stay, Grandpa. We need to be here whatever happens. We need to be here for Da and Ma."

My heart ached for them. They had already lost one mother and even the smallest chance they could lose another was too much to bear.

Pastor Collins offered to take all the rest of Mattie's students back to the school until someone could come get them. With far less people in the room things seemed a little calmer for a moment.

Mr. Mobley took in a long breath and blew it out. "Everyone, stop panicking. Everything will be fine. We're going to deliver a baby here today and no one is going anywhere but home to celebrate it. And that's that."

I reached my hand out for his and he took hold of it. No matter how old she was, Mattie was still his baby and he wasn't entertaining the thought of her going anywhere. There was so much love and family in this room that the walls themselves were sighing from the fullness.

Daniel came out onto the landing above us. "We need to get a nurse. Now."

Chapter 24

Cole

"I'll go with you," I said, putting my hand on Daniel's shoulder and then slipping past him so I could rush downstairs to Ruby.

She saw me coming and went straight into action. By the time I got to the bottom of the stairs she was already laying out how it would go.

"We've got most of what we need here, and I'll get the rest," she said to me as if we were a team. Then in quick succession she gave directions. "There's a frontier nursing outpost not far from here. If her usual nurse isn't available, they'll send someone else. We'll do what we can from here. Go."

"I'll call it in," Mr. Gibbons said, already heading for the door. "Maybe I can get someone headed this way and you can meet her."

"I'll go with you," Mr. Mobley said. "No one goes anywhere alone in a storm like this."

When he opened the door, the force of the now icy wind on the other side blew it back almost knocking him down, but he stayed on his feet. The sky had been whispering of snow but since it seemed way too early for that we hadn't taken her seriously. Now she was raising her voice to scold us.

Just then Pastor Collins came up the steps. "I've got someone watching the kids. I'm here to help. What do you need?"

"We're going to make a call for the nurse," Mr. Gibbons said, pointing toward the grocery. "Cole, you stay and help Daniel."

I nodded. "Hurry and be careful," I called to Mr. Gibbons and Pastor Collins as they fought their way out the door and Mr. Mobley and I struggled to close it behind them. I figured Daniel would want to stay with his wife, so I called up to him where he stood on the upstairs landing. "You can stay with Mattie. I'll find the way."

Daniel turned and looked behind him, indecision stretched tight across his face. He wrung his hands together and breathed out hard. He rushed down the stairs, taking two at a time.

"It's OK, Cole. I'll go," he said and turned to Ava and Ruby, pleading. "You two stay with Mattie and don't let anything happen to her. I said I was coming back with a nurse for Emily. I lied. I went out on a run to deliver some shine because I didn't realize how sick she was and I thought we needed money more than a nurse. This time, I'm going to get that nurse come Hell or high water and I'm going to do it myself."

"You shouldn't be riding alone," I said. "The weather is getting bad and you're in no state to be by yourself."

He opened his mouth to protest, I'm sure. I was still getting to know Daniel, but I could tell that he was a man of fierce honor and fiercer stubbornness. I held my hand up and then out for him to shake.

"We go together and we come back together. With the nurse." I nodded my commitment to him.

He looked back toward the rooms upstairs and then turned back and shook my hand. Ava stepped in between us and put her hand on Daniel's chest like she was holding back a bear.

"It's not safe," she said. "Didn't you see that wind and feel that cold? That's snow at best and ice at worst. We can wait here for the nurse. And if she can't come, Ruby and I can figure out what to do. It's not like women haven't given birth without a nurse present before."

Daniel reached out gently and took her hand from his chest. He held it in his and kissed it softly. "Ava." He said her name like a whisper. "There is no way along all the Hell for Certain that I'm going to just sit here and wait. You know that. I appreciate your concern. You're a good sister. But I'm going to be the good husband to Mattie that I wasn't to Emily in the end. There's no talking me down from it."

"You were a good husband, Daniel," she whispered to him. "And you will be again."

Mr. Mobley put his hand on Daniel's shoulder. "I trust you, son."

"Thank you," Daniel said back to his father-in-law.

"Cole," he said to me and let go of Ava. "Let's go. We'll stop by the grocery and see what Mr. Gibbons found out and then head out on the main road."

Ruby was beside me then and I felt her hand slip around mine. "Take Patty," she said. "She knows all the roads. Even the ones that aren't." To Daniel she said, "We'll take care of Mattie. I promise."

I looked at Ruby to see if I could tell how much faith she had in those words. From the look in her eyes, she had total conviction. She didn't give herself credit for all the knowledge she had of medicinals, but she was by far the closest thing to a nurse this town had.

We said our quick goodbyes. Maybe I shouldn't have right there in front of everyone, but I put my hands against her face and planted a kiss on her lips that I let linger just long enough for my fingers to tingle. Then Daniel and I braced ourselves for the wind and pushed our way outside.

The door closed with a thud behind us. We looked at each other for just a second, maybe giving each other a last chance to change our minds, but the steel in his eyes, and I hoped the determination in mine said that wasn't an option.

"Get your horse and meet me at the grocery," Daniel said. He started walking toward his own wagon before I had a chance to say anything.

I'd only ridden Patty a handful of times when I was out on my fake investigative journalism trips and I had never ridden very far since I never went to most of the places I said I was going. Once I rode to Hyden but that was only because Mr. Gibbons had asked me to bring him something and I had to oblige at least that. Otherwise, I'd driven Mr. Mobley's car a time or two and almost wrecked it going over roads that weren't road enough to go over. I was much better on foot, but that was about to have to change fast.

I ran for the pen in between the church and the library. Luckily the wind wasn't blowing at top speed all the time, but the gusts were almost enough to knock me back a step. By the time I reached Patty she was already complaining about the situation. I untied her and looked around for a saddle. I wasn't a total loss of a frontier man, but I wasn't that great. I got the saddle on and was just securing the buckles under her belly when Daniel came riding up. Already he'd loosed his horse from the wagon, saddled up, and ridden over. He'd surely already talked to Mr. Gibbons and was just waiting for me to fumble around and get on already.

"I talked to Mr. Gibbons already," he yelled in confirmation of my relative uselessness over another gust of wind and nudged his horse back down from where it wanted to bolt against the weather.

He was the guy every other guy wanted to be. Handsome, broad in the shoulders, looking like a movie star on top of his stallion. It was a darn good thing for the likes of me that he was married. And very happily so. I put one foot in a stirrup and hoisted myself up into the saddle. In one try even.

"There's a nurse five miles up the creek at the Dodsons," Daniel said. "Outpost confirmed it. Don't know if she's still there, but she's our closest bet."

"Let me guess, we're not going at a trot."

"I hope you can keep up," he said, slapping the reins and giving a kick with both heels so that his horse turned like she had the map in front of her and took off.

I pulled on Patty's reins and she turned in a full circle. I gave a small kick and she swished her head like she was telling me no. "Come on, Patty," I pleaded. "If not for me, then for Ruby and Mattie." I patted the side of her neck and she neighed.

She turned toward the road and the disappearing spot that was Daniel and his horse in the distance and trotted out toward them. I gave another little kick and called out, "Let's go." I had no idea what you were supposed to say to a horse, but for the love of Ruby I guess, Patty picked up the pace and I was holding on tight as we flew back past the newspaper and the grocery and on out of town.

Trying to catch Daniel was like trying to grasp the wind. I just hoped he'd at least stay in sight or within shouting distance. I knew soon we'd reach more treacherous road and I hoped he'd slow down. I feared that he wouldn't. Maybe at least his horse would. I could also imagine him dismounting and running through the forests and up the riverbanks so that his horse and me and my horse would have trouble catching him.

The weather was not letting up and the thick gray that settled in around us was almost touchable. I thought that if I had the nerve to let loose the reins and reach out to the air around me that I could hold it in my hand like a cold damp rag. I was suddenly very aware of how dangerous this trip might be if the weather decided to turn further, or this nurse was not a mere five miles away and Daniel was not able to be reasoned with. That would likely be my greatest challenge. Love doesn't always think straight. I pulled the collar of my coat up and wished I had some gloves. We'd left dressed for late fall, but the dead of winter had made an early appearance.

Daniel rounded a bend in front of me and disappeared. Just before I panicked as I didn't really have a clue where I was going, I heard him yell out a "whoa" to his horse and I breathed out a deep sigh.

"Keep us up, Patty," I said encouragingly. "He's just up a ways."

I rounded the bend to find him waiting for me at the edge of the creek. He looked back when he heard us coming.

"We'll cross here and that will cut some time, but the path is a little rough for half a mile or so behind the creek," he said. None of this was a question. These were instructions and I was to follow them. "Patty doesn't mind water, but Opal here isn't a fan. She'll balk, but you just keep going around us and she'll follow Patty to the other side."

I nodded, shivering violently in the pressing wind. Daniel seemed unfazed.

"How long will it take to get to the Dodsons'?" I asked through chattering teeth.

"If we press on at a good walk when it's rough and a trot when it's open, we'll get there in under an hour," he said, untying a blanket that was fixed to his saddle and tossing it back to me. "We don't have time to freeze to death."

I couldn't tell if he was serious or making a joke, but either way, I agreed. I nodded and wrapped the blanket around me. "What about you?" I asked. "Aren't you cold?"

"I'm too scared to be cold," he said and tried to laugh. "Let's get going."

We both nudged the horses toward the creek and just like Daniel had said, Opal reared up just a tad and stomped around a bit. I could tell she wasn't aiming to throw Daniel. She just wanted him to know she wasn't happy. He waved me around and Patty and I took the lead.

The creek wasn't deep at this spot, but the water cut across a few rock formations here and there making it more treacherous than I wanted it to be. Patty stepped in like she didn't even notice it. Her confidence reminded me of her usual rider and I smiled. I knew Ruby was taking the lead back in town as well. I could picture her giving out instructions for Ava, making sure that Mattie did as she was told, and comforting a worried Mr. Mobley as well. They were all in good hands.

I wondered what my purpose here was other than to lead Opal across the creek. I half expected Daniel to tell me to go on home once he got across, but instead he thanked me and pulled back out in front, nodding for me to follow.

The wind whipped around us, twisting its cold fingers around me, prying the blanket away so that I had to hold onto it with one hand and the reins with the other. I longed for a hat. Daniel at least had that. I guess that was why he gave me the blanket.

We trotted along most of the way, cantering when the land was open enough, and walked when the path got tight here and there. I had the impression that this was not a well-traveled road. We were riding as the crow flew for sure.

When the road was wide enough, I pulled up alongside Daniel. I wasn't sure if Daniel was the comfortable silence sort of guy or if he preferred a distraction. Since there was nothing comfortable about this outing, I opted for the latter.

"I'm sure she's going to be fine," I said and then cringed at my generic and totally unhelpful comment.

"She will be if I have anything to do with it," he said. "I might be a pretty dumb guy sometimes, but I learned from that mistake last time. I won't even come close to letting down a wife again."

"You're far from dumb," I said and realized the opportunity to thank Daniel was right in front of me. "Thank you for not giving me up. I owe you."

He waved the comment off. "That's what friends are for."

"Are we friends?" I asked, surprised.

"Aren't we?" he said and then smiled. "See, like I said, I can be pretty dumb."

"No," I said in reply, "it's me who's dumb. I haven't really had any friends to speak of in years. I guess I don't recognize friendship when I see it."

"Friends help each other out," Daniel said and glanced at me. "You're helping me now."

"Am I?"

Daniel laughed out loud. "I guess we're both pretty dumb."

I laughed too. "Maybe. I hope I'm helping, but I'm not sure how."

"You're keeping me from going stir crazy so that I don't try to gallop Opal through the thicket and injure the both of us so that we're the ones needing a nurse."

I nodded, understanding. "Happy to help."

"You're brave to come back here," he said. "I commend it. It would have been easy enough to just keep those deeds."

"I wouldn't call it brave," I said. "I'd call it desperate."

Daniel chuckled. "Produces the same action sometimes, doesn't it?"

I nodded. "It's all or nothing now. I guess I'll see what happens."

"I'm sure everything will be fine," he said and winked, handing my platitude back to me.

"Do you really think so?"

He looked at me as if giving the notion some serious thought, but not really being sure how to answer. He didn't and we just walked on, winding through the woods and out into small clearings here and there where he'd clap the reins and give Opal a kick and she'd swish her head in protest but then canter as far as she felt comfortable before returning to a walk on her own accord.

"Stubborn horse," Daniel said to her and patted her neck. Then he looked at me. "Yes, I do think everything will be OK."

"I shouldn't have lied that day," I said, shaking my head. "Mostly I hate how easy it all came out. I just opened my mouth and this entire story fell out and not one lick of it was true."

"You're a natural born writer," Daniel said. "I really did like your articles. I bet you could write a good book, too. You'd score some points with Ruby. Not that you need them." He smiled at me.

"I do like to write," I said. "I guess I get my ability to make up a tall tale from my father. I hate that I'm like him."

"Then use your imagination for good and not evil like he did."

"I don't think I'll ever get out from under his shadow."

"I did it," Daniel said. "A father's shadow that is. But he's not the only father you've got. Remember that."

"You mean God, I suppose," I said.

"I sure do," Daniel said. "I also mean Pastor C. and Mr. Gibbons and even Mr. Mobley. I've been the orphan son before, a time or two for different reasons and when the chips were down and with me they always were, I was never alone to fend for myself. Even when I acted like I was."

"I don't know," I said. "I've been alone for a while now."

"You just thought you were," he said. "We think a lot of things that aren't right when we're under pressure. We do a lot of dumb things." He pointed ahead of us then. Up in the distance, a closed gate and the fence it was attached to came into view. "Like this," he said.

I knew what he meant. "We have to jump it?"

He nodded.

"Did you know that was there?"

He nodded again.

"Why did we come this way?"

"Because that's the Dodson farm. The house is on the other side of that open field beyond the gate. We're coming in the back way. It's faster."

"We're going to jump the fence and then run for it aren't we?"

"Yep."

"What's the likelihood of getting shot on the way in?"

"Not zero," he said. "Dodson isn't a fan of unannounced visitors. Me and him go way back though."

"So," I said, urging him to continue with something more reassuring.

"So, he probably won't shoot me," Daniel said. "You should stay back."

"What?" I asked, but Daniel was already picking up speed. "Daniel," I called out, but all he did was wave his hand behind him telling me to follow.

"Patty," I said and slapped the reins, "do not tell Ruby about this."

I closed my eyes and kicked with both feet. I could feel Patty pick up speed. Her feet clomped the ground beneath us and she whinnied in determination. The cold wind whipped harder the faster she went and I held on tight. The blanket Daniel had given me sailed off the back but I didn't dare slow down. Patty was in charge now and I was along for the ride. I supposed that was always the case, I just deluded myself to think that this animal was bowing to my control. I was at her whim. She was just allowing me to call the shots so long as she agreed. It was a scary thought one second but a comforting one the next. I knew full well she could jump that fence. So long as she did too, we'd be fine. I opened my eyes just as we sailed over it. Patty's strong legs held sturdy as we hit the ground running on the other side.

I shouted out triumphantly, sure that I could jump the fence back in Certain and everything would be OK. It would be OK because I was not jumping alone.

Patty and I raced through the field catching up with Daniel just as the Dodson house came into view. I had the deed to this land, too. This was the one that Dad had wanted the most. He acted like it was the Thomas land that mattered, but that was personal because Mr. Thomas was the one who believed him from the start. He wanted to make a fool of Mr. Thomas, but this was the piece of land that Dad thought could fetch a price. The rest of it was just dirt, he'd said. Coming in from this angle, I hadn't realized where we were. But Dad had ridden us out to the house before. He'd brought me with him when Mr. Dodson signed the deed over to him. I recognized the name when Daniel said it. I'd read those names off the deeds hundreds of times. I just didn't realize I'd been here.

This was the last property he'd tricked out of its owner's hands. I suddenly had another fence to jump.

Daniel pulled Opal up to the front of the house and dismounted before she'd stopped good. He was already running for the door calling out Mr. Dodson's name. I pulled Patty to a halt and slowly slipped out of the saddle. My wobbly legs almost gave out from under me.

I went up to the front door standing with Daniel as he pounded on the door and yelled out. The wind yanked his words off the porch and sent them out across the drive, but the pounding got the door open.

"Daniel," the man, Mr. Dodson as surely I remembered him, said in surprise, "what in the world, son?"

"Is the nurse still here?" he said.

I could see there was a horse tied out front but around here that could be anyone.

"She's inside," Mr. Dodson said, pointing behind him. "What's happened?"

"Mattie's in labor."

"Hold on, son," Mr. Dodson said and put his hand on Daniel's shoulder. "Take a breath. Get inside, this weather is awful."

I wondered if Mr. Dodson was another one of those fathers. Did he know Daniel's story as well? He looked at me and squinted. I could tell he was trying to place me but coming up short. I was about to change that. I followed sheepishly as we went in and Mr. Dodson closed the door behind us. Memory roared back as everything here was much the same as it was before. I shivered against the nearness of it all.

"Go on in and fetch the nurse, son," Mr. Dodson said to Daniel. "She's just finishing up. You almost missed her."

Daniel breathed a thank you and slipped past the man. I was left face to face with Mr. Dodson.

"I don't know you," he said and held his hand out for me to shake.

Time to jump. "I'm Cole Cooper. Mack Cooper's son," I said without taking hold of his hand. I saw the recognition in his eyes. "You don't have to shake my hand. I understand."

His hand lowered but his eyes stayed on mine. "Is Mack here with you? What are you doing with Daniel?"

I shook my head and answered the first question first. "My father isn't here. I have the deed to your land and I've come back to return it."

How hard was that, Cole? "I rode out here with Daniel to help him find the nurse for his wife Mattie."

"Is this a trick?" He looked me dead in the eye.

"No, sir." I looked at him right back.

He nodded and stuck his hand back out to me. I tentatively reached out in return.

"You grew up," he said, shaking my hand firmly. "I wouldn't have recognized you. You don't look anything like him."

"I'm glad to hear it," I said, my heart pounding with relief. "I'm sorry for what he did."

"I'm sorry I trusted him," Mr. Dodson said and looked at me sincerely. "Can I trust you?"

"Yes," I said and nodded firmly, finally believing it myself. "I'll have your deed and everyone else's at the church on Wednesday morning. I'm going to send a notice to everyone to meet me there."

"I'll be there," he said and nodded at me. "I can't promise everyone else is going to be so understanding. I'm just a nice guy. Not too humble, but nice." He smiled at me.

Daniel came back into view with a woman dressed in a light blue suit and riding boots that must have been the nurse. "OK, let's head home, Cole," Daniel said, smiling at me. "We did it. Nurse Sanders will come with us. Everything is going to be fine." He blew out a deeply held breath and patted my shoulder.

He didn't know I had just come clean to Mr. Dodson or that his open acceptance of me had probably affirmed to the man that I was a good guy after all. I hoped it had at least. Mr. Dodson smiled a small knowing smile, but then his face fell and he pointed over our shoulders.

"Y'all best ride fast," he said. "That's snow coming and coming in hard."

I turned around and sure enough there it was, like a moving white wall coming in over the hills in the distance. It grew visibly closer as we stood there watching it.

The nurse shook her head and I thought she was going to refuse to go with us.

"If we're going," she said, with a British accent that surprised me, "we better go fast. It's headed this way and aiming to follow us all the way back to Certain I bet."

Daniel nodded in confirmation. "It's moving too fast to turn. It'll get us before we get back."

I looked back and forth between them. "What does that mean? Are we not going? What about Mattie and the baby?"

"Of course we're going," the nurse said and walked past us toward the black mare tied in the yard. "You'd better keep up. I'm not interested in getting stuck out in the woods in a blizzard. It's only five miles from here to there, but that's enough to die in the snow. Especially once the sun goes down, which it's going to do in about thirty minutes."

"This sounds like a bad idea," I said, growing nervous.

"It is a bad idea," the nurse said. "But that's part and parcel for the job."

I didn't realize Mr. Dodson had disappeared until he was back handing us coats, hats, gloves, and blankets. "You can give them back to me on Wednesday."

Daniel looked at him and then at me. He gave me an approving nod.

"Let's head out," Daniel said as we all put on our extra layers and mounted our horses.

I hoped none of the horses were afraid of snow. As if they all three heard me and wanted to make sure I knew they were ready, they shook their manes and stomped their feet.

"They know what they're in for," Daniel said. "Let's go!"

Chapter 25

Ruby

The ride to the Dodsons' and back should have taken a couple of hours, maybe three if you accounted for slow going and having to wait on the nurse to finish whatever it was she was already doing. It had been longer than that. Too much longer. Mattie was resting upstairs with her father and Marie was reading her a book, keeping her distracted. Mr. Gibbons had gone back to the grocery to be near the phone. Pastor Collins went back and forth.

Mattie's contractions were still far apart, so I knew we had some time. She had calmed down and that had been half the battle right there. I couldn't say as much for Ava though who was about to wear a path in the floor.

"Stop pacing," I said. "You're making me nervous."

Ava lifted the wooden blinds on the front window for the hundredth time and looked out. "It's snowing even harder. Where did this storm come from?"

"This is news I don't need, thank you," I said, my heart sinking. I was desperately trying to pretend that everything was OK, but each report from Ava, who was usually the calm one, made that less and less possible.

"They shouldn't have gone," she said, looking back at me with worried eyes.

"Who was going to stop them?"

"Even so," she said and sighed.

Ava went to the other side of the room to check on Ella and Hugh. The story of *Peter Pan and Wendy* drifted to my ears every so often as Ella did her best to keep her little brother occupied. This was the third time Ella had requested that book since I brought it to her all those months ago. I smiled to think that books were working their magic all through the house.

I wished I had my medical books, but the weather between here and the library made me rely on my memory, which wasn't bad. The distraction of turning the pages to look at all the diagrams would have been nice though. The thought of Cole out there in the cold, under a blanket of ice and snow was more visual than my heart could handle. Five miles might not sound very far, but in weather like this with the sun set behind the hill already, it was far enough to get in bad trouble.

I glanced back at the press and our paper stalled out mid process. Getting ink seemed like the last of the unimportant things in a list of unimportant things. All I wanted to see was Cole and Daniel come through that door. Nurse or no.

"Do you think they'll get here in time?" Ava asked, pulling out a chair at the table and sitting next to me.

"I hope so," I said, "but we'll be OK if not. We both know what to do. You've had five kids and I've read every book in the library that even mentions anything about medicine. Between the two of us and with God's help for sure, we can deliver the baby."

She bit her thumbnail and nodded. I had never seen Ava lose composure before and watching her now as she worried about Daniel, who she still considered her brother-in-law, with the memory of her sister's death almost visibly swirling around her head, it was obvious to me how much effort she usually put into appearing unfazed all the time. I wondered who Ava really was behind the face she showed to the world.

A heavy knock vibrated the door and Ava rushed to it. My heart leapt. I hoped it would be Cole and Daniel, but I knew they wouldn't have knocked. Ava pulled the door open and wind and snow pushed their way in like they were there to collect a debt. The papers we had pulled out for the press blew off the table and I rushed to get them. Maybe getting that letter out to everyone was down on the list, but it was still on it.

When I turned back to the door it was closed and a stranger was standing beside Ava shaking snow off his coat and shuddering against his lingering cold the way a person who has been out there for a while might do.

Ava looked at me in question. I shrugged and shook my head in answer.

"Who are you?" she asked the man who was taking off his hat and looking for somewhere to set it.

Normally she might not have let a stranger in without asking that question first, but this wasn't the evening to leave anyone standing at the door or to leave the door standing open. I hoped he was here for good reasons.

"I'm Joshua Hartwell," he said, putting his hat back on for lack of anywhere good to put it, then taking off his gloves and sticking his hand out for Ava to shake.

She did and then put back on the composed Ava face that I knew. "That doesn't tell me much."

"I'm from *The Hazard Herald*," Joshua said and lifted off the satchel he had over his shoulder. "I'm here with ink for your paper." His eyes widened as he looked past me at the press. "She's a beauty," he said, handing the satchel to Ava and walking across the room to the machine. "I had no idea you folks had a Washington." He looked at me and nodded his approval. "Or any press for that matter." Ava and I looked at each other as he kept talking. "Does Certain even have a paper? I've never heard of one. Anyway, Mr. Wooton told me to get over here and deliver this ink and help out if I could." He rubbed his hands together like he was getting ready for something. He took off his hat again and set it on the compositing table. "Let's get printing."

My thoughts were flying all over the room, but when I reached out to try and catch them, they fluttered away. The ink was here! And so quickly. That was wonderful, but Cole was out in the blizzard and Mattie was in labor and I didn't really know how to work the press. I was depending on Cole coming back for that. I was depending on Cole coming back for a lot of things, I realized.

Joshua Hartwell took off his coat and flung it across a chair. He reached out behind him presumably for his bag that probably contained the ink tin.

Ava stood behind him with a very Ava look on her face. Her expression was contained contempt. There was no way she was going to walk over to this man and hand him the bag he just handed her when he could very well come get it himself. A smile cracked across my face. Perhaps I did know Ava well.

"Mr. Hartwell," I began, but he held up his other hand to stop me.

"Josh," he said and dropped the hand he was holding out for the bag, seeming to realize that it wasn't going to be placed there. "No formalities here. I was just told you all were in a bind and needed to get something printed pronto. That's my job."

"We're sort of in the middle of another thing we need to get done pronto," I said, glancing upstairs.

He turned to follow my gaze. "What's that?"

Ava, having set the bag down by the door, walked over to join us. "We're expecting a baby."

Josh's eyes went to our stomachs back and forth, his face showing confusion. I pointed toward the staircase that led up to the loft bedrooms. On cue, Mattie cried out and Marie stepped out onto the landing calm as anything.

"I think the baby is coming now," she said. I admired that kid. Of course, she had no idea what "the baby coming" entailed. The ignorant bliss of youth.

"I guess it's time to deliver a baby," I said and clapped my hands together.

Josh exhaled, puffing his cheeks out. "That," he said and pointed toward the baby delivery area, "is not my job. I hope."

I clapped him on his broad shoulder. "Don't worry, the women have it in hand."

He visibly relaxed. "Good," he said and looked around. "I'll just prepare the ink stone then and let you guys handle the hard work."

Ava winked at me but we both knew we hoped that the nurse would get here soon. Two women would be good, but the three of us would be better. Especially that third one. Ava had been on the birthing end and I'd read all the books, but someone who had been on the coaching and catching side would be most helpful.

"Your ink is by the door," Ava said, but since she was not actually a contemptuous person, she said, "and thank you very much for bringing it. Especially in this weather. It must seem less than a necessity when the snow is blowing like that."

"Printing and delivering the news is always a matter of necessity," Josh said, nodding his head to punctuate his point.

He winked at Ava and something miraculous happened.

She blushed.

"Y'all coming?" Marie called from the top of the stairs. "I don't want to have to do this myself."

"You ladies go handle the hard part," he said, looking away. "I'll get us set up down here. Is the type set already?"

I nodded. "Yes, it's all set, the furniture is in place and the plate is ready. The paper is over there." I pointed to the ruffled pile that had been blown a bit by the wind each time the door had been opened.

He looked at me approvingly. "Sounds like you know what you're doing."

I shook my head. "I'm all book learning and that's as far as I read. The newsman," I said and paused, feeling good about the title, because he really could be, "should be back soon. He's out fetching the nurse with Mattie's husband." I reached out suddenly and gripped Josh's wrist. "You didn't come across anyone traveling, did you?"

Ava stepped closer to me and wound her arm around my other one. "Coming from Hazard you wouldn't have crossed paths until they were close to town. Did you see anyone?"

Josh pressed his lips together and shook his head. "No ma'ams. I didn't."

I let go of his arm, but Ava held tight to mine.

She cleared her throat and spoke with determination. "They'll be fine. I'm sure they hit that road not long after Mr. Hartwell here and they'll be coming through that door any minute."

We all looked at the door, but it remained closed.

"Just Josh, Mrs.--?" he said to Ava in question.

I tried to sneak a look at her. It had been five years that her husband left and never returned.

"Bell," she said her last name without a title. I put my free hand on hers where it gripped my arm. "I'm widowed. I think," she said.

If Ava hadn't been holding onto me so tightly, I would have fallen over. Everyone in Certain knew her story. But this might have been the first time she spoke any part of it to a stranger. Even Mattie knew only because I had told her.

"I'm sorry to hear that, ma'am," Josh said.

"It's been a long time," she said. I could feel her stand up straighter. "Life has gone on."

He nodded and his deep brown eyes lingered on hers. I wanted her to be able to linger in the moment right back, but Mattie cried again and we all jumped.

"I've got things covered down here until your newsman gets back," Josh said.

"Cole," I said, loving the sound of his real name out in the air for anyone to hear. "Cole Cooper."

Josh nodded and Ava and I headed up the stairs and into Mattie's room. She was sitting up in the bed, pain stretched across her face.

"I was trying to hold it in," she said apologetically.

Ava chuckled. "You can't hold a baby in, sweetie. It comes when it comes no matter."

Mattie laughed too. "I meant the pain," she said. "I didn't want you all to worry."

I took hold of Mattie's hand. "It's a friend's job to worry and to take care of you. You settle in and let us do our jobs."

Mr. Mobley looked at us nervously. "I think it might be too much for me." He looked back at Mattie. "It's hard to see you in pain, pumpkin.

217

But I'll stay if you need me to."

Mattie winced against a contraction. "I'll be OK, Pop. I've got my ladies here and I know that Daniel will bring that nurse back. We'll be OK."

"Maybe Marie and I will go downstairs with the kids and help keep everyone busy," Mr. Mobley said and winked at Marie. "That sounds like a good job for us, doesn't it?" He put his hand on Mattie's belly. "While we wait to meet this new one." Tears caught in his throat as he looked at her with more love than I knew how to understand.

"That would be a great idea," Mattie said and reached out for Marie to come to her. "Give me a hug and go on down with Grandpa and help take care of everyone. I'll be fine. And we'll all meet brother or sister soon."

Marie slipped her hand into Mr. Mobley's. Worry showed on her face. I knew showing emotion was a feat for Marie too. She took after her Aunt Ava as far as her stubborn self-sufficient nature went. Strong women, both of them. They both needed to let someone in from time to time, too.

"Go on," Mattie said. "No need to worry."

She was a mother for sure. Making light of difficult things so that her kids wouldn't worry until there was something to worry about. And perhaps there wouldn't be. Surely everything would be alright.

Marie and Mr. Mobley turned toward the door. He stopped and blew Mattie a kiss before he closed the door behind them.

Ava went around to take the seat Mr. Mobley had held and I sat down by the desk on the other side of the bed. We flanked Mattie and were prepared to do our best to see her through this, come what may.

She reached out her hands to each of us and we took hold. She breathed out. "Tell me it really will be OK." She winced again and her eyes filled with tears. "Or at least that you'll be here with me if it's not."

"We're not going anywhere," Ava said.

"And it really will be OK." I wasn't sure if that was true, but that was what she needed to hear and that was what friends were for too, providing irrepressible hope no matter what.

Mattie nodded but then her face tuned up in pain and she yelled so loud my heart nearly stopped beating.

Chapter 26
Cole

It might have been a five-mile ride there but it felt like it had been twenty already on the way back. I followed behind the nurse who followed Daniel. Cold wind howled against the knit cap I wore. My ears were grateful for Mr. Dodson's kindness. I was grateful for his grace.

To keep my mind off the blowing snow and freezing air, I planned out how I might address the inevitable crowd once the news was out and the folks came for what was theirs. I hadn't let myself think this far ahead because facing the reality that the reality might not be what I wanted was not at all appealing. They say that ignorance is bliss, avoidance is too. But it's a false bliss.

What I had now that I didn't have when I came to town was actual hope. Before, I didn't have Ruby and Daniel. I didn't know how easily Mr. Mobley and Mr. Gibbons would take my side. I didn't know how comforting Pastor Collins would be. I didn't have friends. Friends that had taken me in like family.

Suddenly, up ahead I heard Opal whinny and Daniel call out to her. My heart raced with apprehension until I looked around a little more.

Although the snow had made a fast blanket over just about everything, I could make out a familiar place on the trail. That whinny was Opal complaining because we were back at the creek.

I called out to the nurse. I wasn't sure if she heard me. The wind whisked away my words so forcefully I could almost feel them being ripped right out of my mouth.

"I'm coming around to lead," I called and in case some of the words didn't get there, I nudged forward, calling again. "Nurse Sanders, let me pass in front and I'll lead the way."

I was beside her then and she waved me forward. I clapped the reins a bit to keep Patty going and came up to Daniel trying to stop Opal from dancing off into the woods in the other direction.

"Opal," Daniel was calling. Only a word or two made it to my ears. "Mattie…some water…home."

"Daniel," I called, getting his attention more from sight than hearing as Opal turned in her small circles. I waved and pointed. He nodded and pulled up on Opal's reins again.

I walked Patty slowly into the frigid water. Thankfully it was shallow, but I still didn't care to fall in. The banks on either side and even the rocks that stuck up beyond the water line were covered in snow. Somehow snow even seemed to collect on the water itself. Everyone talked about the snow looking like a warm winter quilt, but to me it looked like this was why the Hell for Certain had gotten its name.

I looked behind me and saw that Daniel had convinced Opal to go in and the nurse was right behind them. We were close now. We were going to make it. I felt like Daniel did when we headed out. I wanted to gallop Patty all the way home.

Home. I hadn't dared call it that, even to myself. But now I wanted that more than anything. And the biggest part of what made Certain home to me was Ruby. Even if I couldn't be sure of anything else, I was certain she loved me. I was certain that I was wanted. Everyone wants to know that they're loved. That they aren't too damaged to be accepted. I finally knew that and I had to get home. It was time for the ghosts in the haunted house of my heart to dissipate forever.

I gave a soft kick with both feet along Patty's side and she lifted her head and swished her mane. "We're almost home, Patty," I called and bent forward to rub the side of her neck.

Just then something ran out of the brush up ahead of us on the bank and Patty reared up. I held on as best I could, but she was too spooked from the cold and the wind and whatever little animal had darted past that I couldn't get control of her. Daniel splashed up beside me and reached out for me, but I missed his arm and went tumbling into the water.

I shot straight up as soon as my butt hit the cold creek floor, but I was wet through and through. Patty ran on across the creek without me and honestly, I didn't blame her. Water splashed up against me and before I could figure what was happening, Daniel's hand was reaching down to me from atop an unhappy Opal. I grasped onto his wrist and between my jumping and his other hand grabbing hold and hoisting me up I found myself clambering behind him across the saddle and clinging on as we went the last yards across the creek.

Once on the bank I fell loose and onto the ground in a shivering ball. Both Daniel and the nurse were next to me in seconds. Daniel threw a blanket over me even as the nurse was tugging off my coat and wet shirt.

"He needs to get these wet clothes off immediately," she said, and the blanket whisked itself off me at Daniel's hands I knew, but the sensation was surreal. "Take off your pants," the nurse instructed.

"Me?" I heard Daniel's voice ask and then the sound of his belt.

"Not you," she said, as she tugged this time at my shirt. "Everything wet has to come off, now."

"Everything?" I asked through chattering teeth.

"Everything," she said. "And you don't have anything I haven't seen before, so there's no time for modesty."

"Aren't we almost there?" I asked, my teeth chattering so hard I wasn't sure she could even understand me.

"We're more than two miles out and it's probably no more than 20 degrees out here. This storm has rolled in like the devil himself. We're all in danger just being out, being wet on top of it could be the death of you," she said as she pulled my shirt off and reached for the buckle on my pants. Her English accent made everything she said seem truer. "You can start to get frostbite in about 30 minutes in conditions like this," she said as I pushed her hands away from my zipper. "Especially with wet clothes on wet skin."

"I'll do it," I said, embarrassed, but freezing and she was a nurse after all.

"Here," Daniel said, pushing his pants into my hand once I had my own tugged over my already aching skin. "Put these on. I have long johns on. I'll be fine."

No wonder the weather seemed to bother him less. I guess he'd suspected the storm that evening. I had a lot to learn about being a country boy again.

"Are the both of you aiming to freeze to death?" the nurse asked and then she pointed at Daniel. "Don't take that off, too. I've another blanket."

I don't know what he was taking off to give to me, but she handed me the blanket instead and I wrapped it around me as tight as possible.

"Where's your hat?" she asked me, and we all looked back at the creek. She ran back to her saddlebag and pulled out a knit cap. "Put this on. We need to get back to town as soon as possible."

"Ride with me," Daniel said and I hoisted back up behind him onto his horse. "Patty will follow. Hang on."

We set off at a good clip, but not so fast that I couldn't hold onto the back of the saddle with one hand and keep the blanket tented around me to keep the air off with the other.

Daniel called back to me over the wind, "We're only a couple miles out. Thirty minutes at the most we should be back to town. Don't freeze before then."

"Trying not to," I called, shivering so violently I was probably making it hard for Opal to walk.

"I know I said it was nice to have a distraction," Daniel said, "but you didn't have to go to such lengths."

"Just trying to help," I said, teeth clacking. "That's what friends are for."

It certainly felt like friendship when a man gave you his pants to keep you warm in the middle of a snowstorm. It felt like friendship when he forgave your bald-faced lie and kept your secrets until you were brave enough to share them yourself. It felt like friendship when he took you with him on the most important day of his life.

"Indeed," Daniel said in answer, and I relaxed even through my shivers. "I will need those pants back though."

"They're too long anyway," I said.

The wind and still blowing snow cursed at us the rest of the way back to town and we tried to keep a low profile hoping she would let up. Nurse Sanders led the way, probably knowing where she was going just as good or better than we did as she cared for the woman and children regularly in these parts. She was used to making good time getting from one emergency to the next I imagined.

"We're back," I heard Daniel yell after a little bit.

I didn't want to say anything about it, but I was stinging and burning everywhere. The blanket was keeping the wind off, but even the skin under Daniel's pants was aching. I knew that was a bad sign.

I dared peek up and out of the blanket and sure enough, we were pulling up to the newspaper building and already the nurse was dismounting and tying her horse. She reached up to me and I took her hand to steady my slide down. No time to worry about being manly when you're wearing some other guy's pants and about to freeze to death.

Daniel nudged me toward the door. I knew he was aching to get back to Mattie, so it meant the world that he took the time to make sure I was heading inside before he took off. I was shaking too hard to realize I'd already stepped inside, until I opened my mouth to call something and the nurse's voice rang out instead.

"We need some dry clothes down here and some more wood on the fire." She pulled me toward the wood stove at the back of the room. "Don't get too close too fast. We need to warm you up slowly no matter how fast you want it to happen."

I could hear children's alarmed voices and in the periphery of my vision I saw them running around, like little sprites in a fairy story, jumping up and down waving their arms all around. I was having a hard time putting the whole scene together in my mind.

Ava came out onto the landing then and yelled back toward the bedroom, "They're here but something's wrong."

Daniel was already running up the stairs in his long johns when Mattie cried out and he startled so bad I thought he might fall off the stairs save for the railing holding him in. The nurse called for me to stay wrapped up and then she grabbed her bag and darted past me. She was up the stairs in a flash.

I looked around for Ruby, but my eyes lit on a stranger in the room. "Who are you?" I said, my teeth chattering a little less now that I was inside.

He walked across the room in a few long steps and stuck his hand out for me to shake, but before I could reach for it, Ruby had ducked around him and thrown herself against me knocking the blanket off kilter.

"What happened," she said, her hands running over my bare chest like they were looking for the shirt that should be there. It wasn't an entirely unpleasant sensation despite the chill that still clung to my skin.

She pulled the blanket back up around my shoulders and spoke to the stranger whose hand was still outstretched. "Put some more wood on the fire will you, please?"

"Can do ma'am," whoever he was said.

Ruby dragged a chair from the table up to the wood stove, but not too close.

"Your skin is pink," she said to me, still searching her eyes over mine. "Why are you half naked? Did you get wet? Where's your shirt?" She kept firing questions at me and then began to bark orders. "Whatever you do, don't rub your skin. I'm sure it's stinging and it'll sting more once you start to warm up, but keep your hands off."

At that she knelt in front of me and took my hands in hers gently. Not rubbing but huffing warm air onto them in small puffs. She reached up again and pulled the blanket back around my chest. I did catch her sneak a peek before she pulled it closed, setting my hands against it to hold it in place.

"Like what you see?" I asked and winked.

"Cole Cooper," she said and scowled at me. "If you weren't possibly suffering from early-stage hypothermia, I'd smack you."

"So that's a yes," I said and bit my lip.

"Don't do that," she said and put her fingers against my lips, worry in her eyes.

"You could put something warmer against them if you want to," I said, my teeth clacking, but less so than they had been. I was home. Ruby was here. Everything would be OK.

"This is not the time," she said pointing her finger at me. "I've got a baby to help deliver."

"How's it going up there?" the stranger said, looking up toward the room. "How's Ava doing?"

What did he know about Ava and the baby? And why was he even asking about Ava?

"Who are you?" I asked the man again.

Again, he stuck out his hand and I shook it, careful not to let the blanket fall.

"Joshua Hartwell from the *Hazard Herald*. I'm here with the ink and to help the newsman here get a special delivery printed. Are you him?"

"I suppose so," I said.

"Well once you thaw out and get some clothes on, we'll get going."

Mattie screamed out again.

"She's close," Ruby said. "I need to get back up there. Are you OK?" She looked stricken with indecision.

I was flattered, but a baby on the way was more important than my cold fingers and toes.

"I'll be fine," I said and touched her hand. "Toss me down some clothes and I'll send Daniel up his pants. Although, I doubt he cares too much about them right now."

She looked at the trousers I was wearing and smiled just a bit. "That explains why he's up there in his underwear practically. I knew Mattie was still doing OK because the first thing she said to him was 'where are your pants?'"

I smiled back at her. "Go," I said. "I'm sure the nurse could use someone else with some medical knowledge. Go do your thing. I'm OK."

She stood up and touched the top of my head, then leaned down and did in fact put something warmer on my lips, hers. I knew this wasn't the time, what with Mattie laboring upstairs and just about everything all around us in limbo, but on the other hand, uncertain times are the most certain times to kiss the woman you love.

Blanket be damned, I stood up and pulled her to me without breaking the kiss. I put my cold hands into her warm hair and felt her warm hands rest ever so gently on the cold skin of my back. Both our mouths were hot with the kiss that we had been meaning to kiss all the other times we'd kissed. All the stars had aligned now. No matter the busted-up path it took to get me back to her, I was here and I wasn't going anywhere. This kiss meant to tell her that in no uncertain terms.

"Understand?" I asked when we finally let the kiss fall away.

She reached up and touched my face in answer, giving me a long look and then rushing for the stairs.

I watched her all the way to the top until she was gone inside my room where all hell was breaking loose by the sound of it.

Joshua cleared his throat. "That was some kiss."

The door opened upstairs and Ava came out tossing my clothes over the landing.

Joshua waved up at Ava like she was Juliet on the balcony. She nodded back to him. I cleared my throat then and he looked away as she ducked back in.

Joshua and I stood there looking at each other for a moment. Until he pointed at my clothes and said, "Put your clothes on man and let's get to work."

Chapter 27
Ruby

Still very aware of Cole's kiss, I rushed back upstairs to help Mattie. Ava and I had done the best we knew to do between the both of us which was quite much considering her actual experience and my studying. Still, I was very grateful the nurse was there.

Already she was laying out her equipment. I was smitten with the very idea of her and everything she was doing. She wore a smart white collared shirt and a tie with a blue vest over the top, the same color as the blue pants that flared at the thighs and were tucked into a pair of tall riding boots. Her hair was tucked up in a low, folded bun that stuck out the bottom of the rounded cap that matched the vest and pants. Her blue coat had already been taken off and was folded nicely across the chair near the desk. I had seen the FNS nurses dozens of times, but standing here in the room with one while she prepared to deliver a baby was a new thrill.

She took off the vest and tied on an apron as she talked to both Mattie and Daniel in a calming voice. Once she tied the strings behind her back, she reached into her bag and retrieved another rolled up apron that she handed to me as if that was always the plan.

She spoke in her regal sounding accent. "I don't have a courier with me," she said. "I'm hoping you will assist. I'm told by Mattie here that you have some medical knowledge."

Couriers were assistants to the FNS nurses. They carried medicines to homes and outposts. They assisted the nurses when needed. They cared for the horses and did all manner of chores in whatever way they were needed. It was an honorable post and I was happy to do it.

"Of course," I said, my own voice not nearly as crisp and smart as hers, but it was strong. "I'm happy to help."

"Brilliant," she said. "I'm Nurse Sanders. I'm called Sandy. You are?"

"Ruby," I said. "I'm called Ruby."

She smiled at me and nodded approval.

I unfurled the apron and tied it on. She had laid out a series of metal nesting bowls on the desk already and she handed me one of the larger ones.

"Warm water," she said like she was confirming something I already knew, nodding to me.

I was at once nervous and completely ready for the task at hand. Where I might have felt fearful doing some other work, assisting the nurse was a rush of excitement like I hadn't felt before. The nurse called instructions to me and I followed. When she called terms and procedures and what to expect next it was all familiar to me and what little wasn't seemed to make perfect sense. We worked in tandem to help Mattie deliver. Ava worked with Daniel to help him not pass out.

"She's going to be alright?" I heard him asking. "Something seems…"
He stopped himself, looking at Ava so that the fear in his eyes was turned away from Mattie.

Ava reached her hand across Mattie's stomach to take hold of Daniel's hand. I glanced at Mattie to see her eyes closed in concentration and pain.

The nurse pressed one hand on Mattie's belly, feeling around as if searching for something. "The baby is in a breech position," she said matter-of-factly.

Daniel looked at Ava and then at me.

I answered his unspoken concern. "The baby's head isn't pointed down. It's not unheard of." But it wasn't common. Most of the time a baby will position itself like it should before labor sets in.

"But it's not the way it should be," Daniel said and focused his gaze on Mattie whose eyes were still closed.

He wanted us to tell him everything would be alright. Hopefully it would, but a breech delivery was not how it should be and there were certainly complications that could occur.

Ava spoke up. "Is there time to turn the baby around?"

"We'll have to at least a little," the nurse said and nodded to each of us as everyone was on the same team at this point.

Daniel nodded back and looked between me and Ava both. "This baby will come out and everything will be fine." He said it not like a command to us or like a desperate hope spoken in fear, but like a man certain life would not do to him again what it had done before. "Mattie and the baby will be OK."

When he looked at Mattie, her eyes were open and filled with fear. He had let go of Ava by then and now took Mattie's hand in both of his. "You and the baby will be fine. This will all be fine. Do you hear me?"

Her eyes locked onto his. If he had any doubt or worry it did not for one fleck of a second show on his face. No twitch of his chin, dart of his eye, nothing. His certainty did not waver and she wrapped herself around his faith, nodding her head at him and pressing her lips together with determination to carry on.

The nurse called for more warm water and I dashed downstairs. Cole and Joshua were hard at work at the press. They spoke to each other regarding the process of printing like they had been working together for years. Roll this, press that, lift, place, crank. They seemed to have things in hand. I let myself watch Cole for a moment. His beautiful face was set in concentration, but his body was at ease. He was in his true element. Back then I knew he had worked on the press with his father and that he wrote articles from time to time and that he was a good writer, but he never really wanted to talk about it. Something about his work on the paper made him sad.

"I know how to do it," he had said. "Maybe one of these days I'll print a *real* paper. I think I could be good at it."

I didn't understand what he meant at the time. It all made sense now.

I smiled to myself and thought *You're doing it now, Cole, you're printing a real paper. Perhaps there will be more after this one.* I could tell from the letter he wrote me and the one he'd written to the town that he was made for reporting, for writing, for reaching people with his words. His father might have set the wrong example, but Cole had a talent for this and a desire to do it the right way. I already knew how I'd support him. I'd make sure he got to run the *Certain Phoenix* from here on out. His words, his paper. The truth. I breathed in deeply and tore my gaze from his strong frame and deep eyes. I needed to bring hot water upstairs. Today I was an FNS Courier. Time to see if I had what it took.

Back upstairs with the water, I continued to follow Nurse Sandy's instructions. I hadn't read much about breech deliveries other than they were difficult.

Mattie labored and Nurse Sandy instructed and time both stood still and flew by all at once. I could tell by the shortening of the space between contractions and the deepening of the pain Mattie showed that the baby was coming soon.

"Is it time?" I asked, looking at Nurse Sandy.

She nodded and spoke quietly to me. "You'll see that we're in a bit of a pickle here."

I looked to see that where there should be a head crowning, it was the baby's bottom instead. I looked quickly back to Nurse Sandy. She nodded again as if telling there was nothing to do but continue to get things done.

"Mattie," Nurse Sandy said in a calm voice, "we're going to do this a little differently than you might have heard about, OK?"

"OK," Mattie said, her voice a quiver of pain.

"First things first," the nurse said–her British accent making her sound like the authority she was, "I want you to try very hard not to bear down when the pressure comes. Do you hear me?"

Mattie nodded but didn't speak.

"She hears you," I confirmed.

"Good," Nurse Sandy said. "We're going to let this baby do its best to be born without us trying to deliver it."

I looked at the nurse in confusion.

Daniel asked my question. "What does that mean?"

Mattie started breathing heavily, almost panting. Daniel breathed out purposefully and closed his eyes very briefly, his lips moving in what I knew was a prayer before turning his solid gaze back to her.

The nurse spoke again in her steady and calm voice. "We're going to let gravity help the baby get into a better position and we're going to try to stay out of the baby's way for a moment until the parts that need to present well enough for us to help do, in fact, present."

I understood what she meant then and I looked from Daniel to Mattie. "Mattie, we need you to get on your hands and knees instead of on your back like this."

"That's right," the nurse confirmed. "Gravity will help the baby get itself out. Little nugget here needs a moment to find his way."

Daniel eyed the nurse. "And that will happen? He'll just come out?"

She took a deep breath that I instinctively recognized as the breath of telling the truth.

"If we don't intervene until we're needed, and he's able to do the maneuvers he needs to do, and Mattie doesn't push until he's making his way, he'll come out. We don't have too long though. That's the difficult part. Once he's coming and coming for good, he needs to find his way out in about five minutes or so, otherwise we'll have some complications."

I reached for Mattie's hand. "But we're not going to. We're going to be fine."

I knew that might not be true, but what she needed along with the truth was hope. The nurse nodded at me.

"We make a good team," she said and then straightened herself tall. "Now, let's get Mattie into position and let this little nugget find his way out."

Mattie scooted up in the bed and we helped her turn over and get on her knees. While we moved blankets here and pillows there she asked between ragged breaths, "You keep saying he. Can you tell if it's a boy?"

The nurse chuckled. "Well, he's coming out tushy first right now and he's showing me enough to know that if you've got a boy's name in mind, you'll be using it."

Daniel's eyes suddenly welled up with tears. "It's a boy, Mattie." He laughed. "Of course, I don't care what it is, but something about knowing one way or the next drives it home." He kissed the top of Mattie's head from his position beside the bed. "We're about to meet our son."

"We're close," the nurse said to me. She spoke softly, so that I could hear her but so that our conversation might be more confidential. "I've done a few breeches before and Mattie's in good shape so far. This position," she said and indicated what we could see, "is preferable."

I could definitely see the little baby's behind instead of his head. My heart beat a little faster at the understanding of all the things that might go wrong.

"The cord could get caught," I said, not wanting to say out loud that it could be around the baby's neck and we wouldn't know that right away.

She nodded. "Yes."

"What do we do?"

She ran me through the procedure quickly as somewhere in the far distance it seemed, Daniel spoke to Mattie and she groaned and tried to speak back to him. I hoped they were oblivious to us for the moment.

"Once it starts it will depend on whether Mattie stays in this position or if she needs to turn back over. Hands and knees is hard when you're exhausted."

"And she is."

We both agreed on that.

"His buttocks will come first," the nurse said, continuing and I nodded along, "and we'll need to help his little legs to unfold. I'll take hold of his midsection and help guide him out a little more. We'll reach the arms next and unfold them."

I knew having the head come last was not a good thing and although I felt I was taking it all in stride as the nurse's assistance, as Mattie's friend I was nervous.

"Then we're down to his head." She looked at me and our eyes locked on the seriousness of this part. "I'll manage the cord as best I can and help turn him so that I've got a safe hold on him. If she's on her back, I want you to press firm but slow and steady on Mattie's pelvis when I give you the call, OK? Not before."

Mattie did want to turn back over and with Daniel's help it was no trouble. Mattie's eyes were a bit wild, but Daniel's were solid. He whispered to her and kissed her head again. She gripped his hand.

"I need to push," she said in a pleading voice.

"We're on," the nurse said to me and then she turned her attention to Mattie. "Try to wait. I'll tell you when."

"I don't think I can wait," Mattie said desperately, her voice soaked with pain.

"You can." The nurse was so calm it almost made me think this whole thing was an easy everyday procedure. Like we were baking bread or something as painless and simple, instead of this amazing feat of nature.

Next the nurse spoke firmly and clearly to Mattie, telling her what was happening, what she needed to do and when and what not to do and how. It all went just as she said it would.

"Cloth," she said to me and indicated the items laid out on the desk.

I handed her a small towel which she put around the baby's midsection after his little legs were unfolded. She turned the baby ever so gently one way and the next as his arms came into view. She pressed and pulled with firmness but care as she unfolded his arms and moved the cloth further up his body to make sure she had a good hold. Before long, his shoulders were out.

"The cord looks good so far," she said to me. "But this is the tricky part. We need him to get his head out and we're hoping that cord isn't wrapped around him."

My heart lurched.

"Now," she said and nodded toward Mattie's belly. "With a flat fist."

I moved into place and pressed firmly and slowly and lo and behold the baby's head came out and praise the Lord, the umbilical cord was not around his neck, but resting against his cheek as if it was nothing but a day's event not to have been worried over.

"He's out, Mattie," I called, my voice breaking in excitement and relief.

From there it was everything else I knew from my books. I handed Nurse Sandy more towels, set the water basin close, and assisted as she directed. We all rejoiced when the baby cried just like he was supposed to. I knew there had been so many possible wrongs that could have occurred, so many dangers, but just like Daniel had promised Mattie, everything was alright and soon enough, Nurse Sandy was handing the swaddled baby over to Mattie and she and Daniel were kissing his cheeks and kissing each other. Tears were shed by us all.

As the nurse was washing up and putting things away, she smiled at me and said, "That will be your favorite part."

"Pardon?" I asked, trying to hide a growing excitement at her understanding of my secret desires and moreover her validation of it.

She winked. "Handing the healthy baby over to its parents," she said. "When you're a nurse midwife," she said in confirmation, "that will be your favorite part."

"Oh," I stammered. "I don't know about that. I'm a librarian."

She chuckled and nodded her approval. "Good then," she said. "You're already used to traveling by horse and dare I say you know these hills and creeks and the people here like the back of your hand."

I continued to help her bag her belongings, my insides all but tingling at the thought of it all.

"You know," she said, once she was all packed and we were just standing there watching Mattie and Daniel gush over their baby boy. "Mary Breckinridge has been talking about starting up a nursing school right here in Kentucky. It's all but a done deal if you talk to her about it. She's got it all planned. Maybe in a year or so at the longest. When she sets her mind to something, she gets it done. That's why I'm here. She's the one who got the Frontier Nursing Service started."

I knew about the nurses of course and knew about Mrs. Breckinridge, but I didn't know about a school in these parts. There was a nursing school in New York, but to be a certified Midwife you had to train overseas so far as I knew. That's why most of the nurses had accents from overseas.

"A real school for nursing?" I asked. "Where?"

"Right here in Leslie County."

"Really?" I asked. I was about to jump right out of my skin.

"If she gets her way, which she usually does. She's an amazing woman."

"Maybe I could go," I said, allowing myself to say it out loud like a dream made real.

"You could be in her very first class," Nurse Sandy said. "I'll put in a good word for you as soon as I'm back at the hospital."

I couldn't help but break into what might have been the biggest smile of my life.

She winked at me and said, "Now of course, we need to give you a nickname. All couriers have nicknames and you're officially an honorary one at the very least."

I didn't know about nicknames. She had said they called her Sandy. That must be short for Sanders. She put her finger to her lips and eyed me carefully.

"Ruby is a beautiful name," she said. "We can't call you Rubes, that won't do." I waited anxiously as she continued. "If you were a ginger, I'd call you Red, but that's not quite right either. What about Roo? RubyRoo. I quite like it."

I smiled even bigger. I'd been given a nickname and all those on the inside of FNS apparently had them. I'd been taken into the fold. My dreams had left my head and were now standing tall and proud right there in the room with me.

Chapter 28
Cole

Every time Mattie cried out, Josh and I eyed each other over the printing press. When no one came running out the door upstairs, we'd go back to work.

I could technically do the job on my own, but it was much more efficient with two people running it. The two of us together could get about four copies per minute. Of course, it was less on the minutes that Mattie yelled out.

While Josh inked the plate with the brayer, I attached the sheet of paper to the lid of the bed and then closed it. We talked to each other while we worked. Doing the job with an actual newspaper man made the work seem honest and worthwhile. I tried to keep my hopes in check as I still didn't know how the town would react, but I could feel myself starting to imagine a real life and real job of creating the news here.

Mr. Mobley paced around by the front door, glancing nervously up at the room about every ten seconds. Several times he headed for the stairs, but then seemed to talk himself out of it and went back to his pacing.

"Should we do something?" Josh asked, nodding at Mr. Mobley.

I ran the bed under the press and shook my head. "He just needs some space, I think." I reached for the figure-four toggle and pulled it toward me which lowered the press onto the ink and the paper. I loved this machine. I knew there were newer models out and of course the bigger papers used them, but the idea that all by myself I could push and pull that toggle and put about three hundred pounds of pressure down onto the paper was a feat of engineering that had to be admired. When I was a child, it felt like pulling the trigger, but now, it was the straight arrow of truth.

Josh rolled more ink from the slate onto the brayer as I ran the bed back out from under the press, opened the lid and removed the printed sheet.

Josh turned back to me to roll the plate again starting the process over. "The page looks good, Cole," he said. "I can tell you've done this before."

I hung the newspaper up on the clothesline we'd strung across the room. "Compositing was my job as a kid. There was a lot I didn't care for when my father ran this press, but I did like styling the paper."

Josh nodded as I put the next sheet of paper in, closed the lid and carried out the rest of my job.

"You did a good job," he said. "The top's a little wonky, but the rest is clean as a whistle. It's hard to read backward and place the pieces so that it looks sharp as well. You got your words out and it's a nice flow and design. I'm impressed."

"Ruby did the top part," I said, wanting to make sure he knew all the credit wasn't mine and that she'd done well. "It was her first time ever. Not too shabby, huh?"

Josh nodded his approval. "Indeed."

As I ran the bed back out to remove the current sheet, we heard a baby cry and Mr. Mobley took off running up the stairs calling for the kids to wait there. They all jumped up and down squealing and carrying on.

I breathed out heavily. "That's a good sound to hear."

We continued printing while sounds of happy voices and laughter came from upstairs. They were probably all exhausted, Mattie the most, but I imagined you couldn't help but celebrate. As Josh and I worked, I kept stealing glances at him. He seemed so familiar, but I didn't want to stare into his face like I was some oddball. But the more we worked and talked, I was sure I'd seen him somewhere and the nervous feeling I got in my gut about it told me it wasn't somewhere good. I'd been a lot of places and done a lot of things to get by. I'd had a grift or three go wrong. Which was why I tried for the most part to do things on the up and up, but when you're only shown the wrong way of doing things, lessons on how to do things right come hard. I looked around the room at all the papers hanging. All the pieces of truth and consequences. My heart jackhammered in my chest. This was getting very real, very quickly.

Josh and I kept working and sooner than I was ready, we were through. There weren't that many families in Certain, so our print run was small.

"Looks like that's it," Josh said and tipped an imaginary hat to me.

"I guess so," I said, looking around for a distraction.

Ruby came rushing out the door and down the stairs. I could always count on Ruby.

"It's a boy," she said as she launched herself into my arms. "He's perfect and healthy. A little small, but the nurse says that's OK. And I helped deliver him and it was amazing." She let me go and spun around in a circle. I chuckled. Seeing Ruby this happy was amazing.

Daniel appeared at the top of the steps then with the biggest smile on his face I had ever seen in the kind but serious man I knew Daniel to be.

"Congratulations," I shouted up at him.

"Thank you, Cole," he said. "How are you doing? Everything OK?"

He'd come out to check on me? I was flummoxed. "I'm good, thanks. The prints are done and we're just letting them dry. I'm warm. Nothing froze off."

"Good," he said smiling and then pointed back at the bedroom. "I'm needed." He nodded and went back in.

Needed. That was a good thing.

Ruby reached out and grabbed hold of my wrists, shaking my hands, and almost jumping up and down. She suddenly let go of me and made a face.

"Your skin," she said, gently reaching back out to take hold of it. "I forgot."

I shook my head. "Me too," I said. "I didn't rub it, just like you told me. I'm all warmed up and everything seems fine. You took good care of me. Just like you did with my hand. You're a good nurse."

She put both of her hands over her mouth then, but I could see the smile in her eyes. "I'm going to get back up there." She paused like she might kiss me, but then she looked over at Josh, nodded to him and went back upstairs.

"What happened to your hand?" he asked once she was gone.

A flash of memory jumped in front of me but jumped away too quickly to catch.

"I feel like I know you from somewhere," I said, pretending to rearrange the newspapers so that I'd have something to do.

"Doubtful," Josh said, turning to the ink slate preparing to clean it up. "This is the first time I've been to Certain, if you can believe it, with it being so close and all."

"This is the first time I've been back in fifteen years," I said, rubbing my hand. Nothing was left of that injury but the memory of it. I had the sinking feeling I did, in fact, know Joshua Hartwell. "I've been all over. I've even been to Hazard recently," I said, pausing, memory returning. "Didn't we get into a fight?"

"Could be," he said and shrugged. "I get into a lot of fights. Blowing off steam after a hard day's work. Little trouble here. Little fun there."

"Trouble just seems to find you?" I asked, remembering our encounter now. The one that injured my hand so badly I could barely use it until Ruby helped me.

"Certainly does," he said with a jovial sigh.

"But you're not a bad guy?" I asked.

He was finished cleaning and I was finished pretending to rearrange things and we just stood on opposite sides of the printing press looking at each other.

"Depends on who you ask," he said. He tilted his head and pointed at me in recognition. "I remember you now. You had a beard." He made a circle in the air with his finger indicating my face. "You tried to punch me and ran into my pocketknife instead."

"I might say you pulled a knife on me, and I tried to defend myself." I pointed back at him, but the fault had been mine. He'd only pulled the knife because he'd caught onto my scam. I'd tried to hold up my hands in surrender but he'd thought I was moving to attack. He slashed, I tried to punch, and somehow the blade had gone into my palm.

He nodded. "I remember," he said. "What were we fighting about though?"

I shrugged, even though I remembered.

"It wasn't Hazard," Joshua said. "It was a bar in Lexington. That's what I get for volunteering for a story nobody else wanted."

"You were pretty soused," I said, remembering that part too. We talked to each other calmly as if we were just exchanging ideas on a project or working the printing press.

"It happens." He folded his arms in front of him. "Do we have a problem now? I sure hope not. It was nice running the press with you."

"I don't see why we should," I said. "It was pretty much my fault anyway."

"You were trying to steal money from me," he said and winked. "I guess I wasn't that soused."

"Sounds like me back then," I said, hating that I'd resorted to my father's tactics over the years. I admit I had tried to relieve a man of his wallet a time or two when things were tough.

"What about you now?"

I waved at the papers hanging all over. "That's what this is about."

"I read some here and there between that lady screaming upstairs and you taking your sweet time to put the paper in." He smiled.

"Like I said, it's been a while."

"Sounds like you're trying to set right some old wrongs," Josh said. "That's a commendable thing."

Mr. Mobley came striding down the stairs then calling out to us. We met him at the bottom of the staircase. The kids crowded around with us. Josh looked at them as if he'd just now seen them.

"Gentlemen, we celebrate," he said, holding out two cigars when he reached us, then he noticed the kids. "Children, I'll have to get you something from the grocery soon."

"I don't smoke," I said.

"You don't have to smoke to smoke a cigar," Mr. Mobley said, handing them to us.

I took it and nodded my thanks. Josh smelled his and closed his eyes obviously enjoying the sweet smell of the tobacco.

"This is a luxury," he said, using the cigar to point toward Mr. Mobley. "Where'd you get something like this?"

"From a past life," Mr. Mobley said and clapped us both on the shoulder. "Come on up and meet my grandson."

Upstairs my little room was getting crowded. Ava stood at the head of the bed on the opposite side from the desk. Mattie sat up in the bed holding the baby wrapped in a blanket. Daniel sat on one side of the bed next to her and Ruby sat on the other down by the foot. The nurse seemed all packed and ready to go on the far side of the room.

"Come on in," the nurse said when we just stood in the doorway. "It's alright. I'm going to ride out before evening sets in any deeper. It sounds like that wind has quieted. Mattie," she turned to the new mother, "I'll be back to check on you tomorrow."

The nurse waved us in and we all moved around each other to find somewhere to stand. The kids were wiggly and took up more space than the adults. The nurse paused at the doorway on her way out.

"Roo," she said to Ruby, "you and I should talk."

A smile as wide as the creek broke out across Ruby's face.

"We will," she said.

The nurse left us all staring at each other. Mr. Mobley, Joshua, and I stood at the foot of the bed smiling at Mattie and congratulating Daniel. We heard the front door open and the murmur of excited voices just outside it.

Daniel's eyes went wide. "That's probably Gibbons and the rest of our family." He put a hand on Mattie's arm. "Are you ready for them all?"

"I might need a minute," she said.

Ava moved past the bed and around us. "Mr. Hartwell," she said.

"Why don't you and Cole and Mr. Mobley come down with me and we'll tell them all the news and give Mattie a moment."

"I think we're being dismissed, young gents," Mr. Mobley said.

"Pop," Mattie said, "Come on back up in a bit, will you? You're part of this too."

"Of course," he said, then turned to us. "OK men, follow Ava."

"Happy to," Joshua said, his eyes meeting Ava's and holding them just a moment.

She cleared her throat and pressed past us.

"Going to be sorry to leave, aren't you?" I nudged him.

"You bet," he said.

Downstairs Ava was being mobbed by a bunch of new kids all wanting details.

"You all have a new cousin," she said to them. "He's a healthy little boy."

"I bet he looks just like me," one of the younger girls said.

"Why would he look like you," a boy I didn't recognize huffed. "For one, you're a girl, and for two he probably looks like his own mama or Ella or Marie at best."

"We're all family," the girl said indignantly. "He could look like me."

The kids all started chattering about who looked like who and how everyone was going to be the baby's favorite cousin. I didn't know all these kids by name, but I figured they were Daniel's nieces and nephews.

Josh looked at the little precocious girl and smiled. "How old is she?"

"Eleven going on thirty," Ava said, meeting Josh's eyes and holding them.

I didn't call it out, but there was something there. That would be a story for another time though as right about then more people burst through the front door.

Mr. Gibbons shrugged at Ava. "Sorry," he said. "Liam came in while Daniel was gone asking about where everybody was and I told him the whole story. I guess he went back home and brought everyone back with him."

Liam and Zachary pushed forward asking about Daniel.

"He's upstairs," I said and they headed that way.

Ava put out a hand to stop them. "Visiting hours haven't started. You two stay here. Your brother is busy."

"Alright, boss lady," Liam said and bowed to his sister.

The room was filled with Mattie's and Daniel's family and all the kids were running all over and it felt exactly like the home I longed for. I couldn't claim it as such just yet, as there was a big fence yet to be jumped, but I was hopeful.

Mr. Mobley found Josh and me hanging out by the press. "Well now, fine gentlemen," he said and pointed to the papers hanging around the room. "Looks like the two of you made a good team."

"We did," I said. "I'm grateful for you, Josh."

Mr. Mobley pressed forward with his obvious agenda. "You know," he said as if he was just coming up with an idea, "this town really could use a newspaper. Some good news in fact. Don't you think?"

Josh and I glanced at each other, but Mr. Mobley kept talking so that we couldn't derail his train. Not that I wanted to.

He clapped Josh on the shoulder. "My buddy Charles over at the *Asheville Citizen* told me he was going to contact Wootton at the *Hazard Herald* to see about getting the ink here fast. Said Wootton had raved about a Joshua Hartwell and that he'd request you if he could. Seems like you've got quite a reputation."

"You could say that," Josh said, his voice apprehensive. "They know my name at the *Citizen?*"

"Oh yes," Mr. Mobley said. "Told me you were one of the best."

Josh looked relieved. "Good to hear."

"You know what else he told me?" Mr. Mobley asked, again not stopping for anyone else to speak. "Charles said Wootton claimed you were good enough to head up your own paper. Said he thought you might be looking to strike out on your own."

"He did, did he?" Josh said, not really answering to Mr. Mobley's implications.

"I think Cole here is going to find that he'll be sticking around," Mr. Mobley said. "I get the impression that writing and printing is in his blood."

"I'm sure he'll do a fine job," Josh said and looked at me affirmingly.

"I'm sure he will," Mr. Mobley said. "But having a business partner would make things a lot easier." He looked at Josh, reaching out to put his hand back on Josh's shoulder. "I know we're small potatoes next to Hazard, but maybe you'll think about us."

I followed Josh's eyes across the room where they lingered on Ava.

"I'll be thinking about you alright," Josh said.

"Good man," Mr. Mobley said, clapped Josh's shoulder and walked away.

"I hope you are a good man," I said and folded my arms across my chest. "These folks may kick me out yet, but I've got their back nonetheless."

Josh studied me and stuck his hand out for me to shake. I looked at him quizzically.

"Truce?" He asked. "Just in case we meet again."

I nodded and shook his hand this time instead of trying to punch him. "Truce."

Chapter 29
Ruby

Across the room I watched Cole and Joshua Hartwell talk to a very excited looking Mr. Mobley. Then Josh and Cole shook hands.

"What do you think that's about?" Ava asked sidling up to me.

"Not sure, but it looked strangely like a deal being struck."

Ava watched Josh and I watched Ava watch Josh. I smiled slyly.

"Stop it," she said and elbowed me.

"I didn't say a thing."

A passel of kids ran by soaking up the excitement in the air. The Council, as I called Mr. Mobley, Mr. Gibbons and Pastor Collins, met at the dining table.

"Anyway," Ava said with a sigh, "Cole was probably just thanking Mr. Hartwell for his help."

I raised an eyebrow. "Mr. Hartwell?"

"I don't know the man well enough to call him by his first name," she said indignantly.

"You mean Joshua," I said, trying to make it sound all sweet and swoony. "Josh. Tall, blonde, brown-eyed, handsome Josh."

Ava turned three impressive shades of pink. "Stop that right now," she said, but there was humor in her voice. "Anyway, we still have work to do around here. We have a paper to deliver and a baby and family to get home."

I was listening to her, but I was watching Cole approach from across the room. My heart fluttered. I loved that everyone was here to celebrate with Mattie, but oh boy did I wish they'd all go home so Cole and I could have a moment alone.

"I don't think folks will be going anywhere tonight," he said as if reading my mind.

The snowstorm. It had all but slipped my mind. "Is it still bad out? I thought Nurse Sandy said the wind had died down."

"Come see."

Cole took my hand with the pretense of leading me to the window, but Ava winked at me knowingly.

He lifted the blinds onto the now dark sky. The snow had stopped and the wind had subsided, but the town wore a white blanket that sparkled in the light of the full moon.

"Mr. Gibbons said the storm stopped a few hours back, but it's still pretty cold out and I imagine it would be best to wait for the sun to melt some of that snow tomorrow before anyone heads out."

I looked back into the room full of people. "What are we supposed to do?"

Josh, who had come to peer out the window as well, offered an idea. "Inside campout of course." He turned and called loudly across the room. "Hey kids, who wants to do a campout at the newspaper office tonight?"

Eight little voices screamed out together proclaiming the popularity of Josh's idea. A steady chant of "Campout, campout" sounded across the room.

Josh's eyes opened wide. "Oh no," he said, but he was smiling. "What have I done?"

The kids jumped up and down and Josh made a point of counting them out loud.

"Eight," he said. "Who are all these kids anyway?"

I pointed at Ella, Marie, and Hugh. "Those are Daniel's kids with his late wife Emily who was Ava's sister." Josh nodded along. "And the other five are Ava's."

I watched for his reaction. He had one, but it wasn't the one I thought.

"She cares for them alone?" He asked, his voice soft with sympathy. "She's not wearing a ring."

She had taken it off years ago. I knew because she had given it to me for safekeeping. *So I don't toss it in the creek, just in case,* she'd said.

I nodded. "That's right, her husband has been gone for about five years."

"She said she thought she was a widow?"

"Oh, he's alive, I'm sure," I said, trying to keep the bitterness out of my voice. Even though Pastor Collins told me I should forgive, I admit I had an angry heart for Christopher Bell. "He's just been gone. Left town to work in the mines five years ago and never came back."

Josh turned and looked at me with incredulous eyes. "Why?"

"We don't know," I said and folded my arms across my chest. "Never sent a letter, no word at all. Just gone. We looked high and low thinking he might have gotten hurt or killed or something, but there was no trace of him."

Cole put his arm across my shoulder and side-hugged me to him. I appreciated the show of support. Josh looked back and forth from Ava, who was headed our way, to me as if I might change the story. I wish I could.

"Well," he said before Ava reached us, "that is one stupid man." Changing his face from incredulity to humor he pointed to the children and said to Cole, "You in this with me, friend?"

Cole shook his head and laughed. "It's friend, is it? I think you just realized what a mess you got yourself into and are in desperate need of help."

Josh shrugged in acquiescence. "You've got me."

"I owe you," Cole said, kissing the top of my head as if he didn't care that the show of intimacy could be witnessed by anyone. My heart fluttered again.

Ava walked up as the men took their leave, sending themselves into the fray of excited children. Josh looked at her over his shoulder and smiled. I was impressed that the five children didn't scare him off. He had gained a new level of respect in my eyes.

"That was most probably a very bad idea," Ava said and pointed at the kids. "Although they'll love it. The kids that is. Cole and Mr. Hartwell may feel differently after a few hours."

"They brought it on themselves," I said and then I nudged Ava again, winking. "Mr. Hartwell must really like kids to take on such an ill-advised plan as a sudden slumber party."

Ava watched him with the kids and again I watched her watch him. He seemed genuinely interested in his campout and was eating up the attention the children gave him. They were already sitting on the floor in a circle making plans.

"I suppose it is best that everyone stays put," I said. No one, least of all Mattie and the new baby, needed to be headed home after dark on a snow-covered night. A shot of panic ran through me. "What about Nurse Sandy?" I asked. "Did she leave?"

"She said she was only going as far as Hazel Moody's house," Ava said. "She has cousins there. She was planning to stay the night. That way she'll be close enough to come back and check on Mattie as well."

I put a hand to my heart in relief and a note of excitement hit me as well. She had family here in Certain. I knew Hazel. The idea of having a contact kept the fire of possibility burning in my heart.

Ava smiled slyly at me. "So, I need to hire a new librarian soon."

I feigned ignorance asking, "Why would you?"

She put her hands on her hips and smirked sweetly at me. "From what I saw upstairs with Mattie, it looks like you have other dreams inside that heart of yours."

I bit my lip against the nervous excitement it caused me to speak of it out loud. "It's a crazy thought isn't it? Me being a nurse?"

"Or maybe even a doctor one day," she said, stoking a deep desire I hadn't even let spark on my own.

Mr. Mobley touched my shoulder, saving me from answering Ava for a moment. "I'd love to see my daughter and my grandbaby if you ladies think it would be alright," he asked tentatively.

Ava grabbed his hand and pressed it between both of hers.

"Absolutely."

"Yes," I echoed. "Let's go see that baby."

Upstairs we opened the door quietly in case Mattie was sleeping, but she and Daniel were wide awake looking fondly at their new baby boy and at each other. Ella, Marie, and Hugh were sitting quietly in the corner listening to Ella continue the tales of Peter and Wendy. Perhaps Ella might be a librarian one day. She never went anywhere without a book, even up here to meet her little brother.

"Pop," Mattie said excitedly and reached out her free hand to him. The other held the new baby cradled against her.

"My baby with her baby," Mr. Mobley said and settled himself in the desk chair beside the bed. He took hold of Mattie's hand and kissed the top of it. "Are you happy, pumpkin?"

Mattie's smile was answer enough, but she looked Mr. Mobley directly in the eyes and said, "I know you must think I'm crazy for leaving the comforts of Asheville and taking a job out here in the middle of nowhere, but yes, Pop, I am happy. Happier than I've ever been."

I glanced quickly at Daniel whose eyes were closed as if giving his wife and her father as much privacy in this moment as he could. Maybe he was worried what the two would say. He didn't need to be.

Mr. Mobley looked at Daniel although Daniel didn't know it. "I can see that, pumpkin. I don't think you're crazy. I think you're very brave. I'm proud of you."

"Pop," she said quietly, "Daniel and I have been talking and there's something I'd like to ask you." Daniel opened his eyes then and nodded to Mattie who continued. "Perhaps it's a silly notion, but what do you think of staying here for real and for good? Even if you don't think me crazy for leaving, I know it's crazy to ask you to leave the comforts of home and move to a cabin in the middle of nowhere, but I'd certainly like you to."

"Oh, sweetheart," Mr. Mobley said, and I thought he was surely going to let her down easily. "You are my comfort of home. From the moment I got here, I never had any desire to go back to Asheville because wherever you are is home to me. I've just been hoping you'd ask me to stay."

Mattie looked happy but genuinely shocked. "But what about the house? What about your business?"

He laughed. "I thought you wanted me to stay? Now you're already trying to talk me out of it."

Daniel's voice spoke deeply. "Sir, we understand you've got better places to be than here, but we'd love to have you close by. Family is important. Other than knowing God himself it's near about everything."

Mr. Mobley drew in a long breath and looked around the room with sheer embarrassment on his face. "Might I confess something?" He asked and then went on without answer. "I already have the Asheville home put up for sale. If I'm lucky it will bring price enough to pay my debts and leave me a little left to build my own cabin and not be too deep in your hair."

Mattie's hand went to her heart. "Your debts? Pop, I thought you were OK."

"Oh, I was for a while, but when the economy started to look up again before this latest recession, I got a little too happy with my dealings and got in over my head. Your mother was the one who was good with money. I've only ever been good at talking." He shrugged his shoulders. "So here you are asking me to stay, as if I had a choice, and here I've been hoping you would because I don't. And because there's nowhere else I'd rather be."

I thought of Cole downstairs wrangling the children and smiled to myself at how Certain had become the home for wayward souls of late. Maybe this poor little scratch of ground was richer because of it. There was worth here after all.

"I'm ashamed I didn't tell you sooner," Mr. Mobley said. "I didn't want to admit I'd lost all the money."

I thought of the very expensive medical books and all Mattie's mother's jewelry. The pin I wore on my overalls even right then.

"Your things could have brought a good price," I said taking off the pin and holding it out to him. "I could bring back the books."

"Don't you dare," he said, waving my offering away. "I saved those out of the sale of the house because I knew they would be appreciated here far more than the few dollars they'd fetch. And you put that pin back on, young lady. I like to see it being worn. It makes me happy."

Ava held out her hand to him. "Welcome to Certain, Mr. Mobley."

He stood from his chair and reached out to shake her hand. Daniel stood as well and stuck his hand out too.

"Welcome, Mr. Mobley," he said. "You've made my wife very happy."

"And you've made my daughter very happy," Mr. Mobley said, shaking hands across the bed. "And you can call me Pop. Well, I know when to take an exit and leave on a high note. Ladies," he said and gestured to me and Ava, "let's go see how our newsmen are holding up against those children."

Mr. Mobley kissed Mattie on the forehead and then kissed his grandbaby. "Oh, what's this little fellow's name?"

"Matthew," Mattie said.

Mr. Mobley put his hand to his heart. "Well, that's my name, too."

She chuckled. "I know, Pop."

"Another little Matt," he said, his eyes welling just a bit. He took in a deep breath. "OK, no one wants to watch an old man bawl like a little baby. Downstairs we go, ladies. Into the fray. Let's see if any of those kids are interested in visiting the *Magical Land of Noom*."

He turned then and winked at Mattie. I knew Noom. The other side of the moon. I sometimes felt that's where I was. Or rather, that's where I felt I had been. Searching the far reaches of the universe for Cole. Lost in my books. Riding my flying ship made from old spools and wooden boards. Landing it along the Hell for Certain Creek where I'd been waiting for him all this while.

Now he was downstairs. Probably getting attacked by a pack of wild monsters. I hoped the wild monsters of tomorrow would treat him with the same smiles and laughter. That was probably a more fantastical wish than any found in the children's section of the library.

From the landing I watched Ava and Mr. Mobley join the indoor campout that Josh and Cole had remarkably in hand as a matter-of-fact. Liam, Zachary, and Pastor Collins were milling around happily, but Cole and Josh were running the show. Cole looked up and waved me down. I raised my hand back to him but hesitated for just a moment. All around the room the newspapers hung in weighted anticipation of delivery. Tomorrow, we would roll them up and deliver their message throughout the town and all around the hills. Tomorrow would be a long day. Tomorrow would be the measure of everything.

Tonight, though, we'd imagine we were under the stars, warm in our bed, lost in the stories in our heads—tales of adventure and possibility told by two librarians, two newsmen, and one grandpa and all the other grown-ups around—soaked up by the imaginations of little children yet to know what the world was capable of.

Chapter 30
Cole

Sunlight cut through the lingering magic we'd let last night become. I had needed that. That spot of hope and home had been the resolve I needed not to run out into the cold night and disappear again and forever. For the sake of what might be, I stayed. I sat up, awake long after everyone else had drifted off to sleep here and there on their pallets of coats and blankets.

Everyone was still and quiet and I sneaked up from my pallet bed, careful not to wake them. In my stocking feet I wandered the room, reverently touching the newspapers where they hung like curtains to other lives I might live. My heart raced so hard it made me sick to my stomach. I found that I couldn't breathe the air that I sucked into my lungs. Getting lightheaded I put my hands on my knees and let my head drop below my heart. That usually worked. It was working much less well this time.

I gasped as quietly as possible and then jumped at a hand on my shoulder.

"Cole?" Ruby's voice was a balm. "I'm here."

Not *are you OK* because it was obvious I wasn't. Not *what's wrong* because she already knew. Not *everything will be alright* because maybe it wouldn't. But whether it was or not, she was there. There was nothing more perfect to say.

I dragged myself to standing and turned around to wilt into her embrace. Her arms wound tightly around me, and my heart calmed. She held me steady all the while.

When I could bear to pull away, I did. "Today's the day," I said with trepidation.

"Finally," she said in a strange affirmation.

My eyebrows raised. Hers countered.

"Today we set things straight and start again," she said and before I could even offer my dismal view of the potential outcome, she held up a finger to stop me. "Let's get these things rolled and ready to go."

I nodded and we began to take down the dried papers and roll them up for delivery. On the last ones Ava and Josh stirred from their spots on opposite sides of the pile of sleeping children.

"Just in time not to help at all," I said jokingly to Josh as he reached for the last paper I had already begun to roll. My heart was still shaky, but an attempt at humor helped keep me upright.

"Just the way I like to do things," he said.

I could tell that wasn't true by the way he'd stepped in with the kids last night. He was a natural with them and his generous spirit made me sorry I had tried to scam him all those months ago. Perhaps he was not as bad as he tried to make himself out to be. Hopefully.

Ava went to the front door and pulled it open. Snow still covered the ground, but the sun was bright and promising. One storm was over and another of a different sort threatened on the horizon.

We had all discussed the plan for the day. Ruby and I would deliver along one side of the creek and Ava would deliver along another.

"I'll go with Ava," Josh said as we were divvying up the papers. She seemed to want to protest but he continued, "I've read what's in that paper and even without the full story I know you all are on a dicey mission to tell a truth some people might be angered by. Let me help."

"I know the people and the route," Ava protested after all. "I don't need your protection," she said, pegging what he was offering. "No one is going to hurt me."

"People get mad when they get swindled," he said and looked at me. "I should know."

"Ava's not the swindler," I said. "I'll be the one they're after."

"Then let me stay for that," he said.

Daniel appeared behind Josh. "I'll be here for that too."

I shook my head at them. "I can't ask you both to fight my battles. Daniel, you've got a baby to care for and Josh, you barely know me."

Ruby slipped her hand in mine. "Then ask me," she said and squeezed tight. "I don't know if you remember, but I'm pretty feisty."

"I wouldn't tangle with her," Daniel said, stepping forward to put a hand on my shoulder. "Friendship is seldom requested and when it's real, it's freely given. Accept it."

I nodded firmly so that I wouldn't have to speak around the lump forming in my throat.

"It's settled," Daniel said and then looked plaintively at Ava. "Please let Josh ride with you. For me."

She sighed and nodded. "For you, Daniel. Because you're my brother and so that my other brothers don't give me flack."

Josh raised an eyebrow. "How many brothers do you have?"

"Worried about something?" she asked him, but there was a playfulness in her eyes.

Ruby called us all to attention. "It's time to go." She called over to Mr. Mobley who was now awake and pretending—not very convincingly—to mind his own business. "Can you watch the kids, Mr. Mobley?"

He startled as if he hadn't been listening and I smiled at his attempt. "Of course, of course. You kids go have your fun. And I've got Pastor, Gib, Zach, and Liam. We've got things handled."

I didn't know that it would be fun, but I appreciated him trying to make it sound easy.

"I'll help with the kids while Mattie is sleeping," Daniel said and kissed the top of Ava's head. "There's plenty of us here to manage."

We bundled up and headed out into the snow on horseback, up through the hills, around the bends, across the creek and along its banks handing out the first true newspaper Certain had seen in a very long time.

My heart pounded with each delivery. They mostly went the same.

"Hello, sir," I said, my heart beating so loud in my chest I could barely hear my own voice. "I'm Cole Cooper. You might have known my father Mack some years ago. I hope you'll read this announcement and join me in town tomorrow. Thank you for your time."

Short and sweet so that I wouldn't have time to falter, and no one would have time to fully grasp the situation before Ruby and I could safely ride away. She'd offered to do the delivering for me, but I needed to do it myself. She was there to make sure I found the houses and so that I wasn't alone. And her standing beside me probably kept me from getting shot as several people did answer the door with a gun in hand.

"I'm here," she kept telling me when I'd return to my horse looking like I had eaten some bad soup and was about to toss my tummy.

It was enough to keep me going.

We made fast enough time, but it was nearing dark as we rode back into town. Claire's deadline was tomorrow morning. I thought I'd have the night to recover and get ready for the coming confrontation, but I was wrong. Just like the last time, a mob was waiting outside the newspaper door, their voices carrying across the still cold air, chilling my heart in an instant. Why had I thought they'd wait for the following day to come claim what was theirs and to get a chance to put a Cooper in his place?

I looked at Ruby and she gave me her refrain.

"I'm here."

Claire was standing on the front steps of the newspaper building holding up her copy of the newspaper we had just delivered. Light from inside the building shone behind her in the growing darkness, lighting off her red hair like it was fire. I had wanted to leave her out of the delivery, but it didn't seem right. She had been on Ava and Josh's path, and I was glad they'd given her one, even though I knew she was going to make things difficult. I hadn't told the story she wanted me to tell. I don't know why I didn't expect her to turn up right away as well.

I wanted to turn around and run, but it was time to face this and get it over with. I dismounted and handed Ruby the reins. Pushing on ahead through the crowd on my own, I made my way up to the door where Claire was fuming. She stood her ground as if she wasn't going to let me have space beside her. I caught her eye and tried to plead my case with a sincere look. It didn't get me more than about six inches of space on the landing, but it was enough.

I raised my voice above the low rumbling din. "Everyone, can I speak please?"

Most people quieted at having seen me take the stage, or at least that was what it felt like I was doing. The part of me that was my father's son wanted to get ready to put on a grand performance, but the greater part of me that was my other father's son was ready to be honest once and for all. I tried not to get lost in memory. Everything, even right up to the deep dark blue color of the night sky pulled me back into the past.

Claire tried to preempt my address by balling up her copy of the paper and tossing it on the ground. "Why should we listen to you, Cole Cooper," she said, spitting out my name like it was a vile taste she was removing from her mouth. "Everything you've said has been a lie since you came into town." She glared at me and then turned to the crowd with a pained look on her face. She pulled the ring off her finger and held it up. "I suppose this was a lie as well since you're not Henry Hall after all."

My father had nothing on Claire when it came to performances it seemed. What was I to say? The ring was a lie, but it was one she told. I wasn't interested in getting back at Claire, though, and I wasn't going to turn this into a fight.

The crowd rumbled and I figured they were glad to get their shot at calling me out. My father had managed to leave before the crowd formed, but I was here to take the brunt of their anger then and now. As they grumbled again amongst themselves, I turned to Claire and tried to explain.

"I'm sorry I didn't write the story you wanted me to about your father," I said. "He was a good man. I'm sorry he believed my father, but I have to tell the truth now. If I printed your story, it would be more lies."

I tried to reach out to her, but she jerked away from me. "Did you hear that," she said to everyone. He just said he printed more lies."

My mouth fell open. "I did not."

Claire scoffed. I could see what was coming. She knew she wasn't going to get what she wanted so all that was left was to make sure I didn't either.

"You own half the town," she said and clucked her tongue at me. "What makes any of us think that a Cooper is going to give it all back? This is probably just step two of your father's long game."

The crowd rumbled a little louder.

"As a matter of fact, Claire," I said, shivering from the cold or the fear, I wasn't sure. "This Cooper does aim to just give it all back. Just like the paper says." I held myself steady.

A voice shouted from the crowd. "I thought you said you were a reporter searching for the deeds."

Another voice echoed the obvious line of thinking. "Yeah, you said your name was Henry Hall and now you're Cole Cooper. Figures a Cooper would come to town lying to everyone."

My heart sank and my stomach rose to meet it.

"Fair enough," I said, scanning the faces. Glad the darkening light dimmed them a bit. "You're right. I did come into town on a lie. I was afraid to say who I was because I feared this right here." I waved my hand forward at the angry mob. "I didn't mean to lie. I just found myself telling a fib to cover my cowardice and it just got bigger and bigger."

The door opened behind me then causing me to jump, but when I turned to look it was Daniel. He put his hand on my shoulder for a moment and then stepped beside me, nudging Claire over.

Claire scoffed. "Of course, you'd be in on this, Daniel Barrett. You probably knew it was Cole all along."

I shook my head at Claire's careful statement. She knew Daniel knew, but saying that would mean that she knew also.

"You're right, Claire," Daniel said. "I did know."

The crowd gasped like we were in a movie and the big admission had been made.

Daniel continued, "And I know that Cole isn't responsible for what his father did to this town. Sometimes we pay for other people's mistakes and that's what happened to you and your family and that's what's happening to Cole."

Daniel spoke so calmly and confidently. I admired him greatly and wished I had told him. I'd have to make sure to do that.

"Folks," I said loudly to gain people's attention back from where they were starting to talk amongst themselves. I patted the breast pocket of the thick jacket I wore. "I have your deeds right here."

That was the wrong thing to say if ever there was one, because about three different men from three different directions pressed through the crowd toward me. Each of them wore the same angry face.

"Why didn't you give that to me when you came to my house?" one man asked.

"Yeah," another said. "If you aimed to return it, you would have already. This is just part of your game."

I didn't flinch, but it was also a welcome sight that Daniel stepped forward and put his hand out to stop them before they went further. Daniel must have held more clout or instilled more fear than he thought because all three men stopped at once.

"Let the man finish his sentence," Daniel said, "before you make any rash decisions."

Claire scoffed again. "Like the one where Cole decides to keep the deeds."

"What are they worth anyway," Daniel countered. "Nobody here has anything and nobody out there wants what we don't even have."

But I knew what they were worth. That's the whole reason I came back to return them. Sure, you might say that the value a piece of land has is only what someone else is willing to pay for it, and like Daniel said, nobody out there wanted anything in Certain. But when you don't have anything, the one thing you do own means everything. And these people owned the land they lived on. Most of the people staring up at me from the street lived on land passed down to them from generation after generation and it meant something not just to own it, but to keep it in the family. Those pieces of paper I had in my pocket meant more than gold itself. They meant pride and self-worth and that was about all anyone had these days. To lose that, was to lose it all.

A voice shouted from the street. "So, what do you want from us?"

I wrinkled my brow. "Pardon?"

Clarie spoke for the lot of them. "What do we have to do to get the deeds back?"

"Nothing," I said to Claire and to the rest of them. "I know what these are worth to you. I know what Certain is worth to me. The plan was for everyone to show up here tomorrow and I'd give them back." I reached into my pocket and took out the leather pouch that held their pride. "I guess tonight will do."

Beside me Daniel pointed at someone in the crowd who had started to push forward and the man stepped back. From the other side of the crowd, Mr. Gibbons and Pastor Collins edged through and came to stand on the now crowded stoop beside me.

"Brothers and sisters," Pastor Collins said, "We know it was not Cole who stole from us. It was his father, and we can't blame Cole for that. We can be grateful that he's here now because he didn't have to be. Returning these deeds is not another scam and I know that's what you fear. What will you have to do now to get them back? What bigger thing does he want?"

"Yes," another man spoke up. "What can you possibly want from us now?"

I scanned the crowd and found Ruby's eyes on me. She put her hand over her heart and nodded to me to tell them the truth.

"I want you to let me come home," I said. "I want you to forgive me for what happened. Even though it wasn't me who did it. I have lived with the knowledge of this and of everything else my father did for a long time. I want a chance to be better than the man he showed me how to be and I hoped that coming back here would give me that chance."

I don't know what they thought I was going to say, but that must not have been it, because a low murmur of confusion rippled through the crowd. I became very aware of Claire's hot stare on the side of my face.

"I'm sorry, Claire," I said. "I was never trying to scam you, and I wish your father had found the deeds and given them back, but it is what it is and it's about time I told the truth of it." To the crowd I said. "I know you've read my letter, and I hope you'll believe it. I know my father used this paper to trick you all. I wanted to use it to tell the truth. Everything in there is the truth. I did know at some point what he was doing, but

I was just a scared kid. Now I'm a scared grown man and I just want to start over. Here in Certain. This is the only place I've ever considered home."

I opened the pouch and called out the first name. They were in no particular order as I had often flipped through the stack and wondered for a while at one and then another until the papers were all one mass of names that I feared.

"Mr. Zeb Wolfe." I held out the deed and a man I had seen a time or two in town stepped forward and took the paper from my hand. He studied my face for a long minute and then stuck his hand out for me to shake.

"I'm sorry for what your father put you through," he said and took the deed reverently after we shook hands.

"Thank you," I said. He nodded and stepped back into the crowd. I called the next name. "Mr. Jackson Greenup."

One man after the next came up to claim their land until I neared the end. "Mr. Percy Laurel."

Most shook my hand and looked at me kindly. A couple were less forgiving, but that was to be expected. I noticed that no one left after receiving their document and I worried as to why. They all just huddled around talking to each other and comparing papers.

"Mr. Homer Dodson," I called and the first man I'd come clean to just last night came up the steps.

"I take it you and Daniel made it here with the nurse and that Mattie and baby are fine?"

Daniel spoke beside me. "Healthy baby boy."

"Congratulations," he said, took the deed and shook both mine and Daniel's hands.

The last deed I had placed at the end for a reason and when I called it, I called it by the family representative that was here. "Miss Claire Thomas."

I held the deed out to her, but she didn't take it. She just pinned me with steely eyes.

"This doesn't make things right," she said, not taking the deed.

"I know it doesn't," I said. "I can't undo what was done. I can only make the amends I came to make. I'm sorry, Claire."

She took the deed from my hand in a huff but like the others she didn't leave.

I looked at Daniel and asked him, tilting my head at the crowd of people still hanging around. "What do I do now?"

I had envisioned being run out of town like last time, under the cover of darkness no less, just like now. But the townsfolk all stood there looking at me. I didn't know what else I was supposed to do.

Daniel leaned in and whispered, "Give them a chance to forgive you." Then he turned toward the crowd and spoke to them. "Why don't we all go over to the church and have a moment to let this settle in. If anyone has any questions, I'm happy to address them." He held his hand out in a motion toward the church across the street.

Mr. Gibbons spoke as well. "Pastor and I will come along as well. Between the lot of us we can sort out what to do."

What to do? Maybe I was still to be run off. I sighed deeply and Daniel put his hand on my shoulder.

"We'll handle it," he said to me. He tilted his head toward Claire and asked me, "Are you OK here?"

I nodded and he walked out into the crowd waving them to follow him which, thankfully, they did. I turned back toward Claire. She was still fuming and although I wanted to be mad at her for blackmailing me, mostly I just felt sorry for the whole thing.

"When did you realize it was me?"

"That day I came to your office and spilled the coffee on you," she said. "Remember?"

I nodded.

"While you were making it," she said, "I saw your journal on the table. I just wanted to get to know you better and thought I might sneak a peek while you were taking forever to make the coffee."

I sighed. "And you read something in there that gave me away."

She nodded. "At the time, I thought it was divine intervention. It was open right to a passage about hoping Ruby would forgive you after all these years and hoping the town would see who you really are."

I looked away.

She tsked and said, "And you, like an idiot, had written in the front of the darn thing 'Property of C. Cooper.' It was easy to put two and two together. I was just shutting the book when you came back over with the coffee and I knocked it out of your hand."

"On purpose I guess."

"In shock more like it," she said. "But I knew then and there that I was going to get you back for what you'd done."

"But—" I said, but she stopped me.

"I know it's not your fault what your father did," she said. "But I felt like a prize idiot because I had believed there was a Henry Hall. I had been taken for a fool by a Cooper again."

"I'm sorry," I said again. "What now?"

She sighed and gestured toward the group of folks filing into the church. "We'll see."

She turned and walked down the steps. The rest of the crowd was gone by then. The street was empty except for Ruby who hadn't moved an inch. She waved at me.

I smiled at her and felt the tiniest bit of hope.

Claire stopped next to her and looked back at me. "We'll let you know what we decide."

Claire might have thought what I said next was meant for her, but my eyes again found Ruby. "You know where to find me."

I went back inside the newspaper office where I was sure people thought I'd be until they had decided my fate. But I went straight out the back door headed back where I came from.

Chapter 31
Ruby and Cole

Ruby

Cole was right. I knew exactly where to find him. After Daniel, Mr. Gibbons, and Pastor Collins had all made their appeal for forgiveness, which most people had done before they even got into town, I was tasked to let Cole know the outcome. I had gone into the newspaper office, but I knew that's not where he was. I didn't even call out for him there. I went straight out the back door and followed the moonlight to the creek. Snow still covered the ground and the chill lingered, but the storm had long stopped.

I grew up along the Hell for Certain, I delivered books along its banks, and I foraged for my precious medicinals through the brush along its way. Finding the creek in the dark was as easy as walking through town on a sunny day. Especially finding the spot where Cole and I would meet up all those years ago, where I had discovered him when he returned to town, and exactly where I knew he would be waiting for me now. My gramma's thin spots came back to my mind. She was right. They were everywhere. Anywhere you wanted to see past this world and into the next. But I didn't need a portal to another place. I was happy here. In this spot. Heaven was right here for now and so was Cole.

I let out a low whistle. Our adventurers' call. I waited only a second and he returned the call to me. My heart fluttered just like it had all those years ago when we'd sneak out from our homes late at night and meet along the creek just like this. Where we'd run to after school or church or just on a Tuesday with nothing better to do, just to spend time together. And where I had waited for him to come back to me that fateful night that his family left town.

I rounded the little bend and break in the creek that we used as our landmark and there he was, waiting for me. I shivered just a bit as I approached him. The air was still cold, but I think my shiver was mostly from relief and anticipation of what came next. Because anything could come next now that he was staying.

I smiled widely at him, and he sighed deeply, doubling over just a bit to put his hands on his knees.

I reached out my hand to him when I was close enough to touch him. "They forgive you of course. And, of course, they agree most of it was not yours to ask forgiveness for."

He straightened up and then seeing my hand gripped it and pulled me tightly to him. His breath was a ragged jangle of released nerves causing his chest to heave against me. "I thought they might not." He said, his voice a breathless whisper into my hair.

I had worried about that too. Claire had held out as long as she could and it seemed like her vote might hold some sway since the town pitied her because of her father's death. In the end, Daniel, of all people, convinced her to let old hurts go. That he was the one to calm her anger was quite a show of forgiveness given that she usually hated Daniel's guts. Maybe they too could call a truce.

Cole pulled back from me then but held both my hands in both of his. "You just did what I had hoped to do all those years ago." I must have looked confused because he shook his head and spoke again. "Come back to the creek with news that everything was alright." He let go of one hand and wound his arm around my waist. "I told you I was coming back, and I meant it. I didn't mean to leave you here waiting for me. I should have come back years ago, but I was too afraid."

"You didn't have to be afraid."

"I know that now," he said. "But the longer I stayed away and the more lies I was caught up in with my father's scams, the less real everything seemed. I wasn't even sure I was real. What if nothing had been real? What if Certain was a dream and if I came back, you wouldn't even be here. It would have been my imagination and it was better that it stayed there than to find out I couldn't really come back." His eyes were so pained. "I don't know what's real and what's not sometimes. What if I don't know how to be Cole? What if I don't know who he is?"

"I know who he is," I said and let go of his other hand so that I could touch his face. "I have always known who you are. And God knows who you are. And we'll both help you figure it out for yourself."

Cole

"You're not make-believe," she said snagging right at the thing I feared the most.

That maybe I wasn't real, that all my dad's stories and all my tall tales that I claimed I just told to get me through had turned me into a make-believe person. A real sort of phony and I feared that most of all.

Ruby reached out and took my hand "Do you hear me, Cole? I need you to hear me. You are not made-up. You are the real thing, even if you don't yet know what that thing is. God knows and he'll tell you in time. But until you hear from him, you listen to me. You are real." She moved closer to me, and closer still until I c.ould feel the heat from her lips inches from mine. She kissed me firmly and purposefully like she was sending me a message and she was.

"Did that feel real to you?" she asked.

I nodded because it felt so real that I couldn't speak. My insides rattled like a supernova about to blow and all that was holding it in was the existence of the universe itself and the very skin that I could feel on fire from her touch.

"Wait a minute," I said and pulled back from her, trying not to let a sly smile creep across my face. "I was supposed to come back here and kiss you, not the other way around."

She sighed and gave a little roll of her eyes, but then bit her lips in a way that told me she was pulling my leg in the best of ways. "A girl can only wait so long and then she just has to take matters into her own hands."

I nodded and pretended to begrudgingly concede. She laughed and punched my arm.

"Now this is the kind of pretending that the real Cole does," she said. "The real Cole is kind and funny and makes me smile. He doesn't have a lying bone in his body, not really–Henry Hall notwithstanding–because you and I both know who Henry is."

I nodded. "Yes, Daphne Dandelion, we do. Although I suppose I'll just go by Cole from now on."

"Good," she said. "Because that's who I've been waiting for to come back through the moonlight and kiss me."

"Close your eyes," I said and when she did, I darted away. I shouted from my short distance. "Open them."

I could see her looking around for me. "Cole?" she called out, but she was smiling. Ruby had me pegged and it felt good to be known.

I sauntered back toward her with my hands in my pockets like no big thing had happened at all. The moon shone across the creek and lighted on her hair. She really was beautiful, then and now. Inside and out.

I spoke ever so nonchalantly. "Turns out everything is fine. Nothing to worry about after all. Now where was I?"

She sighed and her breath fogged against the cold. "I think you were going to kiss me."

"Yes," I said. "Our first kiss."

She raised an eyebrow. "I do believe we've kissed several times already. Believe me, I remember them all."

"But this is our first kiss with everything set straight," I said. "Everything from here on out is just me and just you."

"It always has been," she said and smiled. "But you can still kiss me."

We closed the gap between us, both stepping closer, both winding our arms around each other. She stood on her toes so that her face was inches from mine. I leaned in like I was going to kiss her, then moved my head back just a bit.

"So, when you become a nurse, who's going to help me run the paper?"
She gasped a little. "Who said anything about me being a nurse?"

"A good newspaper man can scope out a story," I said. "And that one
is plain as day."

"I don't know," she said. "Do you think I could be a nurse like Sandy?"

"If you can deliver books on horseback, I have no doubt you can ride
horseback to deliver babies too," I said. "You can do anything you want
to, Ruby. And you usually do."

She smiled at me then. "I do like to get my way."

"I remember that about you," I said and winked.

"The only thing I never got was you," she said.

"You've got me now," I said, and feigned an incredulous look of pride.
"What more could you want?"

"For you to stop talking and kiss me already," she said and before she
could say any more, I did.

And then I kissed her again.

I remembered every moment of my time in Certain when I was a
kid. It had been false words on paper that dragged me away, but it had
been another written word read in the lamplight on darkened nights that
had given me the courage to come back. I had counted on the chance that
love was indeed patient and kind. I hoped that it didn't envy or boast,
that it wasn't proud and that it might not be easily angered. I hoped
mostly that it hadn't kept a record of wrong and that it would delight in
the truth and that it would protect me.

Ruby sighed sweetly beside me and pulled gently on my hand.

"It's cold out," she said. "Let's go."

I nodded and we started back toward town following along the Hell
for Certain into a heaven I was just now beginning to accept. Moonlight
glittered off the patches of snow that clung to the rocks along the creek.
Ruby's hand warmed around mine, her hold on me steady and sure. The
water whispered a welcome and I knew that I had finally come home.
Faith, hope, and love were all that remained, and the greatest had indeed
been love. Even if nothing else was certain, I could be certain of that.

Acknowledgments

I've always wondered what authors said in their acknowledgments when they were on their third or in this case, fourth book—not to mention those people who are on their 50th! What if there isn't anything new to say? What if I still, four books in, forget someone? What if I say something silly? There's always something new to say, I hope I don't forget someone, and I'm sure I'll say something silly. But the fact that I get to write this page is an honor—one that never grows old.

This page means so many things.

It means that someone thought my story was worth publishing. Thank you, again, Fireship Press/ Cortero, Mary Monahan and the ever patient Jacquie Cook for allowing the story of Certain, Kentucky to continue! I'm so thrilled to have Ruby's and Cole's story out in the world and to be able to continue Mattie's and Daniel's along with them. Thank you for putting up with all my changes and suggestions and ramblings. Writers need all the help we can get and I'm so appreciative for all you do for me.

This page means that I have the best agent in all the land! Thank you, again, Julie Gwinn of the Seymour Agency, for always being a champion for your authors. You create a sense of partnership that is truly wonderful. I know we're in this together and in this big world of publishing, I'm so glad I don't have to chart my own course and sail the ship there all by myself. I would be lost on a deserted island, failing to make a fire, and most likely eating a poisonous mushroom. Thank you, my agent and my friend.

This page means that people are reading my work. Thank you so much, dear readers for loving the people of Certain and wanting more of their story. Thank you for supporting me as part of my street team, for following and engaging with me on social media and in the real world, for offering laughter and love in all the areas of my life—for allowing me to be part of your world and being such an important part of mine.

This page means I'm part of a larger writing community that has helped me immeasurably along the way. Writing might seem like a solitary job and in some ways it is, but in many ways, it's a group effort and I have the best group supporting me! Thank you to my writing community—my fellow writers and colleagues whom I am blessed to call my dear friends. Your words of encouragement are invaluable. Novel writing is a long haul activity and we all need to be lifted up along the way. I hope I do the same for you. Special thank yous to Heather Bell Adams and Bill Spencer for reading this novel and for loving it and helping me to make it better. Thank you to Elizabeth Genovise who reminds me that we're not writing for ourselves, but to share the love of our God who cares for us more than we can imagine. Thank you, as always, to my Wildacres Writers Workshop family for all your love and care along life's way. Thank you especially to Judi Hill, whom we lost recently but will be forever in our hearts, for starting Wildacres Writers Workshop so many years ago. I would not have so many of the people whom I love most dearly and experiences that mean so much to me were it not for her. Rare is the person to whom the phrase, "My life would not be the same without you," actually applies. In Judi's case, it does.

This page means I have the most supportive family a girl could ask for, especially, the most supportive and encouraging husband who always makes sure that I have time to write and who understands all the ups and downs along the way, and who doesn't expect me to be anyone else other than who I am. Thank you to my kids who are my every reason for living. I'm not perfect and I mess it up all the time, but I love you so much the force of it would knock you right over if you could really feel it. I hope you do and that you're just really good at not falling over what with being young and all. Thank you to my extended and immediate family as well for not thinking (or at least not saying so out loud) that I'm a nut for having stories dancing around in my head and then writing them down in the hopes that other people will read them.

And most importantly, this page means that I am loved just like I am, mess-ups and all, by the One who cares for us the most, our precious Lord, Jesus Christ. God sees all our mistakes and missteps and welcomes us home no matter how many times we flub it up. I hope this book shows you that. I hope you feel the force of His love calling you home no matter how far you stray, how long you've been away, or what mistakes you feel like you've made. Truly, when nothing else is certain, God's love is.

Thank you all so very much,
Amy

About the Author

Amy Willoughby-Burle grew up in the small coastal town of Kure Beach, NC and now lives in Asheville, NC with her husband and five children. She teaches creative writing and works as a freelance editor when not working on her own fiction. She is also the director of Wildacres Writers Workshop.

She is the author of the novels *The Lemonade Year*, *The Year of Thorns and Honey*, and *The Other Side of Certain*. Her award-winning short fiction has been published in numerous journals and in her collection, *Out Across the Nowhere*. Her fiction focuses on the importance of family and friends and centers on the themes of forgiveness, second chances, and finding beauty in the world around us. She likes to write about the wonder and mystery of everyday life.

Visit her online at www.amywilloughbyburle.com

*If you enjoyed **Even if Nothing Else is Certain**, please leave a review where you purchased the book.*

Other Titles by Fireship / Cortero

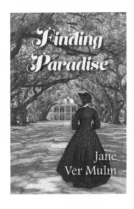

FINDING PARADISE
Jane Ver Mulm

To what lengths must they go in order to discover a paradise of their own?

Ellen Schmidt finds herself out of step with the world around her. Considered a spinster in her community, her closest friends are the slaves that her family owns. After her father arranges her marriage, she must face a cruel set of circumstances and the beginning of the Civil War, setting her on a path that seems to be out of her control. Strong and independent, Ellen continues in her own unique way to forge a future that can include a paradise of her own.

"Finding Paradise grants a fresh perspective on the meaning of family, friendship, love, loyalty and what it takes to build and strengthen 'the ties that bind.'"
—MaryBeth Thayer, journalist and creative writer

UNDER THE INFLUENCE
J. T. Kunkel

Sometimes the truth can set you free and sometimes it can imprison you. And it's not always your choice.

When thirty-year-old Cordelia Corbett returns to Point Pleasant Beach, New Jersey and rejoins her boss at Kohr's Frozen Custard after a sixteen-year hiatus, they immediately run into a crime scene at the Food Shack down the boardwalk. Cordelia is drawn to a handsome stranger as they both lend a hand.

Soon, love may be in the air between them, if they can stop butting heads long enough to let it grow. Or will Cordelia's new obsession with crime-solving stand between them?

"A cozy mystery that entertains and has you cheering by the end!"
—Jane Ver Mulm, author of *Finding Paradise*

For the Finest in Nautical and Historical Fiction and Non-Fiction
www.FireshipPress.com

Interesting • Informative • Authoritative

All Fireship Press books are available through leading bookstores and wholesalers worldwide.

Milton Keynes UK
Ingram Content Group UK Ltd.
UKHW042225180324
439698UK00005B/459